The Scent of

Eternity

Alan T. McKean

BLACK ROSE
writing™

ISBN: 978-1-61296-379-2

PUBLISHED BY BLACK ROSE WRITING

www.blackrosewriting.com

Printed in the United States of America

The Scent of Eternity is printed in Perpetua

Dedicated to the memory of my Texan stepson the late
Major Luke Gains Parker USMC (1976-2013)
Semper-Fi. Brave, godly and faithful to the end. Much loved and missed.

The Scent of Eternity

PART 1

PROLOGUE

Rome 9th/10th June 1940

We were six Vanguard operatives fleeing in two taxis from the Il Termini train station in Rome, pursued by the Nazi Abwehr and the evil Professor Reynolds, organizer of PATCH. PATCH—People Allied Together to Change History—was a dangerous rival time travel organization that attempted going back into history to change what appeared to be small events, but which were events that, if changed, would prove disastrous. They had already attempted to drag England into the American Civil War so that the United States would be divided into two countries, which would render it ineffective in World Wars I and II. They had tried to assassinate George Washington. Thankfully, Vanguard had countered both of these attempts.

I'm Major Drew Faulkner, a former under-achiever working a dead-end job who risked it all to improve my future by agreeing to time travel. So far, praise God, I had stayed alive—barely. My second in command was Lt. Angus McTurk, an arms expert and unarmed combat instructor who makes the British Special Air Service (SAS) nervous. Operative Mike Argo is an Oxford graduate and Kendo master, as well as a top-grade soldier and linguist. He rescued his fiancée Hera from a Roman gladiatorial arena in First Century AD. Hera is a capable fighter who fit into modern life without losing her skill to survive in dangerous situations. Angus McTurk and I had rescued Sebastian, a slave in 1863, and offered him a career as a Vanguard operative. Sebastian accepted our offer and had proven himself invaluable. Then there is the most colorful member of our team, Anton Devranov. Anton is a Russian émigré from 1867, who had saved my life in China, and who had an endless stock of "old Russian sayings" for every occasion—and to hear him tell it—a girl in every town. His fast reactions and linguistic skill had proven themselves. Our Vanguard team was a mixed bunch, but it worked. Usually it worked. Except now, Hera had been shot.

With Hera wounded, we had to first escape Rome with our lives intact, and then find and apprehend PATCH organizer Professor Reynolds and his associates. PATCH made the *Scarlet Pimpernel* look like an amateur.

'They seek him here they seek him there, those Frenchies seek him everywhere
Is he in Heaven or is he in Hell that damned elusive Pimpernel.'

We were starting to wonder how someone could scheme up so many problems and stay so hidden, a modern day *Sir Percy Blakeney*, but with evil intent.

More frightening to me was the chilling possibility that Caleb Bryant, the Nantucket sea captain who had murdered my wife of ten minutes in cold blood because she would not marry him, was still be alive and working with PATCH. Bryant was a murderer and a terrorist—evil and dangerous. He had proven as slippery as a conger eel and had exhibited the same charm and personality.

Apart from my wife Lucy's death, the thing that weighed most on my heart was Mi-Ling's illness. Mi-Ling was my adopted Chinese daughter. I had rescued her from a child brothel in Foochow, China and she had repaid that kindness by saving my life aboard the *Night Arrow*, China to London in the great tea clipper race of 1867. I wanted to be the best dad I could be for her. Resolutely, an illness for which nobody could find a cure or even a clear diagnosis stalked her, sucking the life and fire out of her heart. Chinese linguist Dr. Lucy Francis was improving Mi-Ling's Mandarin, which kept her mentally alert – but did not bring physical healing to her frail body. Dr. Lucy was also helping former slave Sebastian develop better communication skills.

The Vanguard operative missing from our two taxis during the harrowing chase through Rome streets was Meryl Scott, my former girlfriend. We had very nearly married at one time. Meryl was an Olympic swordswoman and expert in combat. Former or not, I suspect Meryl and I still held deep feelings for each other – deeper than either of us cared to admit.

In a vital time traveling organization like Vanguard, there were other teams, but we were Vanguard Alpha. I keep a journal of events to record everything that happens to our Alpha Team. If you find this journal, what you will read actually took place, and is written from first-hand experience, whether you believe it or not is up to you.

CHAPTER 1

Aberdeenshire, Scotland, 1868

I went out into the estate to find the sons of Jock Shepherd. Bryant had murdered their father, and they wanted Bryant brought to justice as much as the rest of us did and might be happy to cut a few corners in the process. Andy and Tam had just finished lunch.

"Andy, Tam, can I get a quick word with you outside?" I asked their mother, Meg who was busy, but took time to greet me. Since Jock's murder, Meg had kept herself active, but she was still overwhelmed at times with waves of grief.

When we were outside I asked, "Do you know anyone who has a boat that I can hire?"

The boys thought for a minute or two before answering, "Sandy Hammond. His boat isn't jist big, but it's not wee, either. Can we ask what you want to do with it so we can tell him?"

"Do you know where Crawton, south of Stonehaven, is?"

"Aye, sir," Tam replied.

"I am quite happy to pay for the use of the boat and for the two of you to attempt to locate a sailing ship that might be anchored there, the *Allegheny*. It belongs to Caleb Bryant, the man who shot your father. I need to know where it is. If it's not at Crawton, I think it will be north of there. If you can find it, I will be grateful. Take as long as you need. Please don't approach the ship and try not to be seen. Bring me word. I need to know if it's flying a flag. Do you know what the United States flag looks like?" They nodded. "Send me a telegram if you locate the ship and please take care of yourselves." I gave them money and they headed off eagerly.

I called out after them, "Remember send a telegram if you can't get back or if you think you may have located the ship." They waved cheery hand and something reassured me that I had put the two right men on the case.

Bryant was an American citizen and he was wanted there by the law, but if his ship were raided, it would probably need to be by the Marines. The times Bryant had appeared with his PATCH helpers, his ship had not been far away. I had formulated a theory to present to my Uncle Adrian, a physics genius. He and Reynolds at one time had been colleagues and had worked together on time travel. Now they were the brains on opposite sides. I submitted my ideas to Adrian in writing and a meeting with the team was organized. I left Bellefield in the time car and arrived in modern times, somewhat confusing since Vanguard Headquarters were at Bellefield in modern times! When everyone was assembled, I put my idea to them. Meryl was there. I had to admit, I was pleased to see her.

"Proceed, Major," Colonel Carlisle invited. When the word 'major' was mentioned, Meryl looked up from her notepad and flashed me a quick smile.

I took a deep breath and explained, "It seems to me that when PATCH puts in an appearance, it's within a hundred years of 1868. We've been able to go back two hundred years. Maybe their time travel car has a range limit in time. Nobody seems to have thought of going a hundred years forward of 1868. This, if I am right, is bound to limit PATCH capability, although granted, they can cause enough trouble just with the short range they have achieved. Now, suppose the thing they wanted from Bryant was simply the use of his ship? They use the ship, as a kind of signal-booster station. That might be how they got the two assassins on location to attempt murdering George Washington in 1755, during English General Braddock's expedition in Virginia. How do we know that the visions and incursions from PATCH have not centered from Bryant's ship? If we impound or destroy the *Allegheny,* then we might limit what they can do."

Silence sat heavily in the room. At least my ideas were not dismissed out of hand.

Vanguard Head Colonel Carlisle responded, "We need to find out what, if anything is going on aboard that ship. I was going to suggest NASA, but the ship exists in a time frame about a hundred years before NASA came into existence."

Captain Carter of the USMC entered the conversation, "There are cameras that can be used to see through objects. They'll tell you what's inside. The challenge is to get close enough for them to work. They're used a lot to search for illegal immigrants, but it's easy to get close to a big rig. If the camera can't penetrate the hull, then there is only one thing left, that's to board the ship, but reconnaissance first. The moment we do board, we tip off Bryant and maybe PATCH, and let them know we suspect something. That might cause them to change their *modus operandi*."

"I have two locals keeping an eye out for the *Alleghany*," I informed the group. "They know they're to observe and telegram me about anything suspicious. The trouble is I have to get any telegrams they send in 1868."

The colonel assured me, "We'll work on a stealth team and try and get the results we need. Until then, we must keep an eye and ear open for PATCH. For them, *the game's afoot*, as a famous British Detective once said." With the recollection of Sherlock Holms, whose help we could certainly have used had he been flesh and blood, the meeting broke up.

Sebastian would stay in 1868, at the house in Bellefield, and Angus would come and go. I walked back in the direction of the time car and heard a soft voice behind me. "A penny for them!" it said.

I spun around to face Meryl. "Meryl, I'm sorry for what I said about not wanting to be friends with you anymore because you fell out of love with me and in love with someone else. It was inexcusable. How is Kitchi?"

She was silent. We sat down on a couple of chairs. "What happened?" I asked.

The scent of coconut came to me, that lovely fragrance of hers that had always spoken the language of love to my heart. Meryl shrugged.

"I didn't seem to fit in to Kitchi's Native American culture. There's a trial period of a couple of months before any marriage. It just didn't work. It seemed that when there was no danger for Kitchi and me to face together, we had little to say to each other. I like the strong silent type, but he was too strong and silent. We didn't seem to have that much in common; perhaps I was having a foot in both camps so to speak. We wanted to be perfect in each other's eyes, but we're human. We needed room to have a bad day and didn't know how to make it. Maybe I did not try hard enough." She sighed and looked out of a window.

"I'm sorry. I really want you to be happy." I looked at her. I guess inside I wanted to take her in my arms and hug her. Instead, I quipped, "Well, at least we have something in common."

She perked up, "Let me guess…"

"*SavaJava,*" we both said at the same time, naming our favorite coffee house. We laughed.

"Congratulations on your promotion, Major," she added.

She tucked a lock of blonde hair that had fallen over her face back behind her ear. The blue eyes looked at me. I wanted to say something, but the next time I said anything romantic to her, I knew I had to feel it and mean it. "*Amigos?*" I asked.

She smiled. "*Si, amigos.*" Then as I walked away, there was a slight pause and she softly added the phrase I don't think I was meant to hear, "*para siempre.*" My Spanish was practically non-existent. Later I found out that *para siempre* meant 'for always.'

The truth was, I missed Lucy. She and I had shared real hope for a future. But now, Lucy was in Heaven. She was happy and at peace - but I was left behind to wallow in grief and despair and loss. Lucy and I had not been intimate. Bryant had murdered her before we could spend even one honeymoon night together. Every time I closed my eyes, my mind returned to the church and Bryant's arrogant self-justification for cold-blooded murder. I suffered anew like an old wound opening at the memory of Lucy's lovely face and the spreading blood stain on the bridal gown that she had so looked forward to wearing – "just for you, my darling." Then, as my beloved Lucy lay dying in my arms with her blood spilling out on the ground, she had held my hand and promised, "I'll love you through eternity, my most beloved."

Hatred for Bryant ate into me. I wanted to punish him. I wanted revenge! Then I realized that I wanted to punish him beyond death, and that was God's territory. I was treading on dangerous ground. Yet over and over in my mind, all I could hear was his self-righteous death sentence on Lucy. He had had no right to murder her. He had had no right to take her life just because his blasted pride had been hurt. The light of my life had been extinguished because of his vanity. I wanted to kill him with my bare hands—take away his life as he had taken away my Lucy's life. Yet, a voice inside me said, *If you kill him because of your pride, what is the difference between you and him?* It was as if I could hear God's voice saying, *Justice or revenge? Vengeance is mine. I will repay.*

Sometimes I thought I would be justified in killing him. As long as Bryant was alive, Mi-Ling lived in danger. In Bryant's sick mind, Mi-Ling was guilty of his crony Lancaster's murder and he wanted her punished for it. I was Mi-Ling's protector. I had to keep her safe. Bryant's death would accomplish this. Then that same voice of God in my mind whispered, *Drew, who do you think has been keeping and protecting Mi-Ling? You? You will find that Bryant has a daughter just about Mi-Ling's age. Mi-Ling needs a father without blood on his hands.*

Had I imagined that voice -those words? Did Bryant really have a child the same age as Mi-Ling? Even if he did, what did that have to do with me? Bryant's daughter would be someone else's responsibility. So why would God tell me about her?

Here I was kicking around in the same modern times I had left, exchanging the nothingness of my life for adventure. Now I wanted to get back to 1868, to be with my daughter and to see if there was any word from the boys watching for Bryant's ship. Was the ship still at Crawton, or had it been moved somewhere else? Bryant knew where I lived. Why was he still around? I couldn't see PATCH being happy if Bryant concentrated on personal revenge. Lucy's death had not advanced the PATCH cause.

* * *

When I got back, Sebastian and Doctor Lucy had finished their lesson for the day. Mi-Ling had cut her lesson short. She was too tired to continue. Her fatigue was worsening, and with it, my anguish and worry increased.

Dr. Lucy said, "Mi-Ling is such a bright girl. Her Mandarin is really coming along. She misses Lucy, which is only right. To her, Lucy was Amma. Maybe a talk with you would help. She needs to know you still love her. Ill health takes away a person's confidence and strength. I guess we all need a little encouragement. You're doing very well with Mi-Ling." Dr. Lucy was not being patronizing. She spoke seriously and seemed genuinely concerned about Mi-Ling.

Before dinner, I talked to Mi-Ling. She was enormously pleased to see me. "When Papa talks to me, it makes me very happy. Mi-Ling feels so tired sometimes, as if my spring has run-down. I would love to be in the hills. There are so many animals, birds and pretty flowers to see. Do you think there will be animals in heaven, Papa?"

Alarm exploded through my mind. Mi-Ling was still young. Talking about heaven was not a good thing from someone who should have her whole life ahead of her. "I'm sure there will be," I managed to say around the obstacle blocking my throat. "But when you get better, you can see the animals and the flowers here."

She looked at me with a young face filled with wise eyes. "Papa, why do I not get stronger? I used to run and play and laugh. Now, Mi-Ling forgets how to laugh."

I tried unsuccessfully to change the subject. "You used to laugh at me when I made funny faces—look!" But my face was so stiff with fear of losing my daughter that it hardly seemed to move. Mi-Ling did not laugh. "Is there any present I can get you, sweetheart? Anything?"- I asked hopefully.

She looked up at me and said, "Time. If Papa knew how to put it in a bottle like perfume, then Mi-Ling could breathe in *The Scent of Time* each day and get better."

We ate in the kitchen that night. Mrs. Fraser had left food, and the stove was on, keeping the place warm. I must have been morose at the meal and the subject of Mi-Ling came up after she had left to rest. Dr. Lucy told me not to worry - that I was doing everything I could.

"Everything is not enough," I cried in despair. "Doctors can't treat her. The medics don't know what's wrong. She is dying on her feet and I feel so awful and so helpless."

Anton said, "Old Russian saying. When you come to the bottom of the herb cupboard, then only *The Scent of Eternity* is left."

The conversation struggled. No one seemed hungry. Sebastian had waited for a lull in the conversation. "What about God?" he asked suddenly.

We looked at him. "I've been asking God to heal Mi-Ling," I responded, "but so far, nothing's changed. It makes me wonder if He's even heard my prayer. Where is He now? Why isn't He helping?"

Sebastian said, "You don't understand. Hasn't God given you the ability at the press of a button to summon the time car and go and get the prayer answered?"

We must have all looked blank.

"Go back in time to Galilee," Sebastian explained. "Go meet with the Main Man. Go talk to Jesus Christ. In my Bible, it says that folks were always going to Jesus to get healed and He healed all of them. Why should Mi-Ling be any different?"

"But we've never gone that far back before," I protested.

"Well, ain't – aren't – isn't there a first time for everything?" Sebastian asked.

It rattled through my mind and I said, "Sebastian, Mi-Ling is dying and the journey might kill her."

He took a deep breath. "Dying through a journey is one thing. Dying through your excuses is something else."

"Okay. You're right," I replied. "I'll have to go ask the boss if we can do this. Maybe we can outrange PATCH and protect ancient history. If Colonel Carlisle doesn't agree for Mi-Ling's sake, then he may for that reason."

Sebastian grinned at me. "Just show me where I sign on the dotted line! That's one trip I've gotta make!"

I looked at the big guy and warned, "You might not get back if anything goes wrong."

He burst out laughing. "When you've done been a slave and didn't know whether you was going to get back at the end of a day, then you ain't worried about things that might could go wrong. Besides, seeing Jesus is going to blow all that away."

* * *

There was no use in asking anyone else if they wanted to come along yet in case our boss, Colonel Carlisle, refused, so I went to headquarters alone. When I got back to modern times, I went straight to the colonel's office and explained my plan.

"Yes, Drew," he said. "I can understand you wanting to help Mi-Ling. But suppose when you get there you can't find Jesus? Or have you thought of the implications if you find instead that He didn't exist?"

I hadn't thought of that. Yet, I knew in my heart that Jesus was real even though my prayers for Mi-Ling had gone unanswered. Still, I had to respect Colonel Carlisle's objections. "I know, sir. But think of the implications if we find Jesus and find out that He is real."

"Some people won't believe you," he countered.

"With all due respect, sir, 'what's new' about people not believing Jesus is real?"

"Well, Major. Choose your own team. But I would like a detailed report. If this comes off, we will have blocked an access door to history against PATCH."

"If it doesn't come off, sir, you may not get to know about it," I reminded him.

"Yes," he agreed. "It's a big responsibility, Major."

"I'll have a good team and I would welcome any recommendations you want to make," I replied.

"I'll let you know if any names come to mind."

I kind of floated back outside. It might mean a number of injections for the team, including anti-malaria and prophylactic against leprosy. I hoped Meryl might be in the canteen. She was. She hadn't eaten breakfast and was having muesli and yogurt and coffee. She hadn't seen me. She seemed to switch off at HQ, but a spring could not remain taut all the time.

"Two pence for them," I said as I came to her table.

"Two pence?" she said in surprise.

"Yes, to allow for inflation."

She smiled and seemed pleased to see me. Meryl had the kind of smile that you could get lost in — like filling your tank with gas and getting distracted so it spills over onto the forecourt. She started to speak, then remembering she was holding a spoonful of Muesli decided that eating it first was the best solution.

"Do you want to go to first century Galilee?" I asked her. "Blink once for yes, and twice for no."

She blinked once and then cleared her mouth. "You want me with you?" she asked in amazement.

I smiled my reply. The hair she had tucked behind her ears fell across her face. "Well, you see," I added in words, "it was either you or Rambo, and you hold one good thing over Rambo, apart from being a lot better looking."

"What's that?" she asked, crinkling her nose.

"You're real and Rambo isn't. Please come with us. The boss has told me to choose the team, and you're in — if you want."

She smiled fully and naturally then, and it reminded me how beautiful she was. "Let me check my diary."

"Buy you a *SavaJava* when we get back," I offered.

"And a chocolate brownie?" she asked, looking serious.

"Ohhh, well, I suppose so," I teased, pretending to take my billfold out and check the contents.

"Done," she said. "I'll go pack my bag for first century Galilee." She skipped out of the canteen, kissing me on the nose as a pleasant afterthought. She passed a window and the sun shining through it lit up her hair. I was reminded of Kitchi's name for her *She who has Sun in Her Hair*. Suddenly, my confidence began to return.

Angus McTurk was my next stop. He was in the gym, sparing with a Royal Marine Commando. They looked as if they were going to kill each other.

"I hope you two have done a risk assessment," I commented.

They stopped, "a what?"

"Yes," I said. "You have to decide who is going to kill who first, and then make sure you don't."

"Okay, Mike," Angus said. "That's enough for today."

"Yes, sir," came the reply.

"Let me introduce you two," said Angus. "Major Faulkner, meet Lieutenant Mike Argo."

I wasn't in uniform, so I extended my hand and we shook.

"Glad to meet you, sir." We chatted amicably for a moment before he excused himself, realizing that I had come to see Angus. He went off singing a tune I hadn't heard in years, *The Minstrel Boy to war has gone, in the ranks of death you'll find him...*

He had a good tenor voice and I was to discover over the next few days leading up to briefing that he would sing that song when he thought nobody could hear him. When Angus and I were alone, I asked, "How do you fancy a trip that we may not survive?"

"Oh," he said. "Same old, same old. Where? Or perhaps it's more like — when?"

"First Century Galilee to meet Jesus Christ and ask him to heal Mi-Ling."

Angus whistled in surprise. "And home in time for tea, I suppose?" he quipped.

"Come on, Angus. I need your expertise and Mi-Ling needs help. Meryl and Sebastian are coming, along with the linguist Dr. Lucy Francis. Don't suppose Mike Argo would fancy a trip? How is he with a knife or sword?"

Angus smiled. "I would want him guarding my back."

"If we get there first," I explained to Angus, "it means we can cut off an alley that PATCH may attempt to use to change history. Any forays they have to ancient times might be intended to change a victory won by one side to another; like the Persians instead of the Greeks winning at Marathon."

"Okay, sounds good," he said. "I take it the chances of surviving are about thirty percent?"

"Probably less," I replied thoughtfully.

Angus nodded and shrugged his shoulders. "If we don't survive, Abigail will kill me. Okay, I'll have a word with Mike. The experience will do him good."

"Fine," I said. "I appreciate that. Remember, you taught me everything I know."

He laughed. "Well, you've earned your pips, or you will have by the time this is over."

"What would I be doing if I wasn't doing this?" I asked jokingly.

"Probably lazing around on a beach somewhere writing a book about time travel and sipping Sangria," he said. "Nah, nobody would ever believe it or buy the book."

I left Angus and concentrated on the upcoming mission, one which I prayed with all my heart would save my daughter's life. *What could we take with us and how should we dress?* I wondered. We were going to an occupied country with Romans ruthlessly roaming about. In history books, the Romans' favorite subjects were civilization, taxation and extermination. It was an odd trio that seemed to work for them. I reckoned once we had seen Jesus – if we did – then we would hightail it out of there. It made me wonder why Jesus picked a place like that or a time like that to be born and begin His ministry.

* * *

For the next two weeks it was more injections, medical checks and classes on First Century religious beliefs. There were also meetings with a Roman historian and re-enactor, as well as a crash course in Latin for those who didn't speak it. Meryl and Dr. Francis were warned to keep their hair covered. The surprising news was that Mike Argo had achieved a first class degree in Latin, Greek and Byzantine studies from St John's College, Oxford, had been a rowing blue, and was in the choir. He was also a Kendo practitioner. He also turned out to be a good portrait artist. When Mike and Dr. Lucy met, they broke into Latin, sharing Latin jokes.

Mike didn't believe Jesus existed or ever had. He expected us to meet "a bit of a chancer," a good public relations man. "Look at the damage religion has done," he argued. "I prefer a short life, but a happy one. A good song helps. One wrong cut from a Kendo blade, and life is over."

I asked him, "Suppose you're wrong?"

"If I am, and it's a big if, then I won't have a leg to stand on." He thought for a second or two, and added, "I would like to take my Katana with me - my Kendo sword. It may prove useful."

"Okay, I agreed, "but as best you can, try not to make it obvious."

I felt confident that the big guy would be handy to have around.

Mike was still thinking things over. "I suppose there is a chance that not all of us will get back."

"I promise you," I responded, "Nobody will be left behind." Mike nodded but as I looked into his grey eyes, still waters ran deep.

* * *

"Mike is a dishy guy," Meryl remarked to me when I met her two days later and she heard he was coming on the trip. "But he always seems to underestimate himself. This will do him good, confidence-wise. I can think of someone else who has come on confidence-wise."

I smiled at her. "I take it that in your subtle fashion you are referring to me. I still remember what I was like before I left for China. You helped me a lot. I couldn't have done it without you."

Meryl shook her head. "No. I didn't keep my word. I fell for Kitchi. He's gone now." She looked out of the window. Meryl's blue eyes mingled with the sky, as her heart worked back to 1755.

Has he? I thought. *Is he hidden in the quiet of Meryl's heart, or is it just my imagination?*

"When I was younger and boring, I grew up near the sea," Meryl said suddenly.

"You never told me that!" I interjected.

"You never asked," she pointed out.

"No, I guess I didn't."

She sighed, those blue eyes traveling to a faraway past that I couldn't share – time traveling without a machine. "I would go down to the beach and feel the sand in my toes and the wind in my hair, it was down my back in those days and you could taste that salty tang off the sea. The dolphins jumped, the gulls cried – and I felt safe. There was so much going on all around that nobody would notice me."

I found it hard to believe that nobody would notice her.

I looked at her and said, "You can take your children to the beach and sing them sea shanties—*yo-ho-ho, let's have an ice cream.*"

Tears welled up in Meryl's eyes, but she didn't cry. "There's something else I didn't tell you. I can't have children. Not just what the colonel told you. I knew I couldn't have children before I joined Vanguard. That's one reason I joined. I didn't have to make that sacrifice. It had already been made for me." The diamonds of her pent-up yearning ran down her cheeks. "Sorry," she apologized. "I'm being goofy."

I wanted to let her talk. Her words were hitting home. She hadn't intended them to; - she was simply telling the truth. "I would take a book of poetry down to the beach," she mused. "One poem I loved was *Sea Fever*, by John Masefield." She quoted softly:

I must go down to the sea again
To the lonely sea and the sky
And all I ask is a tall ship
And a star to steer her by...
And all I ask is a merry yarn
From a laughing fellow rover
And a quiet sleep and sweet dream
when the long trip's over.

We were silent for a few minutes, each lost in our own thoughts and in the wonder of being together again. Meryl sighed. "I wonder what Jesus is like? At least we won't have to wait till *'the long trip's over'* to find out."

"We'll find out soon enough," I assured her. "Perhaps when we see Him, the trip won't be over, but just beginning."

She nodded and her hair moved from behind her ear and gave her the appearance of having one blue eye.

I had heard and seen a side of Meryl I had never expected. She had opened her heart and taken out her box of treasures and shown them to me. I felt deeply touched and honored. I remembered the sophisticated woman who had spoken to General Lee at Gettysburg. I had only known Meryl on the surface. She was a deep well of many unchartered waters.

"Oh!" She exclaimed. "I have to dash!" Then she suited action to her words.

I watched Meryl until she vanished from my view. After a while I realized that I must also, in her words, "dash." It was time to explain to Mi-Ling where we were going and what was going to happen. What I had not reckoned was Mi-Ling's reaction and her self-sacrificing request on behalf of a friend.

CHAPTER 2 - Preparation

How do you tell a young girl that she's dying? How do you tell her that there's only one hope? How do you cope when that same girl puts the need of her friend before her own?

Dr. Lucy accompanied me to Mi-Ling's room. Mi-Ling was delighted. Her pretty face beamed with a radiant smile. That was one thing about Mi-Ling; no matter how sick she looked on the outside, there always seemed to be an inner light like someone had lit a candle and put it deep in her heart and the light reached her eyes and her smile. "Mi-Ling, sweetheart, you know I love you, don't you?" I asked.

She smiled again, like the sun coming out from behind a cloud that had passed over its face. "Mi-Ling loves you, too, Papa." Then the eyes looked into mine and read the words that were in my mind, but that I found so hard to speak. "I am not being well, Papa, am I?"

"No, sweetheart, you are not being well," I said, trying not to cry.

She looked at me with her beautiful pure eyes."Is Mi-Ling going to die like Jasmine and Amma?"

I took her in my arms. She rested her head on my chest. "Mi-Ling is not afraid when Papa is here."

"We're going to take you to see one more doctor." I told her, kissing the top of her glossy black hair.

"Does he live in the big city?"

"No, sweetheart, we are going to take you to see Dr. Jesus. We can take you to where He was when He was on the earth. We can travel back through time." I did not expect her to understand.

She thought for a moment. "Papa, do not be unhappy. If Jesus and Mi-Ling meet, Mi-Ling will be well again. Jesus will make me weller than well." She added, "Father God will open all the doors that will get us back to where Jesus is and He will make Mi-Ling well." She thought carefully, as if she was being shown something and was putting it into language that I could understand.

"Every year has a door and at New Year, the door of the old year is shut and the door of the new is open. We cannot go back to an old year because Father God has shut the door on it. He alone can open it again to let us through to Jesus. Papa, Jesus can do anything. I don't want to go without my friend Connie. She has that red mark on her face that makes all the children laugh at her. Jesus can take that away. I don't want to go without Connie. Papa, she has been so kind to me." Little tears emerged from the corners of her eyes. The evidence of her willingness to sacrifice ran like polished diamonds down her cheeks.

I didn't need to go back to the first century to find out if Jesus existed. His Spirit was in my daughter, and her unselfish attitude - proved it.

I looked at Dr. Lucy, and she nodded her head. "To Connie's mother," Dr. Lucy pointed out, "it will be like Connie being over for a day's schooling or play with Mi-Ling. Drew, do you realize the one important thing that this will mean for Connie?"

I shook my head.

"This is 1868, not our time when women can stand on their own and build their own lives and futures. If Connie's face is healed, it will improve her chances of making a happy marriage. Think about it. Not only that, but getting a job." Dr. Lucy added. "Women in 1868 find jobs like teaching or running shops. Some even own their own shops."

"In the law's eyes, its kidnap," I said pompously.

"And when she comes back healed? You can say you were taking her to a foreign doctor, who might be able to help, or miracles simply happen when Jesus is around, her mother will follow that.

"Suppose something happens to her and she doesn't get back?" I asked dolefully.

Mi-Ling shook her head. "Papa, not to worry; Father God will take care of us all the way there. Peoples not know what Jesus did for us if we didn't all get back again."

Lucy stayed with Mi-Ling until she fell asleep. I suspected that Lucy was learning as much from Mi-Ling as Mi-Ling was learning from Lucy.

Sebastian was downstairs and inquired about Mi-Ling's health. He was hoping for word of improvement, but honestly, she had not improved. "Drew," he said. "There's one thing different about this trip. It ain't to prevent PATCH- although they shore 'nuff need preventing. It ain't about machines and gadgets and guns. This trip is about faith. The reason is different. We're trying to stop that daughter of yours from dying. We're trying to stop your heart – all of our hearts – from breaking. It's like a time – aw shucks! I can't remember the word for the wagon that takes sick folk to hospital."

"Ambulance" I suggested.

"Yup, that's the one. You're running a time ambulance to make a little girl well again."

"Two little girls," I corrected. "Mi-Ling doesn't want to go without Connie. She wants Jesus to remove the red birthmark from Connie's face so kids won't laugh at her anymore."

"Drew, you is one lucky feller to have a daughter as special as Mi-Ling. Hey! We can have a party when we get back and take the kids to *McDoubles* for something good."

I laughed. "I think they would likely prefer *McDonalds*, which is probably what you meant."

"Maybe I do, but we's gonna be celebratin,' an that's the main thing."

Before we could celebrate, we had to get there – not just get there – but try to arrive where Jesus was at the time. We consulted with some experts and tried to narrow a time frame for the time car. We decided to focus in at Capernaum, by the Sea of Galilee. There would be seven of us. Meryl was blonde and Mike Argo had fair hair. Both agreed to dye their hair black. Mike said he would flatten anyone who made remarks about dyed hair. However, all of us realized how important it was to look as local as possible. Dr. Lucy was getting contact lenses, as glasses hadn't been invented yet. The other obvious fact was that Dr. Lucy and Mi-Ling were oriental and could be taken for mother and daughter.

Mi-Ling began calling Lucy "Mama" straight away so she wouldn't forget. Mike agreed to pose as Lucy's husband. I noticed it only took about ten seconds to convince him. Angus was quite happy to be single on the trip; besides, Abigail would kill him if he did anything else.

I walked beside Meryl. "I guess we need to be married on this trip, too. It will save you from getting pestered."

She looked at me, with inquiring eyes.

"Meryl," I said, "I want love to mean something to us this time. For that to happen, it must be in the context of marriage."

"Are you asking me to marry you?" she asked.

I shook my head. "No. Not yet. When I do, I want it to be serious. I want us to know that we can both carry it through. I don't know if you can love me after what we've both been through. If you can…Meryl, let's see how things go. Just now I need your friendship, to trust and rely on you. *Amigos*, remember? And maybe if things go well – it could turn to '*amores.*' "

Anton asked about going to HQ to see what life was like in the modern world and find out if he could try time traveling. He couldn't recall any First Century Russians.

He wanted to investigate bits of Russian history he wasn't sure about. He wanted to see (in the interests of science, of course) how women had developed from 1867 to 1967. "From the days of my youth in St Petersburg," he told us, "I have sought to lead by example. Old Russian saying; it may be tough, but on a journey to a new place, someone has to take the first step into the unknown – because nothing is yet known. Besides, we might be able to get after Bryant and PATCH and I am only too happy to offer my services. Without this excitement, there would only be vodka, women, and having to write my memoirs." He put on his philosophical look and sighed.

"What makes me think is that when someone writes their memories, how do they know they haven't forgotten anything unless someone reminds them? Here now there is travel and vodka and women and something to put into the memories. One day I will be married and it will be such a loss for them, such a loss; one happy girl, and the rest all their hearts- breaking."

Anton was adamant about not coming with us. There were enough in the party already and he didn't think there would be a need for a French speaking, Russian Czarist Émigré in first century Palestine. In case the need for one came up, he was perfectly willing to volunteer. Especially since Dr. Lucy was going.

We had attended our last briefing and everyone had moved through to 1868. To take care of the house and stop PATCH from taking it over, some SAS operatives would guard it and the grounds. Tomorrow we would go.

I walked out the front of the house and sat on the steps. Meryl came up behind me. She was dressed in the same outfit that she had worn the night before I set out for China in a quest to win the tea clipper race and Lucy's heart. How long ago it seemed since then.

"Isn't that the same dress that you wore that night when it all began?" I asked.

She smiled broadly. "Well done, Major."

"Meryl, I'm scared." I reached for her hand. "At least this time, I don't have to leave you behind."

She smiled at me. "This time I can promise and keep it. I'll be there for you."

"I wish we were on that beach of yours. Take me there when we get back. It does exist, doesn't it?"

"It was there long before I arrived and it will be there long after I'm gone," she assured me, it was at Morar, and its white sands

Early the next morning, everyone was ready to go. Even Anton was up early to see us off. For once, he seemed to have run out of *Old Russian sayings*. I suspected he regretted the need to let Dr. Lucy out of his sight.

Connie was the most excited about the trip. She said she did not "really ken" what was going on, but it sounded like fun and she would be happy to see Jesus anytime.

"Poor kid," Mike remarked. "She's in for a letdown. He probably doesn't exist."

Mi-Ling overheard him. "Oh, no, Mr. Mike. When I was in that terrible place in Foochow, I used to pray every night for someone to come and rescue me. Some days I cried when nobody came, but I never give up. Then one day Father God answers my prayer and Papa walk in and want to set me free. When Papa left that terrible place, Mi-Ling left too, and Mi-Ling learn to smile again. Jesus will do the same for my friend, Connie. Then when you see, maybe you will smile again." Mike was big and tough, yet Mi-Ling had found the chink in his armor and discovered he really did have a heart.

We crowded into the time car and got as comfortable as possible. I threw the switch. There was no going back.

CHAPTER 3

Capernaum, Galilee, About 4th April 31AD

The journey took longer than it had on our previous experiences, but as we had not been this far back in time, that was to be expected. Mike sang *The Minstrel Boy* to himself, but loud enough to be soothing to the rest of us. The scanner showed that we had entered the right time scale. We exited at an outcrop of rocks to the east of Capernaum.

Angus took charge. "Right, people, we're on rocky ground. When you get outside, - stay together and watch where you put your feet. There are snakes and scorpions and if anyone gets bitten or stung, we have a problem. We don't have anti-venom for first century snakes."

Angus looked at a list he was holding. "Oh yes, if you pass any soldiers, don't look them in the eyes. Look down at the ground as if you were afraid. Try not to do anything sudden or unusual to draw attention to yourself or to the rest of us. Mike and Lucy are the linguists. Let them do the talking. It's better that they think you're a visitor than for you to open your mouths and confirm it. Any questions?"

Angus looked at each of us. We all seemed excited and slightly agitated, probably because we were. Had we known what was coming, we might not have been so casual, Hindsight is a great teacher.

"When we find Jesus ..." Angus continued. I thought, *at least he is being positive.* "The aim is to get out as quickly as possible. People, we are away out on a limb. There are two controls for the time car. If we have to split up, we make sure that one person in each group has a control, for the time car."

When we stepped outside we were hit by the heat. It felt like an oven door opening. Think fish or smoking fires with fish over them and the buzz of flies. Water lapped around the edge of the lake. We heard the hum of conversation and cries from the circling birds overhead.

There were people everywhere, mostly in groups. Fishermen repaired their nets and dried them from the night's fishing. Even though I couldn't recognize what was being said, the sound of laughter was recognizable in any language.

To keep from looking like she was eavesdropping and drawing attention to us, Dr. Lucy purposely tried to listen in to conversations. She was a good linguist and her sharp ears picked up several things. She heard people mention *The Prophet* and *The Healer,* but that alone would not help us find Jesus.

Anton had had an Old Russian saying, *if you cannot find the needle, look for the haystack.*

Where were the haystacks of people located? How did people refer to Jesus – identify Him? *Jeshua Ben Joseph, the teacher, the prophet?*

Not knowing where to go, we decided to stick to the shore. It was at least cooler for Mi-Ling, who looked frighteningly frail and tired.

Angus had gone off scouting. We decided it would be better if I were Mi-Ling's father and Lucy her mother, which meant Mike and Meryl, would team up. Mike joked, "I'm doing better on this mission with girls than I do in real life."

Then we hit gold. Angus came back from the other side of town saying there was a crowd and somebody who looked as if he was healing people.

We pulled the others together and I kind of wished that Mike were not so tall. He might attract the guards' attention. Thankfully, the guards were looking bored and sleepy. If they had just looked bored, we might have had a problem. The discipline of the Roman Army broke down in the east, and when they were bored they entertained themselves at the expense of others. Additionally, they were always looking for gladiators. Mike's height might make him a likely candidate.

The sun began to darken slightly as we found our way to the crowd. Many of those gathered looked sick. Even more looked joyful – as if they had been sick but were now healed. Discarded crutches and the cloth bindings of bandages were strewn about everywhere. Cries echoed from one man who held his hands up to the sky and shouted in Aramaic, "I can see! I can see! Thank You, Lord!" Others tested healed limbs. Outer garments that had once hid leprosy had been ripped off joyfully and abandoned. Many people walked around in clothes that still held the detritus and stains of wounds while the flesh beneath glowed in healthy olive and brown.

One couple examined their fingers, counting them in disbelief. A man felt his nose as if he could not believe it was there. Tears streamed down his face. We worked our way through the crowd. Suddenly, Mi-Ling gave a little gasp and fell to the ground. She lay motionless. I picked her up and panicked. "Please, God not now, not so close," I cried. I was unashamed of the tears nearly blinding me as I pushed my way through the crowd, followed by the others. What to do? I went up to a big bearded guy in the center of the group, screaming, "Jesus, Jeshua! Help me. I beg you! My daughter, help her! Help my Mi-Ling."

God we are so, so close, I thought. *Please don't turn us away! Please help!*

Mi-Ling moaned and stirred in my arms. She looked around as if she had just roused from a deep sleep. She looked up at the big, bearded man in front of us, regarding him curiously. Then she spotted the slightly smaller man behind him and stretched out her hands toward Him and cried, "Jesus, Jesus!"

"Papa," she told me impatiently. "This isn't Jesus. Jesus is behind him. Look! Right over there!"

I thought, *-she's fevered how could she know?* But she had known. She was right. It could only be love that recognized the real Jesus. Then it struck me that it didn't matter what Jesus looked like physically, it was who He was that counted. He was shorter than me, perhaps five-ten or so. He was swarthy and bearded, so unlike all the pictures I had ever seen of Him – and yet so like all the pictures because of the love and compassion in his eyes and on his face.

There were so many people pushing desperately through the crowd to get to Jesus that our group kept getting pressed further away. Summoning up inner resources that would have done credit to a US Marine, I exploded with a cry. "Jesus, Jesus! Let it be You! Please help my daughter!" Tears swept down my face as if driven by gale force winds.

"Drew," Meryl said, attempting to pull me back. "That's not Jesus. It can't be."

Then I was in front of Him. I looked into the eyes of Jesus and I knew He knew everything about me. It was humbling and scary and I wanted to look away – but I couldn't.

Still snuggled in my arms, Mi-Ling smiled trustingly up at him. She was so pure in heart that she lacked the reserve I felt. "Hello, Jesus."

Jesus wore a beautiful smile as He looked down at Mi-Ling, but it was the love and acceptance in His eyes that stilled my heart. I stood amazed.

"Hello, Mi-Ling, you've come a long way to see Me." Wordlessly, He looked at me and held out His arms. I placed Mi-Ling into Jesus' arms. An old hymn my granny taught to me sprang into my mind: *Safe in the arms of Jesus, safe on His gentle breast, there by His love o'er shaded sweetly my soul shall rest.* Someone had taken a key and unlocked a closet in my heart.

Jesus held Mi-Ling in His arms and put His hand on her head as He looked up into the sky. Then He took her aside and spoke to her in Chinese. Dr. Lucy was flabbergasted. "But how?" she asked.

"Because He is God," Mike replied. I stared at Mike. He hadn't believed in Jesus. He hadn't expected to find Him. He had spent weeks warning us that we were in for disillusionment and disappointment; that we were wasting our time and would go home on empty.

Gone was her fatigue and frailty. Mi-Ling was fully animated as Jesus spoke to her. The long black hair bobbed up and down. Her face wore the loveliest smile I had ever seen, and yet, Mi-Ling had always had a beautiful smile. It was clear to us that Jesus was speaking words of encouragement to her.

Jesus then spoke to the big guy, who we now realized was Peter.

"He is telling Peter to give Mi-Ling some bread and fish," Lucy explained in a quiet and reverent voice that reflected her awe and wonder.

"Oh, Jesus,' Mi-Ling suddenly said in English, "my friend Connie. Please help her."

We had been so engaged watching Jesus and Mi-Ling that we had forgotten about Connie. She came forward now, walking slowly and unerringly toward Jesus as if she were mesmerized. The obscene strawberry-colored birth mark across her face almost glowed in the sunlight.

"Hello, Jesus." Connie said. She looked at the ground. Jesus reached out and gently removed the scarf that partly covered her face. "Jesus," she gasped. "It's horrible. It looks awful! Please don't laugh at me."

Jesus smiled tenderly at Connie and stroked the side of her face. Gently, he placed his hands on both sides of her face and spoke so softly to her that she was the only one who could hear His words. When Jesus removed his hands, the birthmark was gone. We were all amazed, - except Mi-Ling. I gasped in disbelief.

"Go look into the water at the lakeside," Jesus told Connie.

"But the red marks on my face?" Connie asked shyly.

Jesus smiled at her, a smile that made me think for a moment that I had just walked into the sun without getting burned. "Go. Look and believe what you see," Jesus told her.

Obediently, Connie walked to the water at the edge of the lake and edged forward until she could see her reflection. Her face became an encyclopedia of emotions. The face looking back at her was that of a pretty young woman with wide blinking eyes and no disfiguring birthmark.

"Oh, Jesus, thank you, thank you!" she ran and fell at His feet. Jesus reached down, took her hand in His and lifted her up. "Thank you, Connie. Not only did you know I could heal you, but you trusted that I would heal you. When you get home, Connie, tell them about Me and how the Lord has had mercy on you." Jesus smiled at her and the smile seemed as endless as a sunny summer sky. I felt warmed inside just watching.

Jesus walked over to Sebastian. "Well done, son. I'm proud of you. You've done well with your life. Now, go and preach My word."

Sebastian's face wore the thrill and reverence of a man who had been given something much more precious than gold. He who had been a slave had become an ambassador, with just a few words from Jesus.

Mike stood like a man pole-axed. He had seen with his own eyes, but it was still so hard for him to believe. Jesus put a hand on his shoulder. "What happened to your sister all these years ago was not your fault. She was called home and you could not have stopped it." Then He stared at Mike more intently. "Greater love has no man than this, in that a man lay down his life for his friends."

Tears ran freely down Mike's face. "Lord," he whispered. "I didn't believe. I called you a con-man. I'm so sorry."

Jesus clasped him more tightly on the shoulders and laughed. "Not to worry, son, the Pharisees call me worse things than that."

"Andrew," Jesus said to me, pointing to one of his disciples. "That's your name sake over there. Your family is not yet complete. You saved Mi-Ling. Well done. But there is another who will need your help. And when that happens, remember that whatsoever you do for one of these little ones, you do for Me. I will guide you in what you should do and what roads you will need to take.

Meanwhile…" He pointed to a hill behind Him and indicated I should climb it. Then He spoke to Angus I could not hear what He said to him.

My soul seemed to flow out in obedience to His will and I felt almost vaporized, as if I were pouring up over the hill instead of climbing it. Light fell and covered me as I climbed. The figure that walked toward me was unmistakable. Lucy came into focus.

"Darling," she said with love in her voice. "You must stop worrying and missing me and find the path back to joy for yourself and Mi-Ling. Heaven is awesome and marvelous and wonderful and Jesus, oh Jesus! You saw Him here, but now you need to see Him as King of kings and LORD of Lords. I'm so happy! Darling, I want you to be happy too. Go live your life. You'll not need to look far for perfect happiness, I promise. You'll see her before she sees you. You're a wonderful man, Drew. You deserve happiness. I love you. The next time we meet, you'll be coming to where I am. Now…I love you. Go be blessed and happy."

"Lucy, I love you! Stay with me!" I stretched out my arm and our fingers touched. Then light blazed down again and like the print on a window of condensation, Lucy was gone. I felt as if I should be hollowed out and devastated by the empty hill. Yet, I realized instantly that Lucy had not given me a goodbye. She had gifted me with a promise of meeting again.

My body seemed to melt off the hill and run down to join the others. The encounter with Jesus Christ had changed all of us. For a moment, we gazed at one another in a hushed awe and gladness that no one wanted to molest with sound. Then I managed speech again and said, "Mike, Angus, Sebastian – we split up. Angus, you and Sebastian take Dr. Lucy and the children back to the time car now that Mi-Ling is healed. Mike, Meryl and I will cover you. If anything goes wrong, get the children home. Sebastian, if anything happens to Angus, get everyone home." He nodded.

"I'm not leaving you and the others behind," Angus said.

"Lieutenant, I gave you an order and I expect you to carry it out."

Angus looked at me with a mixture of emotions that included anger and surprise, then replied, "Yes, sir. I understand." They pressed on and we followed, keeping them in sight.

Out of nowhere, soldiers arrived on the scene; a Decurion with three lancers and a horse archer and three spearmen. I warned Meryl to pull the hood on her cloak over her face. We had to avoid them noticing the others who were well on their way to the time car.

The soldiers surrounded us and the Decurion dismounted from his horse. He walked round us and said something. Mike interrupted. "He wants to know where we live."

I pointed to further down the coast. Something else was asked. I could feel the perspiration running down my back – not all of it due to heat.

"He wants to know what we are doing here," Mike said.

"Tell him we came to see the miracle worker Joshua, from Nazareth."

The Decurion added a word and Mike translated it as 'the troublemaker.' Then he noticed Meryl, who despite her cloak lacked our bulk. It was obvious she was female. He drew His sword and lifted the edge of her robe, exposing her smooth legs. Meryl didn't flinch. He leered, an expression that twisted into my gut. Being a man, I knew what he was thinking. He took the sword point and pushed Meryl's hood back. I noticed out the corner of my eye that the horse archer had seen Dr. Lucy and the others and went charging off after them.

I shifted the bowie knife to where I could draw it.

Meryl's black hair and blue eyes looked back at the Decurion and he licked his lips greedily. He said something to one of the lancers who dismounted. The two of them laughed.

A saddle blanket was brought and Mike translated. "We can go but the girl stays so she can enjoy some real men. We can come - back for her in three hours—before dark."

The Decurion pushed Mike out of the way, and laughing, grabbed for Meryl. His face still had a smile on it when Mike's Kendo katana came whistling out its case. The Decurion was dead on his feet –the lancer followed suit and I got one of the spearmen with the knife. Meryl grabbed the Decurion's sword and killed the other spearman. The three remaining lancers couldn't use their weapons. I got one and Mike got the other. The horse archers' horse, minus the horse archer, galloped up with Angus on its back. An arrow took out the remaining spearman. There was a cheer from people, who then started to make themselves scarce. That meant more soldiers were coming.

"Angus, get Meryl back to the time car now," I ordered.

Meryl tried to protest. "Do as you are told," I barked at her. "How can I marry you if you are dead? Move! " She realized it wasn't the time or place to have a domestic argument,- so she left quickly with Angus.

"Come on Mike," I said. "Double time."

"It looks as if we are going to get away with it." Mike marveled. But just after he spoke, the other lancers showed up.

"If they surround us, sir, neither of us will get away."

"Right, Lieutenant. I'll stay here. You get the others to safety."

He glanced at me and drew the katana. "With all due respect, sir, I'm staying. You go. I'm not going to be responsible for breaking Meryl's heart." He tried a shaky laugh. "Besides, - I've always wanted to disobey a direct order from a superior officer. Now, get lost, sir."

I looked at him in disbelief. *Greater love has no man than this in that a man lay down his life for his friend,* Jesus had said. I saluted Mike. Just as I was leaving, I heard Mike say, "Into your hands, Jesus, I commend my spirit."

If our attackers had been archers and not lancers, neither of us would have survived. Mike had his back to a rock, but seconds after I left, he was surrounded. Four of the lancers fell. I managed to get back to the others.

One of the lancers had ditched his lance for Mike's sword and had pushed ahead of the others. Another lancer was close behind him. The lead horseman was waving Mike's sword and yelling while swinging it round his head. Then one of those irresponsible moments hit me. Had I been a proper officer, I would have got my troops out before the others reached us. But I didn't want that creep to have a trophy of such a brave man's sword. Angus thought the same thing. He shot the lancer coming behind, as he presented the most danger. The lancer with Mike's sword was not a swordsman. He came up and took a swipe at me, missed, and exposed his back. I rammed my Bowie knife into his leg and he screamed with pain, dropping the sword. I picked it up and ran for the time car. Angus had put another arrow to the bow, but the lancer was preoccupied with his wound. Angus and I dashed inside, slammed the door, and threw the switch – just as the sound of a shattering lance crashed against the outside of the time car.

Angus said, "Sir, - that was the stupidest thing I have ever seen, but my Lord, it was magnificent. Remember, Major, you now have a healthy daughter who loves you."

I nodded. "And one without whose quick thinking and action, I would be a pile of coral-encrusted bones in Davy Jones locker."

After Angus and I had exchanged those few words, a hush fell over the time car. Mike's sacrifice awed and saddened all of us. Meryl was especially silent. She finally mused quietly, "Mike did that for me, - but why?"

"He wouldn't go when I ordered him to." I sighed. "He said I was an engaged man and he didn't want to make you unhappy."

Meryl shook her head. "I'm not worth it."

"Don't say that. Mike thought you were. He wouldn't let you get raped even if it meant sacrificing his own life. He was a brave and courageous and loving man and his love for you was deeper than you realized, than anyone realized."

Amazingly, we arrived safely back in 1868.

"That," said Angus "must be the shortest mission on record. A few more like that and I am going for something safe like bungee jumping."

CHAPTER 4

Scotland 1868 & Modern Day

When we arrived back, we let Dr. Lucy, Mi-Ling, Connie and Sebastian off in 1868. I felt I had to go with Meryl and Angus to debrief with Colonel Carlisle. Mike had been our first death in the line of duty.

First we changed clothes so we didn't look like extras from the *BEN-HUR* film set. Colonel Carlisle was grim-faced. He felt Mikes' loss deeply, but realized it had been a long trip into a difficult area and dangerous time.

I explained, "Mike was goaded into action, sir. They were going to rape Meryl and he was having none of that. He acted to preserve the life of a comrade. The Romans were going to take Meryl and didn't expect any resistance. We nearly got away with it."

"You actually saw Mike killed?" the colonel quizzed.

"No, sir," I replied. "I saw him surrounded by enemies and saw one of the lancers in possession of his katana. I assumed he would not have handed it over willingly."

"Suppose he's still alive?" the colonel asked.

"It doesn't seem likely, sir," Angus said. "If they had taken him as a prisoner, wouldn't they have killed him?"

The colonel shook his head. "Suddenly you have a prisoner who's big, strong, and one heck of a fighter. You're a Roman. What do you do?"

Then the penny dropped. The word *gladiator* sprang to mind and I said it out loud. The colonel nodded.

"The poor guy… you never know what they would put him up against!"

Angus exclaimed, "If he's still alive?"

"Suppose it was either of you?" the colonel asked. "What do you think he would do?"

It didn't take much thought. "He would come and get us, sir." Meryl said.

The colonel paced around the room. "I'm going to consult the boffins to see where they would be liable to take him as a gladiator. We go there, and if he's there, get him out. If he isn't, then get yourselves out. If I can, I'm going to get you some help from the American special services; friends of Colonel Butler, Angus." There was obviously something to which I was not party.

"Hmm," Angus reflected. "He hasn't spoken to me since I gave him a hot dog from a tin. I didn't know that Americans detest canned hot dogs. Still, his boys are the best."

"Right," said Colonel Carlisle. "Give me twenty-four hours to get the wheels in motion. Oh, one more thing. While you were in the Holy Land, PATCH tried to stop the assassination of Lenin in 1924. They jogged the shooter's arm. As a result, he was wounded, but not killed. If he had been killed, it would have brought Trotsky to the fore and that would have been worse. Poor, Russia, it has to bleed before it can begin to heal." He paused. "Right, everyone. Reconvene here same time tomorrow."

We got out of his office. Angus wanted to see Abigail, and made his excuses. I didn't blame him.

Meryl and I walked down the corridor from the colonel's office. As she walked beside me, I realized my love for her, had come back to the surface. The impetus had likely been the sight of that lanky, leering, lancer and Decurion licking their lips.

"C'mon," I said to her, "let's go get a coffee at *SavaJava*. Wash the sand out of our throats." She nodded and walked beside me. We went about three steps and I reached down and took her hand. She gave me a smile and then a hug and the scent of coconut trembled up from her hair.

When we had slipped inside the car, she admitted, "I was so scared when that creep started to paw me. Scared that you and Mike would be goaded into action and you would be killed or Mike injured on account of me." She started to cry quietly.

I couldn't think of what to say. "Meryl, you are both brave and beautiful."

The blue eyes looked at me. "If I am beautiful, it's been a curse." She sighed.

I pulled the car off the road. "Why is it," I asked, "that when you're not there, everything is so empty? It's like going through the actions of life, autonomic living. When you're there, everything changes. You're my best friend. We've been through so much. I need your help again. Come to the jewelers with me and help me choose a present for my mother's birthday."

I had caught her off guard. She stopped crying. Wiping away a scattering of tears, she asked, "What do you think she would like?"

"I leave that to your feminine intuition. Then coffee, I promise."

Her nose crinkled as she smiled and blue eyes washed by tears were happy again. Inside, I was hoping that when we got to the jewelers I could make those eyes even happier.

Parking in Aberdeen was tricky, but I found a small car park near the jeweler's on Queen Street. We walked arm in arm. It felt right and good. I remembered Jesus' eyes as he looked at us. What threw me was what Lucy had said about me seeing the woman in my future before she saw me. *Lucy must have been talking in some spiritual sense beyond my male understanding*, I thought, never dreaming how wrong I was.

The jeweler was not busy. Meryl began looking around. I went over to the engagement rings, while Meryl's back was turned, putting my finger to my lips. The girl behind the counter understood. Meryl threw out comments as I studied a blue sapphire ring with a Celtic engraved gold band. I wandered round the shop and asked Meryl as innocently as possible, "Suppose some guy wanted to marry you. What kind of an engagement ring would you want him to get you?"

She pointed to a couple of rings, and then I pointed to the blue sapphire. Her eyes widened, "Oh...it's gorgeous." The girl behind the counter winked at me.

"What gets me," I said, "is how you tell what size is the right size?"

"You get to know," Meryl said. "I'm a size G."

When the girl behind the counter heard the ring size she discreetly retrieved one the right size.

"Right," I said to the assistant in my official voice. "Can we try that blue sapphire ring, please? Size G."

The assistant smiled. "It so happens we have one that size."

Meryl's face wore the twin expressions of surprise and thrill, as if she were standing at the till in a restaurant and had just been told by the cashier that someone else had paid the bill.

Falling to my knees, I held the ring and took Meryl's right hand, then realizing my mistake, dropped it and took her left hand. "Darling, I love you for keeps. Please say you will marry me. Spend the rest of our lives together. This time, I want to do things in the right order." The shop was so silent that I could hear my heart beating in my ears. We held center stage with the clerk, two other assistants, and a customer all watching us.

The West Indian assistant smiled broadly and said. "Hey girl, what you waitin' for?"

"You really mean it?" Meryl asked in wonderment.

"Yes, my sapphire-eyed darling. I really mean it. Please marry me."

Coming alive, she threw her arms round my neck, nearly knocking me over. "Yes! Yes, a thousand times, yes!"

The rest of the folk in the shop let out a cheer and I paid for the ring. We could return later to get my ring.

The friendly clerk observed, "Pardon me for saying so, but girl! You be glowin' like a Christmas tree."

I grinned at Meryl and kissed her. "Sure 'nuff, sure 'nuff." I agreed.

Meryl walked to the front door. Light bounced off the sapphire.

The clerk clapped her hands in glee. "Sir, it's not the ring she thinkin' about. It's the guy who has given it to her. I hope you both will be very happy! God bless you both."

"He already has," I assured her. "He surely has."

We left the jewelers and I could have sworn that we floated to *SavaJava* for our coffee celebration. It made me think of Sebastian and how Meryl had taught him to appreciate not only his freedom, but the added bonus of enjoying a good cup of coffee.

"Mmmm!" Meryl purred, "Can't you smell that coffee?" We went inside and the barista obviously recognized Meryl. "How's the girl who met Robert E. Lee?" he asked sarcastically.

"Hey, friend, she really has met the Confederate Commander and Chief, and so have I. He's a really nice guy."

The barista changed his *you can't be serious, man, expression* to an expression of *what can I get you?*

I ordered our coffee and was about to order Meryl's chocolate brownie when she looked at the barista and remarked to me, "Oh, darling, for a change I would really like one of those butternut-colored doughnuts." She smiled impishly.

The barista smiled and nodded. While he was filling our order, Meryl filled me in on the joke and explained how she had met the barista while I was recovering from the wound Bryant had given me and had told him about our quest to keep Robert E. Lee from agreeing to engage British help for the South in the Civil War. The barista proved to have both a good memory and a good sense of humor. As we were leaving, he said, "Y'all have a real good day now." This proved the old adage that nothing is stranger than truth. He really had served two people in his shop that day who had met Robert E. Lee.

We stayed in modern times that night to celebrate our engagement. Over dinner, we discussed Mi-Ling. We needed to tell both Mi-Ling and Dr. Lucy about our marriage plans. After agreeing on that, we switched to the topic of the mission to rescue Mike.

"Meryl, this is a nasty mission. The special-forces boys won't mess around. If you got caught, we might not be able to help you."

She speared me with a look of frustration. "Would you be saying this to me if I were a man?"

"Ouch! That's unfair. I hope Sebastian goes with us. The main action will be in the dark or by torch light. I shudder to think what will happen to us. If you were to get caught...dear God, I feel sick thinking about what could happen. I've had to plan one funeral already and I don't want another one. We need you to help deal with PATCH and to try to stop Professor Reynolds. And don't forget—Bryant is still lurking in the background like some plague bacillus. There is plenty for you to do without getting into a firefight with a cohort of Roman spearmen."

She sighed, still a bit miffed. "You guys have all the fun."

"Did you play with dolls when you were a girl?" I asked her.

She looked thoughtful, "Yes, why do you ask?"

"Oh, nothing. I just had this picture of you dressing your dollies."

She smiled. "It was a problem whether to give them an AK47 or an Armalite rifle, and whether to give them a Colt 1911 automatic pistol or a Browning."

"That must have gone well at the Teddy Bears' picnic?"

"Oh, no!" she replied. "My dolls were GI Joes."

"You never told me that before!"

Smiling sweetly she replied, "You never asked, sir."

We chewed in companionable silence and then I asked, "If I tell Mi-Ling about us, will you come through and talk to her? Maybe a 'get to know you session'?" Meryl agreed.

It had been a long day – or days. One thing about time travel – slots of twenty-four hours seemed to have less significance. We agreed together that even though it would be difficult, we wanted to save any further lovemaking for marriage. Once we were married, we could make up time. Meryl said she would stay in modern times and sleep at headquarters.

Agreeing, I headed back for 1868. Only ten minutes had passed in their time since we let the others off before seeing Colonel Carlisle. Mi-Ling was overjoyed and praising Jesus. Mrs. Fraser had given Connie a really pretty dress and had done her hair. Connie looked in the mirror, but not out of conceit. She kept saying, "Thank You, Jesus! Thank You, Jesus! You're wonderful, Jesus!"

"Come on, princess," I said to Connie. "Let's go show your mum how wonderful Jesus is. We walked together – or at least, I walked. Connie cavorted around me like a young filly. A couple of folk passed us along the way. One boy turned around to stare at her and walked into a tree. We got to her door and knocked. Connie's mother opened the door.

"Connie? Connie? oh, dear God." Her mother was floored. She screamed, but it was a scream of joy. She gave her daughter a huge hug. Mother and daughter were lost in each other, so I slipped back outside. I could hear Connie mention Jesus repeatedly as she told her mom about the trip. After having seen Connie's face with the disfiguring birth mark, I thought it would be humorous to listen to someone attempt to explain it away by luck or chance.

Mi-Ling was playing a Happy Families card game with Sebastian. She was winning. When I came in Sebastian said, "Do y'all know how hard it is to get Mr. Bun the Baker? You can finish the game, Drew. Mrs. Fraser promised me a cup of tea and I'm still gettin' used to hot tea instead of iced tea."

Mi-Ling smiled at me. I guessed this was our time. Half of me wanted to ask her what Jesus had said to her. Instead, I held back, just loving and trusting my daughter. If Mi-Ling thought I should know, she would tell me.

"Papa?" she said.

"Yes, sweetheart?"

"Is Mr. Mike really dead? Maybe he is alive and bad people are hurting him"

"I'm going back with others to look for him in case he is alive," I told her.

"Maybe he is waiting for you to come back. Papa, it's terrible when you long for someone to come and help and nobody comes. Day after day you pray, and all you have is hope. And then you came for me, and now you are going to do the same for Mr. Mike. I'm glad, Papa. He has gentle, sad eyes. Mi-Ling prays for him that he will be safe and Jesus will keep him."

Somehow to know that Mi-Ling was praying seemed more important than anything else. I hugged her and told her that.

"Mi-Ling," I continued. "I have something else to talk to you about." She looked at me over her cards with that quizzical look that she had picked up from her Amma Lucy.

"I'm getting married again, Mi-Ling."

She nodded and asked, "Is Miss Meryl the lady?"

"Yes."

She sighed. "Mi-Ling was hoping it was Dr. Lucy."

I was astounded. Finally I managed to ask, "Is that because she's Chinese like you, or because her name is Lucy like our Amma?"

Mi-Ling put her cards down and walked over to the window. "I cannot ask Papa to come and live in my dream. One day, Papa, Mi-Ling may come to you and say that she wants to marry."

"Mi-Ling, you marry only for one reason; love. You marry because you love that person and want to spend the rest of your life with them. In fact Mi-Ling love is finding the person you cannot live without."

She nodded and the black pony tail bobbed up and down. "With love, Papa, it will not matter even if the boy is not Chinese like me. His name also will not matter. Maybe he will be like Angus, or Mike, or like Sebastian -the color of black. Maybe he cannot hear or see, will that matter?"

"It will be your heart and your choice, Mi-Ling, not mine. It will be because he loves you, and I hope he and I will be good friends, too."

She smiled and said, "That is what Mi-Ling hopes, too, Papa."

"And I hope, Mi-Ling, that you and Miss Meryl can become friends. Miss Meryl is afraid. She doesn't know anything about being a mother."

"Mi-Ling not know what it means to be a daughter. Maybe we can both be teachers to each other. Mi-Ling wants Papa to be happy."

I don't know how much it cost her to say that. I didn't want her to like Meryl just for my sake. Then I reminded myself that love can't be rushed.

After our usual routine of me reading to Mi-Ling, followed by hugs and kisses, Mi-Ling skipped off towards bed. I decided that bed was a good idea, but found there was a telegram waiting for me. Bryant's ship was still at Crawton, but there was a great deal of activity. I supposed that the SEALS would try to get the information we needed. When and where would be on a *need to know basis,* and I didn't need to know – at least, not yet.

I had been trying not to think about the logistics of rescuing Mike. Having the idea was one thing; putting it into practice was something else. There would be a lot of consultation and hammering out plans. It was a little unsettling that the details for the rescue from the Holy Land were being worked out by folks in Scotland – and those two thousand years later.

Dr. Lucy would hear about my engagement to Meryl from Mi-Ling soon. I wondered how she would take it, especially since it meant that Mi-Ling wouldn't have at least one Chinese parent. I would cross that bridge when I came to it. Hopefully it would prove to be a bridge to nowhere.

The following day, I checked to make sure the SAS guys were still guarding the house. Then Sebastian and I headed for HQ. We didn't have a sense of foreboding, but neither were we stupid enough to think that this mission was anything else but very dangerous. Death often comes first to those who deny its possibility.

Angus was already there. Colonel Carlisle welcomed us and introduced us to the two SEALS. "Chaps, this is Lt. Stanislaus Kowalski, and Sergeant Dick Hanover. They are both SEALS and both speak Latin. Sgt. Hanover also speaks Greek."

A voice echoed from the shadows in Colonel Carlisle's office. The colonel introduced him as Professor Theopolis Dromon. He was one of the world's foremost Roman historians. His books had had the ring of eye witness about them. "Gentlemen," he said, "I would advise you to lay aside any preconceived ideas while attempting this rescue mission. Life as a gladiator was vicious, cruel and nasty. Unless you were very, very good – it was also short. It was kill or be killed - forget Hollywood. When someone is hit by a gladius - the Roman short sword - it is literally bloody and awful. Mike Argo, if he has been in combat already, has had to have fought like an animal."

Professor Dromon produced a gladius. "This is the best replica we have. It's about twenty-four to thirty inches long, including handle. This is not a slashing sword. It's for stabbing - thrusting into your opponent's guts as he attempts to thrust his into yours. This sword in the hands of trained legionaries conquered half the world. The chances are that Mike would be fighting a *retarius,* a guy with a net and three-pronged trident.

He produced another vicious-looking weapon. "This is the other sword you may meet, if you're foolish enough to go. It was particularly used by cavalry. The Spatha is about forty inches long. It's designed for cutting down from horseback. In later centuries, it was used by both cavalry and infantry."

Professor Dromon's words failed to frighten or dissuade our team. Rather, they emphasized the point that Mike needed to be extracted from there as quickly as possible, but first we had to figure out where "there" was.

"Gentlemen, if you would care to follow me?" Professor Dromon took us to another room. We crowded inside and stared at a model of a Roman amphitheatre and a spread of photos.

"This is where we think Mike would have been taken," Dromon explained. "*Beit She'an*, or to the Romans, *Scythopolis.*The name means *House of Tranquility.* It was a biggish town, but the Romans, being of tidy minds, kept their entertainment centers away from their residential areas. They didn't want the noise of the '*vox populi*' upsetting the neighbors. The Amphitheatre and arena are to the south of town. The Latin for sand is *harena.* Drop the 'h' and you have arena, a place of entertainment; entertainment, unless you are the poor blighters fighting for their lives on the *harena.*

"If you arrive late at night, the only citizens you are liable to bump into are those returning from an orgy, or late night drinking party. Soldiers on patrol might be a different matter. You will have to get into the gladiator quarters and find Mike. Remember, some of the gladiators want to be there. Others are slaves or prisoners – they don't want to be there. If they wanted Mike to fight, he would be locked up, but reasonably well fed. Remember, - putting on a good show is the important thing. One thing you may not know is that some of the gladiators are female. If you're familiar with the word *Amazon*, you know what you might be up against."

There was a wry smile from the SEALS.

"Gentlemen, make no mistake," Professor Dromon warned sternly, "you may think of them as members of the fair sex, but they are gladiators first. They will kill you as quick as look at you. They make their living by surviving. Don't forget that."

Lt. Kowalski picked up the gladius and swung it a couple of times. "Should be easy enough," he stated

Professor Dromon picked up another gladius and said to Lt. Kowalski, "Come on! Come for me with the gladius you're holding."

"I don't want to hurt you, sir."

"Come on Lieutenant! Take a swing - unless you're afraid I'll hurt you."

I thought, *that is not a thing you say to a SEAL.* Angus looked interested. "Come on, Lieutenant," the professor insisted. "I'm a gladiator. Now go for me."

So he did. He took a mighty swing. Had it contacted, head and professor would have parted company. The professor side stepped, blocked the lieutenant's arm, and the professor's sword was at the lieutenant's throat.

"It's a sword for thrusting, Lieutenant," Dromon explained, "not for slashing. If you do, you open yourself to attack and some of the soldiers and gladiators who have managed to stay alive won't stop as I did. Lieutenant, you could kill me in about twenty different ways, but for this exercise, this is the one that matters."

One thing about SEALS, they learn quickly.

Angus whispered to me, "FATAL: Fast Attack Target Always Low, remember?"

The professor continued. "We think the prisoners may be in a building to the south of the arena so they could walk into it with the maximum of crowd appeal. It's near there we hope the time car will stop. That part I leave to your experts." He looked toward Colonel Carlisle.

"Another thing," Dromon warned. "We can't allow you firearms. If you shoot someone back then and leave a hole in their skull, it fuels the flame of those who think aliens landed a long time ago, knocked off a few of the locals for reasons best known to themselves and left. Wounds from sword, axe, or ballista leave distinctive marks. Only kill if you have to. One thing with this time travelling business, and going as far back as Roman or Greek times, if you accidentally kill someone,-when you get back, you could find the US president is different."

"Republican or Democrat, sir?" Kowalski joked.

Dromon smiled. "Oh, much better than that; it could still be the British in charge." We laughed. Then the professor turned serious again. "If killing is necessary to save your lives, then it's necessary, but one of these days, the death of someone in the past may cause an effect we don't like in the present."

There were no questions after the professor finished his briefing. Our distance weapons were to be cross bows, but we had to keep in mind that the overriding priority was to get Mike out and home. What we did not know then was that danger wouldn't be the only complication to deal with.

We had coffee with the SEALS afterwards. They had been around and been in many difficult situations, including tribal disputes in Afghanistan. I gave up trying to follow the various political allegiances as they outlined what it was like to fight in Afghanistan. Yet, our upcoming rescue mission would prove totally different. Hopefully we wouldn't be there long enough to get a suntan. It focused the mind to have a fiancée. I wanted to get back to her, and to Mi-Ling. Rescuing Mike would relieve Meryl, since she blamed herself for his capture.

At least when we were shadowing Bryant back from China, or when Bryant was attempting to stop us, there were times of peace. The prospect for this rescue mission lacked any promise of peace. Yet, I also realized that if I were completely truthful, I enjoyed the challenge. Before, I could not understand why in war time guys actually volunteered for hazardous missions. Now I was starting to understand. I hoped I was not becoming an 'adrenalin junkie.' Folk of that ilk usually died young and unexpectedly.

I needed to talk to Angus. I trusted him and his judgment.

"What do you think our chances are?" I asked

"Depends on how many guards there are and what their procedure is for raising the alarm," he replied.

"What if Mike is not the only slave, or unwilling gladiator?" I asked.

He looked at me and sighed. "We're going in to get Mike. We can't rescue the whole lot, and get clean out the arena. We wouldn't have room in the time car, first of all, and we can only afford one trip — to try it once and either succeed or fail."

"Yes," I persisted, "But how can we leave any others we come across to certain death or a life of slavery? Do we lock them back up again? I can't do that, at least getting away from the arena increases their chances of survival. And what happens if we have to split up into two parties?"

"Major," Angus said, "It's really important that we stick together. We'll need to back one another up – keep each other in sight."

"What about stun grenades?" I suggested. "There should be little trace of these after 2000 years."

He nodded his agreement. "That's a good idea."

So that was us, apart from some decent cloaks and the equipment we needed and a good sword and buckler.

I went to look for Meryl. She was in the canteen doing paperwork, eating a snowball and trying to look as if she were enjoying the coffee. She tasted it and her nose wrinkled.

I laughed at her and gave her a brief hug. "When we get married and I get my bonus," I promised, "I will buy you your own coffee plantation in Ecuador. You can sit on the verandah of our home and drink strong dark coffee to your heart's content. Who knows? You might end up importing it to *SavaJava*."

She smiled and said, "Darling, all I want is for you to come back to me. Please come back. Don't be a hero. If anything happens to you, I won't even get a folded flag from your coffin."

I put my arm around her and kissed her. "I think we have been here before."

She fastened wide puppy dog eyes on me. "Before, we were not engaged. Every time I say *I love you,* you keep disappearing. I don't want your body lying in some God-forsaken place and me not even being there for you."

I held her close and muzzled her blonde hair. "Darling, this is a quick rescue mission. I'll be back before you know it. Everything will be fine."

She pulled away and retorted, "You are talking to someone who was lost in Virginia with you in 1750 something, remember?"

I sighed. "It's a risk we both take." Then I added a promise that I was later to regret, "Next mission we get to go together, no matter what."

"Drew, I'm warning you. Any problems and I am coming after you. You don't get away from me that easily."

I kissed Meryl goodbye and headed back to 1868. I wanted to see Mi-Ling before I left in case something happened and I didn't make it back. I had telegrammed Caroline and Myles, asking them if they could give Mi-Ling a home if anything happened to me. They answered immediately, telling me not to worry; they loved Mi-Ling. Taking care of her would be a joy.

I went to Mi-Ling and explained to her that I was going on a mission to rescue Mr. Mike.

She wasn't at all worried because she believed Jesus would take care of us. I told her that I loved her and gave her a big hug. She stopped my hug halfway and pushed me away gently. Surprised, I looked at her. She smiled. "Mi-Ling will give Papa the other half of the hug when he get back. Then it will be a hug of joy and not a hug of goodbye." When I tried to explain about Carolyn, she dismissed my words. "Mi-Ling not need to stay with Carol Lady, Papa. Jesus will take care of you. He will bring you back. And how can Mi-Ling teach Miss Meryl to be Mi-Ling's mother if Papa not come back to marry her?"

There comes a stage in every mission where you have gathered all the intelligence you can. You have gone over possible scenarios. You have contingency plans. Everybody knows what they are going to do or should do. Yet you cannot cover everything. All it takes is equipment failure or human failure from the other side - like a sentry who is after a promotion, and thus is extra alert; or an officer starting his patrol early, when you did not expect him for another ten minutes, - Of course, I thought, the time car could break down like it did when it deposited us in the middle of the Seven Years War in 1755.

On the other hand, things could go like clockwork – like they do in the movies. But this wasn't a movie; it was real life, which is much more difficult, and prone to having things go wrong. Butterflies were starting to take up residence in my stomach, only their wings were beating so hard that they felt more the size of bats. Then I realized that Jesus is Lord of all time and I could count on His help. I was reminded of an old World War II song in the music halls, "*Praise the Lord and pass the ammunition…*"

We decided that, as there were five of us, we would have two teams of two. Angus and I would work together and the two SEALS would work together. Sebastian would be a floater. If either group got into trouble, he would assist. If both were attacked, it would be the job of the pair who could get out of trouble first to get back to the time car and escape.

Time was of the essence. If there were a line of cells, how did we find which one Mike was in? And if the turnkey was not handily dead, he might not want to hand over the keys. Once we found which cell Mike was in, we had small explosive charges to blow the hinges of the door. In 2000 years, the damage to the door would be covered over. An archaeologist would not be thinking of explosives while looking at the remains of a door and how it was opened – truth is always stranger than fiction, if somewhat more dangerous.

Sebastian joked with me, "If you want someone to sneak up in the shadows – I'm your man." I tried to share the joke, but I really wasn't in the mood for light humor. Too much could go wrong too quickly.

The rest of the time before departure was spent studying the model and memorizing the archaeological photographs of Beit She 'an, as well as the projected reconstructions of what the buildings might look like. Sebastian proved to have a photographic memory. He could remember details and plans, figures, and the position of things. This would be invaluable. Once you have found your destination in the dark, you still have to find your way back to where you have come from. Our lives depended on each other. A turn to the left instead of the right could change everything. We had done everything we humanly could, so I handed it over to the Lord. He could do what we couldn't. He could work the miracle we would need to survive.

We got our kit into the car, left our families letters (just in case), and looked at one another, making an attempt to appear confident – and brave in front of the others. "Okay," Stan Kowalski asserted, "we can do this."

I threw the switch. I was glad I had gone to the toilet before we left – how unheroic you may think, they don't do that in the movies – but this was for real. It was no stage set.

CHAPTER 5

Beit She'an or Scythiopolis – Roman occupied Galilee AD 32 about 6th April 2 a.m.

When the time car came to a standstill, we waited. There did not appear to be a lot of noise; no shouting and nobody trying to knock six bells out of the side of the car. We hoped we were unseen. We closed our eyes to adjust to the dark or half-light that we would meet when we went outside.

The scents hit us first; garlic, fish and incense. From Professor Dromon's briefings, we realized the incense was there to hide the odors of the facets of life then best not enquired into. Right, we had to move fast like Ninja.

The place was lit by torches. The torches threw shadows. Sometimes you imagined someone was there, and then realized it was only a shadow. The torches were strategically placed. Fire was an ever-present danger; some drunken louts doing the Roman equivalent of *goofing about* could burn the town down.

"Along here," Sebastian directed, "I remember the pictures." We hoped we had come to the south side of the amphitheatre. Then we heard the tramping of boots. Roman Legionaries and Auxiliaries wore metal-studded, thick leather sandals called *calligae*. The studs were intended to give grip in battle, no matter the ground. They were not made for silence, but grip. We faded into the shadows with Sebastian closest to the light. The approaching men were obviously on their way to somewhere, and I wondered if part of their remit was fire watching. Next, we came upon a drunk relieving himself.

"Somos vigiles," Kowalski said, and the guy looked afraid. As the conversation continued, Sgt. Hanover translated. "He said we were police watching out for Parthian spies. If he said anything it would have serious repercussions for certain parts of his anatomy." The guy replied he would go. He didn't want to get his throat cut by Parthian spies.

Kowalski added that the spies were last seen round the gladiator arena and pointed in one direction. The man pointed in a slightly different direction, telling the frightened man that if he had not known the right direction for the arena, he might have been suspected as a spy instead of a loyal citizen. The man shot off, gratefully, checking how much was left in his flask.

We had mistaken the theatre for the amphitheatre. Now we were at least headed for the right place. We kept close to the wall. I said to Sebastian, "For crying out loud, Seb, remember these roads and how to get back to where the time car came in."

He smiled and responded cheerfully tapping his head, "Once heard or seen… always remembered. Ma's name was Betsy Anne. My Pa was Gabriel." We hurried forward a few steps. Sebastian stopped suddenly. "My Ma's name was Annabel. It was my aunty that was Betsy Anne. I remember so well that I even remember what I forgot! Ain't that good? " Only Sebastian could have made that sound normal.

Angus and I went along one side of the wall, and the SEALS, Stan and Dick, went on the other. Sebastian went ahead, peered around a corner and came back to us.

"Major there's two guys guarding the gate. We gotta get up and over the wall. When I was a slave we used to go into the master's fruit orchard and relocate some of the peaches. Them was good peaches and, considering the work we did, we counted it as wages. One thing, you'd better not get caught – them was not happy getting their fruit relocated, no sir."

We could get over the wall and not be seen. We were hoping there was not a lot of light at the other side of the wall. In getting over the wall, the SEALS were good. We went over one at a time, so if there was anything unpleasant at the other side of the wall the others got a warning.

We all got over and I was happy to be in the shadows again. We started working our way round the inside of the walls to where Professor Dromon told us the more unwilling gladiators might be held. I had Mike's katana. I thought he might like it back and it would be good for him to have if we had to fight our way back – providing he was in good enough condition to fight. My earlier fear had evaporated. I thought that fear often took over after we were away from the hotspot and allowed ourselves to think of what might have happened.

Time was cracking on and we couldn't afford to get caught by the sudden appearance of dawn and people stirring for work, so we decided to cut across the sand diagonally.

We sprinted from one side to the other and came to the place where we thought the gladiators were held. There were two guys on guard, or they were supposed to be, but they were in a corner playing dice by torchlight. They were intent on their game. It must have been pay day. Stan and Dick decided to take the guards' cloaks – and their places. The guards were quickly rendered unconscious and hogtied out of sight. Stan and Dick replaced them and Sebastian and I got inside. The jailer at the door was totally surprised. He, too, went 'night night.' Now I had to put my plan into action.

I walked past the cell doors singing, *"The minstrel boy to war has gone ..."*

Sebastian said, "Don't go giving up your day job now."

We passed one cell door after another, metal monotony behind which lay someone whose only way out was killing. Complaints echoed from behind doors, the Latin, Gallic, or Parthian equivalent of, "Aw, pipe down! Some of us are trying to get some sleep."

My apprehension grew. Suppose Mike was dead or somewhere else? If he wasn't here....*Lord Jesus, You know we are on a mission of mercy to rescue a friend. Lord, if Mike is here, help us find him."*

The cells extended down another corridor. I kept singing. Sebastian joined in explaining, "A 9-1-1 duet."

"In the ranks of death you'll find him, his father's sword..." came a voice out of the darkness.

"Mike, keep singing," I shouted.

We ran down the corridor to where the singing seemed loudest. "Mike, stay back from the door," I ordered.

"Right," came the cheerful reply. Judging by his voice, Mike was fine and I felt so relieved that my legs started shaking. I set the charges on the hinges, which were fortunately wide. Five-four-three-two-one, *BANG*! They went off simultaneously and the door fell forward. I grabbed a torch from the wall and Sebastian and I ran into the cell. Mike was there, chained to the wall and could have benefited from a good shower. He had cuts all over his body that were starting to scab. We broke the chain.

"I knew you would come for me, guys! Thanks!"

There were two more men chained in the cell. Mike ran over and started undoing their chains. "These are the Sica brothers," he told us. "Without them, I would never have survived. They go free, as well. There is someone else we must rescue." Mike shot out the cell and ran two cells down. He said something in Greek, got the door open and went inside. He unfastened the chains of the figure. The figure was female, of that there was no mistake.

"Sir, Hera has saved my life twice in several fights. I told her my friends were coming back for me and promised her that she could come with us, and that she would no longer be a slave. She's a female gladiator and can use weapons, believe me."

Hera was a beautiful woman, well-built, tall, and extremely fit. She had beautiful slate grey eyes. Her black hair fell loose, rippling in the torch light like raven feathers.

Sebastian said, "Man, if I was him, I wouldn't leave her behind neither."

I felt trapped. There was no time to argue with Mike. "Come on," I urged everyone in our growing group.

Mike pointed to a door and said, "Bolt that. It leads to the guard house."

The Sicae brothers joined us and said that we needed to open the other doors.

"Mike, explain to the Sicae brothers that we need to get away first. Tell them to give us till the candle burns to there." I made a mark where I reckoned ten minutes would be. "Then, tell them to go for it. Warn them that if they get trapped here, the guards will crucify them. Tell them to get over the wall. There are two guards outside. If they can get past them and out into the countryside, they'll be safe. But tell them to remember that dawn will be breaking soon. They'll need to hurry."

Mike hurriedly repeated my words and the Sica brothers agreed. We took one of the soldier's cloaks outside and gave it to Hera. She was dressed for combat and not much else. She took one of the guard's swords and swung it and said a word in Greek.

"What did she say?" I asked James.

"Excrement, sir, I also did the colloquial Greek class."

The SEALS were professional. While appreciative of Hera's charms and beauty, they also recognized a professional when they saw one.

As for Mike, he was obviously in love and who could blame him? Hera walked beside Mike and watched his back. We scooted across the arena and scaled the wall. Then the racket started up behind us. We hoped that some of the slaves, at least, would escape. Hera spoke to Mike.

"She wants to know where we are going."

"Tell her Britannia."

Sebastian remembered in reverse the way we had come and the SEALS backed him up. Then we ran into the soldiers we had seen on the way out. There were ten of them and six of us.

When it came to hand-to-hand combat, Hera made the SEALS look clumsy. Mike held onto his katana like a long lost friend. We tried to merely wound the opponents, but Hera had not picked up that nicety. Five more soldiers appeared and Mike and Hera went back to back. The new 'squaddies' didn't stand a chance.

We fought our way to where the time car would come through. I pressed the button and it stuck. "Come on! Come on!" Angus yelled.

Thankful to have a small torch with me, I shone it on the clip holding the box that summoned the time car and managed to release it.

Shouting increased to a manic level, and arrows rained around us. The SEALS grabbed their crossbows. The rain of arrows quit as quickly as an interrupted summer thunderstorm and only one arrow flew towards us where there had been three before.

I sorted the clip, put the top back on, pressed the control box switch, and waited.

The SEALS threw a couple of thunder flashes into the soldiers rushing at us. The time portal opened and the car came out. We piled into the car, but not before an arrow caught Stan in the back. We closed the door, threw the switch and prayed that we'd get back to the time we'd left from.

Dick broke off the arrow shaft. "Come on, sir," he urged Stan, "Keep with us. We'll have you to the medics in a few minutes"

"Dick," Stan said weakly, "I'll never joke about Robin Hood again."

"The medics will sort you. You'll be good as new. Lieutenant, we couldn't have managed without you."

Stan tried to sit up straight and pretend he felt no pain. "Mike," he noted," that's one nice -looking broad. You can tell her from me."

"The Greek for *broad* escapes me at this point, Lieutenant," Mike replied.

I wondered how one could say to Hera in Greek, "Girl, you are in for one big surprise." Dr. Lucy was the only girl we knew who spoke Greek. Hera would need help, so hopefully Lucy could help her. How do you introduce a First Century female gladiator to 21st Century lingerie? Lucy was going to be busy! Hera would also need various vaccinations to protect her from 21st century diseases.

Thank the Lord, we got back safely, without breakdowns, and arrived at the right time in history. The medics met us and whisked Stan away with them. I took Mike and the others to the colonel's office, and then asked Sebastian to go through to 1868, and to bring back Lucy and Mi-Ling. "Ask Lucy to bring her Greek dictionary," I added. "She's going to need it."

Sebastian replied, "Major, I wish I had got myself educated. Then I could have spoken Koine. That's the Greek they spoke in them days. On the other hand, I reckon Mike might object and think I was sweet talking his girl. I wouldn't like to pick a fight with him the way he uses that blade."

Colonel Carlisle was waiting for us in his office. He was astounded by Hera's presence, but quickly hid his amazement. Angus and I saluted. Dick followed suit, as did a smiling Mike. Hera looked puzzled and said something to Mike. She smiled at the colonel.

"What did she say?" the colonel asked. Mike hesitated, then replied. "She asked, 'Is this Caesar?'"

I could have sworn the colonel blushed. "Anyway," Colonel Carlisle said, "Lt. Kowalski will be fine. The medics patched him up. It wasn't a deep arrow wound, but it will still take him a bit to recover."

Dick Hanover chipped in, "He always did have a thick hide, sir."

The colonel directed an enigmatic look in his direction. "Quite so, sergeant, quite so."

Colonel Carlisle's perspicacious character explained his rank. Totally unprepared for the rescued Hera, within minutes of our arrival, he understood where she fitted in. He addressed Mike. "Mike, I'm giving you a couple of weeks off. Well, really a change of assignment. You and Dr. Lucy Francis need to integrate Miss Hera into 21st Century society. She must understand there's no need to carry a sword or dagger with her and that not everybody is out to kill her. She also needs to understand that she's no longer a slave."

"Thank you, sir, I appreciate that."

Colonel Carlisle added, "I would like Professor Dromon to talk to her. I'm sure it will be an interesting experience for him. I would like a written report. You've all done extremely well. When Dr. Francis comes through, maybe she can introduce Miss Hera to the joys of a shower. Perhaps, too, we can get her to choose a second name that we could pronounce."

"If you would excuse me, colonel," I interrupted, "I should meet Dr. Francis before she meets Miss Hera and explain the situation to her."

The colonel gave his permission and I left the meeting. I took a quick shower and changed into modern day clothes. Coming down the corridor, I met a smiling Meryl. She ran to me, embraced me and gave me a kiss of relief. "How's Spartacus?" she asked. "I take it you were successful?"

I smiled back at the glad reflection in her blue eyes. "You won't believe this," I told her. "We brought somebody back."

She nodded her head and sighed. "What's new? I believe it. Who is it?"

I took her hand and we walked outside as I explained, "Mike's in love. The person we brought back is a fellow gladiator – a girl named Hera. Hera is one very fit and active girl who speaks Greek and can use a sword better than some men. Dr. Lucy's going to have to come through to help integrate her into 21ˢᵗ Century living. Mike will be working with Hera, too."

Meryl grinned mischievously. "It should be fun when Lucy starts telling Hera how to cope with her period in the 21ˢᵗ Century. I hope her Greek is that good?"

"Meryl, there's a lot more important issues than that," I replied, feeling that getting-out-of my-depth sensation.

"Not when you're unprepared and it happens," Meryl quipped. Then she added in a mysterious tone of voice, "Maybe Mike can show her what a shower is for."

"I thought a shower is for washing." I replied. "That's simple enough."

The mischievous smile spread and Meryl's eyes sparkled like blue diamond's catching sunlight. She pressed her body against mine. "Mmm…my, my, Major, aren't we going to have fun in the shower once we're married. I promise you, you'll never want a bath again."

I thought it was time to change the subject. It seemed to be getting very warm suddenly. Sometimes it was hard to know where Meryl's quirky sense of humor ended and seriousness started. I told her, "Mi-Ling and Dr. Lucy are on their way here now."

"You should warn Dr. Lucy and Mi-Ling about Hera." Meryl mused. "Will Mi-Ling be jealous of sharing Lucy with Hera?"

"Mi-Ling is, " I reminded Meryl. " one of the most loving, forgiving, accepting, non-judgmental people in the world. But what about scheduling some get-to-know-you times between you and Mi-Ling while she's here? Maybe Mi-Ling would like something out of *SavaJava?*"

Meryl agreed. "That's a good idea. And, as long as Mi-Ling is here, we won't need to worry about her being kidnapped from the 1868 Bellefield. That's a constant danger, even with SAS guarding the house." She brightened, "Although if that happened, it would mean I could get into the action again."

We walked and I told Meryl, "We need to find out if Bryant's ship has moved and whether the SEALS have managed to get any information on what's inside *The Allegheny.*"

She kissed me. "Got to get back to work. I'll catch up with you later. And I'll make some plans that include Mi-Ling for after I'm off work."

As I headed to where the time car portal, I thought, "*Lord, you have excelled Yourself, taking me from dead-end to all this. With You, Jesus, all things are more than possible. You chose me to time travel — who would believe it?*"

Less than ten minutes later, the time car arrived. Sebastian, Mi-Ling and Dr. Lucy scrambled out, with a couple of cases. Mi-Ling hugged me like she would never let me go. Tears of joy pricked the inside of my eyelids. "Papa, I have been thinking about Carol Lady. Mi-Ling wants to see her."

This came right out of the blue, but who can tell what has been going on in a young person's mind?

Sebastian and Mi-Ling went off to the canteen and I took Dr. Lucy to another room. She looked enquiringly at me. Obviously, Sebastian had not said anything.

"Mike is okay. We managed to rescue him. There was one casualty, and thank the Lord, he's on the mend."

"Yes," she agreed. "Thank God for that."

I hesitated. "Lucy, Mike brought back a friend. His friend only speaks Greek."

"That's interesting. Is he a gladiator?" Lucy asked

"Yes, she is."

Lucy was startled and stared at me. "She?"

"The colonel," I responded, "has a special job for you. Hera has nothing but what she stands up in – and that's not much. We think she's about twenty-four. Being a gladiator from the First Century, she's had to spend her life keeping her life intact. She doesn't know what it's like being a girl in the 21st Century. The colonel would like you to basically integrate her into the 21st Century. Clothes, washing, hair and all those feminine facets of daily life, that we guys basically know nothing about. Most importantly – and this is vital, Lucy – please make her understand that she can't kill people who upset her. She needs to learn a new response system. It might be good to get her enrolled at the gym. The doctor is going to want to examine her, also. You had better go along to protect him."

Lucy nodded in a business-like manner. "Probably a visit to the dentist, as well. And she'll need to get used to riding in a car."

"You are excused from all other duties in the meantime," I said, smiling at her. "Hera's introduction into a new way of life takes top priority – for our survival as well as hers! Mike has also been given time to work with her and with you."

Lucy was openly disappointed. "What about Mi-Ling?"

Her concern for my daughter was touching and I smiled at her again. "Well, just between the two of us, I guess that Mi-Ling needs some integration into modern life as well! She adores you and would miss spending time with you."

Lucy's answering smile soured so quickly that it stunned me. With sarcasm in her voice she asked, "Do you want me to help Mi-Ling before you and Meryl get married or after?" The sarcasm turned to sudden anger. "You could have at least told me that you and Meryl were engaged. What about Mi-Ling? Do you ever find time to think of your daughter and what's best for her?"

Somehow, I shook free of the shocked state her words had reduced me to. "Dr. Lucy, please. One step at a time. Let me introduce you to Hera."

We knocked on the door of Hera's room. Hera was there and Mike was trying to talk to her.

Lucy spoke Greek very quickly and Hera clearly understood. Lucy said to Mike and me, "Can you two clear off and leave us alone, please? We have a lot to talk about. I'll keep you posted." Lucy the professional had taken over. In spite of her earlier sarcasm and anger, I felt that everything was okay again.

I had to get back to 1868, to see if Bryant was still there. Angus went with me for back up, should it be needed. Our mission should be safe enough – mostly seeking information about Bryant and his ship, then getting back. The house seemed so empty. There was a good staff and the estate was well managed, but without my late wife, Lucy, it just seemed so empty. Meryl was a modern-day girl, I realized, with dips into time travel when duty called. She had proven she could survive in earlier times, as she had when Angus and I had fought with Braddock's forces in 1755. That trip had turned out to be a blessing for Angus, since that's where he had found his Abigail.

Being back at Bellefield alone gave me time to reflect. Meryl and I made a good team and we loved each other. But what kind of parents would we make for Mi-Ling? That niggling thought in the back of my mind gave me no rest. Three or four others had helped take care of Mi-Ling since Bryant had murdered Lucy – Mi-Ling's *Amma*. But what would happen when it was just Meryl and me?

Walking about the strangely empty and lonely Bellefield in 1868 gave me an idea. Why not turn the house over to Carolyn and Myles? Every time they came ashore when Myles was on leave, they had to hire a house. Why not give them the lease on Bellefield with the proviso that we could still use it as well? Meryl wouldn't want to live here, and because for me it was filled with the unhappy memories of Lucy, I didn't want to live here either.

Angus had his Abigail and her home. Sebastian was going to be a preacher. Anton was more interested in people than houses, especially if the people were feminine. That left Mi-Ling. For the foreseeable future, Dr. Lucy would be tied up bringing Hera up to speed.

I loved Mi-Ling. But when you love someone you have to think of what's best for them, even if what's best leaves you out of the equation.

Bryant's ship was where it was supposed to be. It was after checking up on that that we heard that her majesty Queen Victoria was coming north to Balmoral for a holiday. I told the Shepherd boys to continue to keep watch on Bryant's ship. The SEALS had not been able to document any information on the ship yet. Their best chance would arrive with a full moon. Angus and I had done all we could for the moment, so we returned to headquarters.

It did cross my mind to wonder how the stock of Kairon was holding out. It was a common factor for both us and PATCH. Without Kairon, all time travel would come to a grinding halt. That could mean operatives from both sides being stuck in some inconvenient places at some very awkward times.

Colonel Carlisle called a meeting in his office. Those present included Captain Craig Carter USMC, a slightly reluctant Mike, Meryl, Angus, the colonel, and myself.

"Can I have your attention people? Thank you." Colonel Carlisle looked round the room and then continued in his no nonsense way. "In 1868, her majesty Queen Victoria is coming to Balmoral for a holiday. She's been under pressure to be seen more. She became a virtual recluse after the death of her beloved husband Prince Albert in 1861. We have reason to believe that PATCH intends to either kidnap of kill the Queen. It's our job to stop them and let history take its course.

"The removal of the Queen before her time would upset the balance of power in Europe immensely. She doesn't die until January 1901, and has been the longest-reigning monarch at 64 years, whether any other monarch will ever match that is still to be seen. In her lifetime, Victoria had some seven attempts on her life, all of which failed. These were mainly carried out by disaffected and disgruntled individuals, not by an organization like PATCH. The other thing they may do is try to put in a double – one who has been programmed to force their political slant. They tried this at Gettysburg with General Robert E. Lee." The colonel nodded at us. "Thanks to some of you here, they were stopped."

We were presented with a file on the queen. Much of what the colonel did not say was in the file.

Meryl was the first to speak, "Sir, the problem is not going to be in convincing the Queen of the danger. The problem is going to be convincing those around the Queen that we are not stark raving mad. I mean, think about it! Imagine saying, '*You see, the kidnappers will appear out of time portals, bright lights, and pull the person inside, never to be seen or heard from again.*'Think of how that will sound to them, sir."

"People, I am very much aware of all the questions. What we need are solutions. The hardest job will be getting close enough to the Queen to protect her without being intrusive."

Craig Carter said, "Sir, I have a suggestion. It may seem kind of farfetched."

"Right now, Captain Carter, I'm prepared to accept little red men from Mars if it will get the job done."

"Sir, my suggestion is that you send Major Faulkner, Lieutenant McTurk, and I to Balmoral in 1868. Our cover is that we are part of the Pinkerton Detective Agency and have received word that an attempt to kidnap the Queen will be made while she is at Balmoral by an American gang lead by Caleb Bryant, the instigator of the murder of Sir Charles Gray, the British Ambassador at Foochow, China. Queen Victoria's private secretary at this time is a Sir Charles Gray. I haven't been able to find out if the two were related. We have to convince Sir Charles Gray and John Brown, Queen Victoria's trusted servant, that the danger is real."

Carter paused, and then continued. "Most Brits can't detect a good take off of an American accent. An American can, just the same as you know when a foreigner is trying to be English or Scottish. I'll go along as back up. If we meet an American, I can do the bulk of the talking, with the others chipping in. In that way no suspicion will be raised. You guys will need to remember where you came from and not let your accent drop, especially when you hit your toe."

Angus asked, "Do you think that will get us close enough to the Queen?"

"I hope so," Carter replied.

Colonel Carlisle looked thoughtful. "You know, it could work. Meryl could act as an agent outside. Maybe the Queen will be less suspicious of a woman. If anything did go wrong, Meryl would be there to contact you."

"Alan Pinkerton was a Scot from Glasgow." Angus said. "He was very effective and his agency foiled at least a couple of attempts on the life of Abraham Lincoln. The Queen's ministers will be aware of this. We'll have to think up a reason why an American gang would want to do away with the Queen."

Meryl put in, "It may just be that they were getting paid to do it. A kind of 'ask no questions' type of thing:- we will guarantee to get the job done. We have the advantage of knowing that from 1868, Queen Victoria has another thirty-three years to reign. That's a lot of influence."

The colonel thinking out loud said, "We've have someone in Pinkerton's

Agency, so we can get details inserted into the files in the right place. That way if someone contacts the agency about any of you, you'll be legit. Sometimes the work of an agent is not just what you remove from files, but what you put into files.

"I will get our backroom boys to get cover stories for you. You need to memorize and live them. You have to be ready to go within a week after you get them. It may even be shorter notice than that."

Colonel Carlisle pondered briefly, then added, "Congratulations to you, Meryl and Drew, on your engagement. It's good to get positive news. Okay, people, that will do for now, dismissed."

Meryl and I went outside for a breath of fresh air. We were relieved to see the sun had come out and the birds were singing. Life was going on as normal – normal, whatever normal was for time travelers.

"Oh, well," Meryl sighed, "back to the corsets again. Still, PATCH won't go away without a little encouragement from us."

"I wonder if Sebastian and Mi-Ling are back," I mused, following my own train of thought. "Sweetheart, what do you think of the idea of giving Bellefield to Myles and Carolyn? I can't see us wanting to stay there."

"Mi-Ling might," Meryl pointed out.

"No, surely not! Once she gets her hands on computer gaming stuff or digital music, she'll be like all the other kids. Won't she?" I exclaimed.

Meryl looked thoughtful. "Will she? Mi-Ling's had experiences with adults in her young life that you wouldn't wish on your worst enemy. The kind of garbage she's had to face is part of life now. Childhood seems to be a lot like the lottery. No guarantees on who gets winning parents and who gets losers."

I sighed. "Well, let's go see how she got on with Sebastian in the big wide world of the 21st Century."

Along the way, we had the type of conversation that newly engaged couples do. Where did we want to live? When? We both realized that we wanted to continue working for Vanguard. The thought of a nine-to-five job didn't appeal to either of us. Yet, we both realized that Mi-Ling needed nine-to-five parents. There were too many latch-key children. We didn't want to add to the number.

Mi-Ling and Sebastian came into HQ. Mi-Ling hugged us both. Sebastian was all smiles. "I do like chocolate ice cream," he declared, "it sticks to your mouth and on me, the mustache don't show. Mi-Ling loved her ice cream drink from *SavaJava*. She was one hungry girl. I declare, but what she didn't order her a steak and chips. Ate it all, too."

I asked Mi-Ling if she had enjoyed the shops. She seemed a bit bewildered. She hadn't liked the loud music, even though she saw people her own age enjoying it.

She wore her puzzled expression. "Papa, we went to a commuter shop and they let me try a commuter game."

I jumped in with size twelve shoes. "I think you mean a computer shop."

There was a pause. "Games are more fun when the other person is real. There were five children like me sitting on the ground playing with some kind of a box like the one you call the time car box. None of them were talking to each other. They were laughing at their machines, but they didn't speak to each other. Mi-Ling does not understand this."

I thought; *Join the club, Mi-Ling.*

The young social observer added, "It was their eyes as they played with their machines, Papa. Mi-Ling remembers eyes like that when men had been smoking opium."

She turned to Meryl to include her in the conversation, "You could not hear the birds sing. You could not feel the wind blow. There was so much noise. Miss Meryl, where do they keep all the horses now they are not needed to pull coaches?"

Meryl smiled. "Mi Ling, these new machines replaces horses. Cars and trucks – vehicles – have engines. They don't need to be pulled by horses. Horses are almost part of history."

"Like me?" Mi-Ling wondered.

I laughed and picked her up and swung her around. She screamed with joy. I put her down again and kissed the top of her head. "Oh no, lovely daughter Mi-Ling. You are real and brave and good and so much more than history!" But even as I held her I remembered all she had survived and wondered if she would write a book one day about her experiences coming through time. Like my story, I wondered who would believe it.

Perhaps it was time to take her back to 1868. It had been a big enough change from China to here. Having been rescued had been a marvelous change in her life. She was deeply grateful and expressed that gratitude on a nearly daily basis. Now she had seen in her 21ˢᵗ Century contemporaries a conformity that puzzled and troubled her. She clearly had no attraction for "modern" life.

Meryl and I took Mi-Ling back to Bellefield, 1868. Joy shone bright lights in her eyes. Connie came over to play when she heard Mi-Ling was back. With the disfiguring birthmark gone, Connie was a lovely child. She and Mi-Ling hugged joyfully and ran to Mi-Ling's room, where they could talk and dream without interruption. I would have liked to be a fly on the wall at that conversation. I wondered if Connie would have reacted any differently to the 21ˢᵗ Century than Mi-Ling had, or if Connie would have shared Mi-Ling's puzzlement and distrust.

About two days after we got back, Meryl and I were by the fire. With Meryl's agreement, I had telegraphed Carolyn asking if she and Myles could come through. I sent the telegram for delivery to their rented home in Inverness. We told Mi-Ling that Carolyn might be coming through to visit. She was delighted. I think it was Carolyn's closeness to Lucy that made Mi-Ling welcome her. She had been a stable factor in Mi-Ling's life. Perhaps she could be so again, although I wondered with some guilt if Mi-Ling felt a bit like the parcel in the game *pass the parcel* when I got a telegram back from Myles and Caroline saying they would be there in two days. Mi-Ling had no such reservations. She was delighted.

Meryl felt at loose ends. Mi-Ling clearly preferred Connie's company to Meryl's. Then too, I was spending as much time with Mi-Ling as possible. Time travel had put my relationship with my daughter at risk too many times. I could have been killed, leaving Mi-Ling an orphan. Meryl decided to go back to HQ with the understanding that I would join her after Carolyn arrived to take care of Mi-Ling.

On that last evening before Meryl left, we discussed a plan she had engineered. It seemed odd for the three of us going through to Queen Victoria to be American. Why not portray Craig Carter and Angus as Pinkerton people? I could be just myself, major from the Gordon Highlanders. It would work to my advantage that I had saved Sir Charles Gray the first time at the ball and stopped the kidnap of his granddaughter. Having had my wife murdered by Bryant, and Bryant now posing a threat to her Majesty, was sufficient reason for my being there. The Queen was a woman. What had happened to me might make her more inclined toward empathy, and thus more co- operative when it came to our involvement in her security during her stay at Balmoral.

Meryl's plan had reason and logic to it. I suggested that Meryl tackle Colonel Carlisle when she got back to HQ. It took a woman to think the way a woman would think. We men were just amateurs in a guessing game. Yet how does a Queen think?

Bryant had not moved. The SEALS tried a night recon, but couldn't penetrate the hull of the Allegheny. That alone could have been an indicator that it was a boosting station for PATCH time travel.

Carolyn and Myles duly arrived with hugs and handshakes. Unfortunately, it was late and Mi-Ling was already sound asleep.

"It's great to see you both again," I said, thinking that my words hadn't really expressed how good it was. "Please freshen up." I helped carry the bags up to their room. Carolyn tiptoed into Mi-Ling's room and placed a gentle kiss on the sleeping child before joining us in the dining room for a late dinner. After the meal, Myles said he was going to lie down. "I haven't had much sleep for the last few days," he explained. "The country air will put me right to sleep. That will give the two of you time to catch up on news."

They were both pleased about my engagement. "Life is short and uncertain enough and you are a young man," Myles said, yawning.

"Mmm, listen to Methuselah," I quipped. "You two look even younger than you did last time I saw you."

Carolyn put her hands on her stomach. "Do you notice anything else?" she asked.

I looked and shook my head. "No. Are you okay? What's wrong?"

Carolyn laughed. Myles yawned again. "You tell him, Lynn. I'm off for a rest." He kissed Carolyn goodnight and went upstairs.

I turned to her questioningly and a smile swallowed up her lovely face. "I'm three months with child."

I embraced her. "Carolyn! Wonderful! What great news! How do you feel? Do you want to put your feet up? Is there anything you need?"

"No, Drew," Caroline laughed, sitting down close to the fire. "I'm fine. The physician is pleased with the baby's progress and Myles and I are delighted."

Silence ate into the room, chewed into slivers by the crackling fire. Only the heat and spitting from the fire assured us that we weren't dreaming. It seemed that both our thoughts ran the same track.

Carolyn said sadly, "Lucy would have been delighted. She would have been fussing over me even more than you did. She'd be busy making plans."

I laughed, breaking the fire's monopoly on noise, "and dropping suggestions for names."

The laughter died away like frost brushed by morning sun. I swallowed hard and blinked back tears. "I still miss her, Carolyn." I said, answering her unasked question. "Every time I see a sunrise I think of her and what could have been. Yet, I've seen her in heaven and know she's happy."

"Drew," Carolyn said softly. "Lucy is home with Jesus, Who loves her far more than any of us. Home where you and I and Myles and Mi-Ling," she rubbed her stomach, "and my little one will be someday. What happened to her was not your fault. Caleb Bryant's an evil man, a jealous man. Instead of listening to God, Bryant wanted to be God. My dearest friend, God made us to feel love. It's part of who He is. But our loved ones are on loan from the Lord. Lucy is safe now. She will never get sick again, afraid again, never die again. Nothing and no one can hurt her or touch her with anything other than God's love. She's out of reach of all the Bryant's of this world – all evil. You have your life to live. There's no disloyalty to Lucy in loving Meryl. Lucy's not coming back. She's set you free. If it had been you who died instead of Lucy, wouldn't you have wanted Lucy to find happiness again?"

"Oh, yes! She was too beautiful inside and out to be alone – and so full of love and so easy to love, even though we didn't see eye to eye on everything."

Carolyn laughed. "Oh, how boring it would have been if you had! The important thing is that you agreed together on what was important and most of all about Mi-Ling."

I ran a hand through my hair and bit back a sigh. "That's the problem now. Things have changed. Meryl and I have to keep on working, but Mi-Ling needs stability. Parents who can stay at home with her. I know you love Mi-Ling. Like me, she misses Lucy. The more she misses her Amma, the more she talks about you and Myles. Would you be willing to look after her? I will help financially of course. We want you to have this house when you feel ready."

Carolyn put her hand on my shoulder. "Poor boy, you've had so much happen to you. We'll be glad to help you and dear Mi-Ling. She can stay with me. I can't risk going back to sea until after the baby is born. Mi-Ling can help with the baby."

"That is a wonderful idea. Mi-Ling will love that. She had such a rotten start in life. I think she'll want to make sure your baby will have a wonderful start in life. Your baby is already off to a great start in having you and Myles as parents."

Carolyn smiled a serene smile. "Thank you, Drew. It was very sweet of you to say that."

The silence in the room wrapped itself round us.

Carolyn spoke first. "I think Lucy would like what we've talked about. Myles will be delighted."

Long into the night we shared memories. The great tea clipper race of 1867 aboard *The Night Arrow* had changed us all, especially Carolyn. It had given her Myles, and now the new child within her womb.

Lucy frequented our conversation so doggedly that it almost felt as if she were there with us. I actually felt the warmth of her smile. I was sitting too far away from the fireplace to have been touched by its heat.

"Lucy fell in love with you the first time she saw you," Carolyn confessed. "She never stopped. She wants you to be happy, you know."

My eyes grew hot and heavy with tears. Not only was I a man and supposed to be immune to tears, I was crying over Lucy, who was safely and joyfully reunited with Jesus in Heaven while I was engaged now to Meryl. I wasn't being fair to Meryl, yet I couldn't stop talking about Lucy. "We planned to go to Texas with Mi-Ling to start a new life. There was so much hope, so much to look forward to."

Carolyn saw the tears. "Drew, you still have that hope with Meryl. You're not marrying second best. Meryl nearly died in China saving you in that sword fight. She's the one you need now for whatever God has for you in the future. God needed Lucy for some purpose only He knows – perhaps even because He knew you needed Meryl and all she is." This was later to prove one of the few occasions when Carolyn's wisdom was flawed.

Wiping tears away, I nodded. "We should tell Mi-Ling about our plan in the morning and see what her reaction is. She'll be sorry she didn't stay up to see you, but we didn't know for sure what time you'd get here and she and

Connie wore themselves out playing together."

Carolyn affirmed my idea.

"I sometimes wish we could turn back the clock, or hold back the years," I said.

Carolyn laughed. "That sounds really humorous — a time traveler who wishes he could turn back the clock!" She patted her stomach. "Life moves forward, and don't I know it! We walk towards the unknown with only the sparsest of clues, yet the comfort is that God does know what's coming and calls us to trust Him."

"I guess I am scared of letting God down." I admitted.

Carolyn smiled and said reassuringly, "In history, there must be thousands of folk who have said that, yet God still gets us through. He will do the same for us. It's late, Drew. We should both get to bed. Mi-Ling's an earlier riser. Goodnight and God bless you, my friend."

With the exit of Carolyn's wisdom, I was left to my thoughts. It's funny how long I had tried to keep busy. Now in the midst of the slowly dying fire, I realized I had arrived at a crossroads in my life. I needed to let Lucy go, despite the mistakes I had made and the hurtful things I had said to her. Lucy didn't hate me. God was not condemning me. Any condemnation was coming from God's enemy, Satan. He was just as real as God, although many people who believed in God didn't believe in Satan.

Jesus described Himself as the Way, the Truth, and the Life. I must believe Jesus' own words about Himself. It was more important now than it had ever been because I needed a clear mind for protecting Queen Victoria at Balmoral. And Jesus was also the source of all wisdom.

I finally fell asleep on the couch. Gloomy Victorian bedrooms were not something you raced upstairs to get to, especially when the room was as empty. The following morning when the house started waking up, I washed and smartened up. I was ready when Myles and Carolyn came down for breakfast. Mi-Ling appeared shortly afterwards. She squealed with joy and flung herself into Carolyn's arms. Then she hugged Myles. Unlike her usual polite, docile manner, she monopolized the conversation, recounting her meeting with Jesus and telling them how Jesus had healed Connie. When the joyful story had tumbled out into the room and Mi-Ling paused, I asked her if she wanted to stay with Carolyn and Myles while I was gone.

"That would give Mi-Ling happy time," she assured us.

"Mi-Ling, I'm going to have a baby. Will you stay and help me? I can't go back to sea with Myles before the baby is born. I will need a friend to help me."

"Can Mi-Ling help with the baby? Yes! Mi-Ling would like that much. I think before the baby is born you will need help." Then she turned and asked me, "Papa, will you be here or will you go with Miss Meryl on an adventure somewhere? Mi-Ling is much sad when you are not with her."

"We will come and go," I explained. "But Carolyn will be here all the time. She and Myles are going to move into the house with us. Myles will be here as much as possible."

"Maybe Mi-Ling will be with you," she said to Myles and Carolyn, "when the baby has a birthday. Maybe for many birthdays."

"We would love that, Mi-Ling," Carolyn assured her.

Then to me. "Papa, you do love Mi-Ling, do you not?"

"Yes, sweetheart, of course I do. I always will."

"Oh, papa! Why did Jesus have to take Amma away? Why papa?" Without warning, she burst into such violent tears that her body began shaking. I had never seen anyone cry so violently before. Her sobs filled the house with their fury and for a brief second, - I froze.

Carolyn didn't. She ran over and wrapped her arms round Mi-Ling, cradling her tear-soaked face against her shoulder. She locked her arms around Mi-Ling and rocked her gently. "Come on little one," she whispered quietly. "Let it all out. There, there."

Myles and I looked at one another helplessly.

"Come on, baby, Mama is here for you." To our amazement, the tears subsided. With her head resting against Caroline's shoulder, Mi-Ling fell asleep. It was probably the most beautiful and gentle action I had ever seen. Some women are born mothers. Carolyn was one of them.

It seemed best to go ahead and leave while Mi-Ling was still asleep. I got my kit together and left Myles and Carolyn in charge. Then I headed through to the future by going back to the past. This time travel business can be confusing.

When Meryl met me, she wore American Civil War-style clothes.

"Next place we go," she asked demurely, "can it be warm enough that I can wear a short skirt and maybe sandals?"

I laughed. "Hmm. I'll talk nicely to PATCH and see what we can come up with."

"I do declare," She responded, "I think you're the most forward man I know – but it's sweet of you."

We had our cover stories,-or at least the others did. All that had been done was to switch British papers for American. It was good to be able to keep your own name as much as possible on a mission. If anyone called to you, you were more liable to respond to your own first name. If you forgot to respond to what was supposed to be your own name, you could be in trouble. To sharp-eared security men, mistakes like that were bread and butter.

I had been given a conditional discharge from the Gordon Highlanders, which meant I did not have to appear in uniform. My position in the Gordon's would be reactivated after Bryant had been 'dealt with' and the Queen's safety ensured. The four of us – Meryl, Angus, Craig Carter and I – got into the time car. It had been important to warn Carter of some of the changes he would see and some of the things he would have to do without. He had proven quick on the uptake. Once seated, I pressed the switch for Balmoral Station near Balmoral Castle and hoped we had got everything right.

Above all, we hoped the Queen had a sense of humor and, contrary to popular belief, would 'be amused.'

CHAPTER 6

Balmoral Station, Aberdeenshire, June 10, 1868

The train station at Balmoral had come into existence because of Queen Victoria and the castle. The village was proud of its royal connections. All of the inhabitants   of the village felt themselves part of Queen Victoria's family. The trouble was that because of the Queen's self-imposed mourning, lasting some seven years after her husband Albert's death, people were beginning to feel like a family bereft of their mother. The Queen was alive, but somehow wearing blinkers to their need, seeing only her own sorrow.

Prince Albert had not been King, but Prince Consort. The Prince Consort was the Queen's husband, but did not have the kudos of being King, although Albert and Victoria's marriage had been one of the happiest Royal marriages in history. It must have been, for they had had eight children, which would imply a certain amount of closeness.

Balmoral Castle had been bought by Albert for his young bride and a certain amount of renovation had been required to turn it into the imposing building it was in 1868, and is even in modern times.

In Albert's bedroom, his clothes for the day were still laid out morning and evening. Warm water was put out for shaving and washing. At night, his night shirt was laid out and his Bible and favorite book put by his bedside table. In season, fresh primroses – his favorite flowers – were displayed. All this we knew from our briefings.

We exited the time car at the outskirts of the Balmoral Station and planted ourselves on the platform, along with our luggage, as if we had just arrived by train. We stacked the luggage beside us and Angus went to looking for transport. He had turned away from the luggage toward the exit when a bullet slammed into the second top case.

We hit the deck and then looked around in time to spot a running figure with a rifle disappearing around the corner of one of the buildings.

Craig Carter joked, "I expected this kind of thing in Dodge City in 1868, not the Highlands of Scotland."

"It's just the welcoming party," I said, trying to portray a coolness I didn't feel inside. "Still, one has to ask the question – how did they know we were coming?"

"Either PATCH found out, or someone in the castle is in their employ," Meryl surmised.

"Maybe they didn't like our taste in luggage," Craig cracked.

We got transport, not feeling entirely happy with sitting in an open carriage that would make us an easy target for our friend with the rifle if he was hidden along the way. It was comforting to be in an era when many of the rifles were single shot, unless of course, PATCH had some automatic ordnance to hand.

Our papers were checked at the gate and again at the castle entrance. We were greeted by a tall distinguished, gentlemen, closely followed by a man in Highland dress.

The distinguished man had to be Sir Charles Gray, the Queen's private secretary. He bore a remarkable resemblance to the Sir Charles Gray I had known in China. The second man stood slightly back. Although he didn't immediately identify himself, I gathered he was John Brown, the Queen's personal servant, and also the one who was responsible for a lot of the security. His eyes were everywhere and within minutes had taken in every detail of our appearance. His gaze lingered slightly longer on Meryl, who returned to gaze with an impassive, business-like surmise of him.

"You are Major Faulkner?" Sir Charles asked me.

"I have that honor, sir, and you must be Sir Charles Gray, her majesty's private secretary?"

"I am he. I heard what you did for my cousin in Foochow, I am deeply grateful. May I introduce her Majesty's personal servant, John Brown."

Brown eyed us. For some reason, I disliked him. One thing that had proved itself in history, however, was his devotion and loyalty to the Queen.

"How do you do?" he said, without real liking or interest on his part.

"May I in turn present my colleagues?," I offered, "Miss Meryl Scott and Mr. Angus McTurk from the Pinkerton Detective Agency, and Captain Craig Carter of the United States Marine Corps." They all made acknowledgements and Sir Charles said to Craig, "The fame of the Marine Corps is well known and respected here."

"Thank you, sir," Craig replied.

"It is to my deep regret that I was not on the spot when Sir Charles was murdered," I told Gray. "If it's any comfort, sir, the murderer did not live long after that."

He looked at me and nodded. "Did you see him meet his demise?"

"Yes I did. The murderer was an American by the name of James Lancaster. He was shot in a fight on board a sailing ship."

"Did you witness this?" Gray asked, repeating his question in slightly different words.

"I had a birds-eye view, so to speak. He was shot by an eleven-year-old Chinese girl."

His eyes opened wide. "Goodness gracious! Why?"

"Because he would have killed me if she had not killed him," I explained.

"And your response?" he asked, slightly forgetting his position as he waited to hear more.

"She is now my adopted daughter. Lady Constance Gray may not be familiar with the latter part of that story."

"Goodness gracious! That's a bit of an extreme reaction, is it not?"

"If the girl *is* just your daughter," Brown said in a menacing tone.

I fought back anger. One couldn't afford anger on a job. But I did say to Brown, "I resent your implication, sir."

"Keep the head," he replied icily. "There was no offence intended."

"Therefore, none taken," I replied falsely. He had meant the implication and I was secretly seething. I got the impression that we rather resembled a couple of mastiffs, eyeing each other, unsure who would come out the victor in a fight.

Craig Carter intervened and brought us back to the task at hand. "Unless I am much mistaken, gentlemen, I believe our united task first and foremost is her Majesty's safety?"

He was quite right. I had nearly let Brown's catty remark ruin everything.

Sir Charles consulted a couple of pieces of paper. "The threat that has been passed onto us, is from a man called Caleb Bryant, a sea captain from Nantucket, so I understand?"

"That's true," I replied. "James Lancaster murdered Sir Charles. The man who planned his murder was Caleb Bryant. Lancaster was first mate aboard Bryant's ship. Your cousin was getting close to thwarting Bryant's plans and schemes." I paused, and then added, "Sir Charles was one of the finest Christian men I have ever met. He touched my life more than any other."

The Queen's private secretary nodded. Perhaps we would be able to mend the bad start and forge some sort of tentative friendship – or at least trust.

"Bryant is a dangerous and determined man," I continued. "More than capable of carrying out any threat he makes. While her Majesty's safety is my first and primary concern, along with the aid of my colleagues from Pinkerton's, Bryant is also responsible for the murder of my wife. I have every desire for his apprehension and for him to answer for his crimes." As I was saying this, I purposely switched my gaze to John Brown. He was not an easy man to stare down, but I was not going to allow him to intimidate me. We couldn't mention about PATCH unless they appeared. Nobody would believe us.

Gray shook his head sadly. "The whole situation is regrettable, but when you are taken into the Queen's presence, do not speak to her unless she speaks to you and you are summoned forward. When you address the Queen, it is either *Your Majesty,* or *Ma'am,* the *am* in *Ma'am* as the *am* in jam."

"Now," he added, "if you will be so good as to wait here, I will convey to her Majesty that you have arrived."

I coughed. "Before you do that, you should know that someone tried to kill us on the way here. It was a single rifleman and he ran off behind some buildings. If you question my statement, you will find a bullet hole in my second trunk and, as there is no exit hole, I assume the bullet is still in the trunk."

"I am glad they missed," Brown said.

Angus said, "If that was a telescopic rifle, as used in the recent War Between the States in America and similar to the one that killed Sir Charles Gray, then any exposed position in which her Majesty finds herself may make her a potential target."

"Aye," Brown said. "Her Majesty is very fond of drawing and sketching. That means sitting out in the open. We can't ask Her Majesty to stay indoors.

She would never agree to it."

"I have a possible solution," Meryl said.

"What may that be, Miss Scott?"

"To my understanding, I am not that much taller than the Queen. What if, when her Majesty was going to paint or draw, we changed places? ," Meryl suggested.

Sir Charles shook his head. "Quite impossible."

"Why so? Dressed in black with a veil over my face and seated, who would be able to tell? A rifleman would have to be quite a distance away."

"Miss Scott," Brown said, "you would be putting your life at risk."

Meryl returned his look with a level gaze. "Sometimes we have to take risks if we want to catch the wolf. I prefer to think of it as baiting a trap. The Queen's safety is why we are here, gentlemen."

"Let us ask her Majesty," Sir Charles decided. He went into the Queen's room, and a few minutes later we were taken into the Queen's sad presence and introduced.

"Major Faulkner," the Queen said. "We have heard of what transpired in China and are grateful for your service. If our life is in danger, danger is a monarch's companion. We are gratified that you have come to aid us during our stay here. We also grieve with you over the loss of your wife. How are you?"

I approached the Queen and bowed. "Thank you for your condolences, Ma'am, I am deeply touched that in the midst of your own sorrow you should feel mine. It is the pain and sense of emptiness, Ma'am, and of life cut short. Yet these feelings your Majesty knows only too well."

The Queen nodded.

The others were introduced and the Queen welcomed them. When Meryl was introduced, she curtsied to the Queen.

Much to my surprise, the Queen smiled at Meryl, and when she did, the real Victoria reflected herself in the smile. The eighteen-year-old girl who had suddenly been thrust into prominence after an oppressive and sheltered upbringing, sprang to life before our startled eyes.

"So you are the woman who would be Queen?"

Meryl put on her best Southern accent, "Your life, Ma'am, is the center of all our concerns. If you permit this, perhaps it will remove the danger to your

Majesty a mite quicker than otherwise. The important thing, your Majesty, is that the would-be-assassin believes it's you. Major Faulkner, Captain Carter, and Mr. McTurk have carried through a number of covert operations successfully. If the assassin shows up, we'll stop him. It's important that Mr. Brown act normally and continue his care and attention of your Majesty. I have a bullet-proof cap that I can wear under the veil. The head is what an assassin will attempt, knowing that almost nobody comes back from a head wound.

"May I suggest, your Majesty, that the next time you wish to go out on the estate, let it be known. Just before you leave, we'll change places. One thing, your Majesty, the color black is very easy to duplicate. From a distance, one black dress and veil look very much like another. If I may have one of your Majesty's hats, please? They are a distinctive shape and may be known by the assassin or assassins. I promise I will take good care of the hat and return it to you."

Victoria nodded. "We see, Miss Scott, that you also have the character of a queen, putting your own needs last and the happiness of our realm first. We are indeed most grateful."

"Ma'am," Meryl said with another curtsy, "I thank you for your words, but I will be even more gratified to be alive at the end of the day."

"Do you believe that one of our staff may be co-operating with the assassin?" Victoria asked suddenly.

"I would leave things as they are, Ma'am." I answered. "Once your safety is assured, we want the assassin and will attempt to take him or her alive. If it's not Bryant, and I suspect it won't be – we might get information on where to find Bryant."

"Just leave him to me," John Brown said darkly. "He'll nae be backward in coming forward when I have a conversation wi' him."

Craig Carter said, "Once the assassin is caught, that won't remove the overall threat to her Majesty. The way of killing a snake is by hitting its head. We must find Bryant to ensure her Majesty's total safety, at least from that quarter."

"One came for a quiet rest in the country," the Queen said. "Still, one does not know what a day will bring. My ladies-in-waiting and we ourselves offer you every assistance."

The Queen thought for a moment before asking, "If the assassin is not connected with Mr. Bryant?"

"Then, Ma'am, we will need to reassess the situation," I acknowledged.

The Queen sighed. "Uneasy is the head that wears the crown."

"Ma'am," said Craig Carter, "we will do our darndest to make sure you keep wearing it till the Lord comes for you in His own good time."

Sir Charles and John Brown seemed quite happy with the plan.

"It might be a good idea if it was not generally known you are here," Sir Charles added.

Angus asked, "May we see some of her Majesty's favorite sketching places? That way we can reconnoiter the land and see if there are any obvious ambush points in these loci."

"Well," said Victoria, "we must return to our work. Sometimes one feels as if one is drowning in a sea of paper. Miss Scott, one difficulty may be your accent. If you were overheard speaking, they would know it was not us."

Meryl smiled and said in an accent that was very close to the Queen's, "We are, of course, most grateful to your Majesty for pointing this out and will do our best not to disappoint." I could see by the slight apprehension on Meryl's face she wondered if she had overstepped the mark.

The Queen got up and returned to her desk. We considered this as our dismissal and started to leave. The Queen looked up and said to Meryl, "Miss Scott, you have access to our presence at any time."

We were shown to our rooms, which were fairly close together. We agreed to meet downstairs in the Entrance Hall for a look round outside.

Angus said, "I would like a look up at the top of that high tower to the right of the main entrance. That seems to be the highest point in the complex."

We found John Brown, and asked him about going up to the top of the tower to observe. He had no objections and told us how to reach it.

"If anyone questions you, tell them to talk to me," he added.

We took binoculars up with us and surveyed the castle from the top. There were no trees within what we estimated as 1868 rifle shot range. It would not be the case with an up-to-date sniper rifle and scope.

"If," said Craig, "you really wanted to assassinate the Queen and maybe one or two of the Royal Family at the same time, what would you use? Quick firing, and easily hidden."

"A mortar," Angus responded. "You fire a mortar bomb and land it amongst those rocks, and a whole parcel of people are going to get killed."

Meryl looked thoughtful. "The Queen might get killed, but she could just as easily sustain only minor injuries, in which case it would treble the difficulties for the next attempt."

"I'm for a rifle with a silencer," I said. "If it is PATCH or an 1868-type rifle inspired by Bryant, the noise and smoke would give away the location of the killer."

Meryl said thoughtfully, "If it's a favorite spot of the Queen's, then someone has to guide the assassin, and get them out. If the Queen is killed, does the assassin need to take the rifle back? Why not dispose of it? Then anyone seeing two figures on the estate would assume they are just out for a walk."

Angus scratched his head. "If PATCH were to put in an assassin they would need the co-ordinates of where the Queen would be. They would need inside information. Could there be a transmitter of some kind?"

"What we need," Meryl said thoughtfully, "probably from John Brown, are the names of any staff that have been fired or have quit over the past month."

I attempted a meeting with John Brown. I found him carrying that perpetual look of suspicion that seemed to be part of him. He had a lot of jealous enemies, so who could blame him? I didn't particularly want to be a friend, but I did hope we could develop a working relationship. I asked him if he could provide a list of former employees and explained that one of them might hold a grudge.

"Mr. Brown, the assassin needs a guide and we are after the assassin. So please distance yourself from the investigation for the time being. If it becomes obvious who has ill intent and that person becomes suspicious that he or she is known, then the would-be-killer will disappear into the woodwork again."

Brown fumed. "This is preposterous! I can't believe that someone would kill the Queen just because they had been fired."

I reminded him, "What about John Bellingham in 1812?: the only person to have assassinated a British prime minister. He shot Spencer Percival when the latter wouldn't grant Bellingham compensation for his wrongful imprisonment in Russia. People with an aggrieved sense of right can act in extreme ways."

Brown looked at me with a certain amount of understanding, although no more liking. "Yes, that was only fifty years ago, but regicide? Isn't that a bit farfetched? Very well. I will provide you with a list. I hope it proves worth my time."

He went away, shaking his head.

* * *

While Angus, Craig and I waited, we looked around outside. Meryl left to talk to the Queen. The ever-dour Brown caught up with us. There were four people on the list he grudgingly handed over.

He explained, "Sandy Macgregor was asked to leave because of certain irregularities. He did not seem to mind too much. James Crosby was bothered with rheumatics, poor soul. Could hardly get around, but he has a wee pension. Andrew Sinclair – it has since come to light that he took the blame for someone else. I suppose it was a sense of misplaced loyalty to Sandy Macgregor."

I looked at the list in my hand. "What about Morag Connor?" I asked.

"Noo, that was strange. She was a sensible quean, a hard worker and reliable. She started missing days. Saying she was sick, but she was seen on the estate with a man. He was not one of the estate workers, so we assumed he was from Braemar or Ballater. Nobody recognized him. He was well dressed in good tweeds, looked well off – so those who saw him said.

"Morag's a pretty girl. Her mother is unwell, so the Queen gave them the house so the mother would not have to be afraid of moving. Her mother would like it fine for Morag to get married and "nae be dee'n wi'an auld chave, the likes o' me."

"If the man she was meeting is the would-be assassin," I said, "she might be unaware of his intentions. Would she purposely do something that would endanger her mother's health and cause her such shame as her daughter getting arrested? She may just be infatuated. He may even have money to pay doctors' bills."

I paused. "Would she know the places where her Majesty likes to paint or draw?"

Brown nodded unhappily. "She would sometimes come and help serve the food. But as I've already said, sir, this is preposterous. Morag would never do something like this. I would stake my reputation on it."

My gut disagreed with Brown. I suspected Morag. Meryl had learned tracking skills from Kitchi. She might be able to follow Morag Connor and see if her beau was connected to an attempt to kill the Queen. Then we could engineer a false outing so that the assassin would show himself. I began to think that, Queen or no Queen, Meryl was putting herself at a terrible risk. And I couldn't help wondering what Bryant was doing with himself all this time.

Brown had a group photo that showed Morag Connor clearly.

A little while later, I caught up with Meryl to relay my suspicions about Morag. She listened, and then said, "The Queen is concerned for my safety for when I stand in her place. I think what you're suggesting can be done. Kitchi taught me a lot about what to look for while tracking. He always held about himself a sense of oneness with the land and nature." A far-away look stole into her eyes before she routed it with a toss of her lovely head and bouncing blonde hair. "Morag can't know I'm following her. I wonder if there is a spare Ghillie suit I can use. "

"Be careful," I warned her. "At the first sign of trouble back off and come back. I don't want to lose you – no heroics."

"Yes, Chief," she replied with a wink. "What we need now is the Queen to make an announcement to the household of where the next artistic outing will be."

"Try and get the Queen to announce a place where there are rocks," I suggested. "An assassin can hide there, but so can those trying to catch him. What about near Lochnagar?"

"Okay, I'll ask the Queen. I can track Morag for a couple of days before the expedition's due to leave." She added, "Kitchi could do it so much better than I can, but he's not here."

As much as it annoyed me to hear it, Meryl was right. I wondered if in her heart she still carried a torch for Kitchi. Surely not – we were engaged to one another. Surely that counted for something, even to the sometimes capricious Meryl. Angrily, I ordered myself, *come on! Focus! Concentrate!*

We apprised Sir Charles Gray of our plan. It was duly announced that in three days' time we would be going to Balmoral Glen on an artistic expedition.

Meryl had been going for walks around the estate, which was huge. For the next few days, she planned to tail Morag Connor in the hopes that she could see who Morag was meeting. Meryl was armed and had a small tracking device, but with limited range. A couple of us would be in the woods at a distance. We couldn't get too close or we'd give the game away. Meryl wore trousers and bound up her hair.

If you are in command, all you can do is make a decision based on the best information you have. The only difference was that this was a real person's life, not a figure on a computer screen. This was real life, and the decision I made to allow Meryl to track Morag was to literally change everything, both now and in the future.

Angus and I shadowed Meryl as she went out. It was vital that Morag saw neither us nor Meryl. Morag went directly to the place where the Queen and her entourage normally stopped. Her Majesty had fixed views on painting and liked to paint a particular locus until she was satisfied with the result.

When we talked to Meryl, she described the tracking effort as having been a waste of time. "All Morag did was just go to the spot and walk up and down. She looked around, picked some flowers – lupins and bluebells – then she left."

"Did she keep the flowers?" I asked. "Did she put them anywhere?"

Meryl looked at me and exclaimed, "Oh, Lord! I'm getting old! When she came back to the castle, I thought something was missing! She wasn't carrying the flowers. My focus was on watching her and staying behind her. But you're right, Drew. The flowers were gone. I didn't see where she put them."

Meryl was upset with herself. "It's nearly dark now. I'll go over the ground tomorrow until I find them. You think they are the marker for the assassin? Marking the spot where the Queen will stop to paint? How could I have been so stupid? Stupid! Stupid!"

"Look," I said, "we can't do anything about it tonight. Get some tea and rest and we'll start in the morning. That's an order." I paused. Meryl's usual sparkle was missing. "My question about the flowers was just an idea," I pointed out. "They might not have meant anything at all. She could have just decided they weren't worth keeping. She might have just put them down and then forgot to pick them up."

"Come on," Angus said to Meryl. "I'll escort you to tea. Remember the accent. You're an American on this jolly outing."

She snapped at Angus. "Are you saying I can't do my job?" The blonde hair bobbed in anger that was uncharacteristic of Meryl. "I'm going to get changed," she informed us icily. "I'll join you later."

Angus and I caught up with Craig, who had been surveying the area.

"Where's Meryl?" he asked.

"She is a bit sore at herself," I told him. "She'll join us for dinner."

We headed to the dining area and waited for Meryl. She didn't come.

"Where is she?" Angus finally asked. "I know women sometimes take a long time to get ready but..."

"Oh, no!" I exclaimed. "Now I feel stupid! I have this horrible sinking feeling. I'll check her room."

I ran upstairs and knocked on Meryl's door. There was no reply. I pushed open the door. On the bed lay a dress. It looked like something Meryl would have changed into to have dinner. I looked into the wardrobe. There was no sign of the clothes she had been wearing. That horrible sense of realization dawned fully. Meryl had gone back to retrace her steps and look for the flowers- alone.

I raced down to the dining room (*at least as fast as you could race in the middle of a palace*) and found Angus and Craig.

"Meryl's gone!" I told them breathlessly. I explained to Craig, since he hadn't been with Angus and me earlier, "Morag picked some flowers and left them somewhere. Angus and I think it might have been a signal for the assassin to show him the place where the Queen will stop. Meryl didn't see where Morag left them when she was following. She blames herself. She's gone to look for them. We've got to find her."

Angus said gently, "Drew, its dark now. How can we find her at night?"

Craig suggested, "We could ask Brown and get a search party."

For the next ten minutes or so, we ran word circles around ourselves attempting to formulate a course of action. We were interrupted by a footman who handed me a note. "Major Faulkner, this communication has been handed in for you. I was instructed to deliver it personally." He bowed and left.

I opened the letter and read it. "*We have your girlfriend, boy, Lucy is hardly cold. Didn't waste any time, did ya? If you want to see her again, leave things alone. The*

Queen needs to be dealt with. Once she dies, your sweetheart will be released. You and me can deal with our personal business later. Caleb Bryant."

"We won't find her," I lamented. "That rat won't make the same mistake he did with Mi-Ling. Yet, no matter what, we can't let Bryant — or his cronies — kill the Queen."

Angus paced the room. "You can't ignore this, Drew! Anything could be happening to her. You wanted command. Now you've got it, your decision."

"Meryl knew the risks, Angus. Our job is to protect the Queen and make sure history doesn't get changed. It would be the same if it were it anyone of us. You know that."

Angus said hotly, "You seem to be forgetting something, Drew. There is someone who would stand the best chance of finding her."

"Who, would that be?"

Angus took a deep breath. "Kitchi."

"Kitchi! But he's back in 1757." We were professionals. I fought to ignore the heavy pounding of my heart. I had lost Meryl to Native American Kitchi in the past. If we engaged him to search for her now, would that painful history repeat itself?

"We have a time machine, don't we?" Craig pointed out. "Meryl couldn't have been gone for much more than ten minutes before we realized it."

Resolutely, I found paper and pen and wrote: *Meryl kidnapped. You must stop Queen from art outing. There is danger.*

I handed the note to Craig, "Take this note and keep it in a safe place. If I don't get back, you'll need it to explain things. If everything goes right, I'll be back in about an hour. I must get to 1757 and find Kitchi."

"I'll come with you to the station," Angus said, "and get the horses back here. But I'll hang on at the station for as long as I can.

"Craig, you use your best American charm and fill Sir Charles in on the events. If you get to see the Queen, make things seem as normal as possible. She's safe if she stays indoors. If she returns to London, an assassin can work in a crowd there as easily as here, as her Majesty already knows."

Angus and I got horses and headed for the station. It was a rough road but the moon was in helpful mode. Once we arrived, Angus made himself comfortable. "Hurry," he urged.

I summoned the time car and rocketed back to HQ. I had to tell Colonel

Carlisle. As could be expected, he was very concerned. "Major, you've done the right thing." He went to a console in his desk. "If it's any comfort they didn't succeed in killing Queen Victoria, so your idea must have worked. I don't know how long it will take you to find Kitchi, but I'm not sending you on your own."

Colonel Carlisle pressed a buzzer. A smiling, confident Anton breezed through the door. The colonel told him about Meryl.

"Drew, my friend, all this Russian about is not good for you." He laughed, "See how I have been coming along in your time? Now I tell jokes in English."

The colonel managed a tight-lipped smile, then instructed me, "Get Kitchi. When you and Anton get Kitchi to 1868, I want Anton back here."

"Of course," Anton said, "the pretty girls in 1868, they will just have to do without me." He paused, then shrugged his shoulders. "Difficult for them, I know, but everybody has to make sacrifices in time of crisis. Old Russian saying, when *the wolf is at the door, you do not worry about closing the shutters.*"

"Right," the colonel said, "Get moving!"

We shot off to get some kit for 1757. Anton remarked, "This is the way to travel. It costs you nothing. Food and accommodation supplied. All you have to do is not get killed. Simple."

Going back to 1757, and remembering the terrible battle at Monongahela, where we fought our way back inch by inch, literally hacking and stabbing. I still got nightmares about it. Often my mind had replayed every step, with young Daniel Boone helping us. That was where Angus had met Abigail, the love of his life.

The death of my Lucy hadn't occurred yet, and until Kitchi came along, Meryl and I were getting closer and closer. In a way, he had stolen her and all our golden dreams. Now, after Meryl and I were safely engaged, here I was turning her over to Kitchi again in a bid to save her life. I could already guess what might happen. Circumstances had seemed to conspire against Meryl and me ever getting married. Maybe it simply wasn't meant to be. When God opens doors of opportunity they are generally well oiled and you don't give yourself a hernia trying to open them. However, this was a time for faith and not philosophy. Meryl or no Meryl in my life, I must trust God with the outcome.

When I found Kitchi, he was surprised. "Kitchi did not expect to see such a great warrior again." His greeting was warm and genuine.

"*She who has Sun in Her Hair* has been taken by evil men. They may or may not hurt her. They want to kill the Queen, the leader of all the white men. They are using *Sun in Her Hair* as a threat so we will let them kill the Queen, our chief."

"You must protect your chief," Kitchi said. "It is the duty of a warrior." Then he asked the question that was on his heart, "Does she speak of me?"

Unwillingly, I nodded. "She wished she had your tracking skills. When she made a mistake and missed a signal, she went out alone at night to find it. That's when she got caught."

Kitchi's warm brown eyes shone with admiration – and love? He straightened his shoulders. "Sun in Her Hair is a brave warrior. There must have been at least three enemies to catch her," He left me at the edge of the village and went to speak to the chief. Anton and I were beckoned over and introduced. Anton seemed slightly nervous and intimidated by the Native Americans. For once, he lacked old Russian sayings.

Chief Running Wolf spoke. "You have come far. My heart is sad that Sun in Her Hair is in danger. If she had been the bride of Kitchi, this would not have happened. She said she could not marry Kitchi, for she loved another and her heart was heavy because she had left him behind."

So at least Meryl had not left me as capriciously as I had imagined. Still, that gave me little comfort now.

I introduced Anton, who bowed and said, "I am honored to come to the council fire of Running Wolf."

Running Wolf studied Anton, "Your speech is different."

"I come from the east, far to the east, and I come to learn. I am a friend of this warrior."

Running Wolf nodded. "We may know many people, but a man is blessed if he can count his friends on the fingers of one hand."

Running Wolf turned to Kitchi, "I still do not understand where the journey to Sun in Her Hair lies, but my blessing goes with you. May the Great Spirit protect you."

Kitchi left to collect his things. He had not remarried since his wife's death and since Meryl left, and this further upset me. But Meryl's life counted on me dismissing jealously and being willing to stand back and do what was best for her.

Anton said to me, "Counting friends on the fingers of one hand sounds like old Russian saying. My ancestors were well-traveled, were they not?"

Unlike the last time we left Kitchi's time, we got to the time car in peace.

Grudgingly, I had to admit that I admired Kitchi. He was going into a dangerous situation to rescue the woman he loved from danger. Yet, there was no guarantee that she would love him in return. I looked into Kitchi's eyes and was reminded of the phrase *still waters run deep.* Although he did not show it in his face, Kitchi's ran into the pool of his heart.

I gave Kitchi a cloak to help him blend in. "Kitchi," I warned him, "many here don't know about time travel. They won't understand. They may say things spoken out of ignorance. Please forgive and be patient with them."

Kitchi smiled. "I will keep the picture of Sun in Her Hair in my heart. Her beauty will keep me from anger, except with those who may have hurt her." When he said that, I realized that I would be very fearful if I were included with anyone who hurt Meryl.

CHAPTER 7 - Joy...Sadness

On the way back in the time car, my body reminded me that I hadn't had much sleep that day. When I got tired, I missed Lucy more. I wondered what Lucy and I would have been doing now had she been still alive. Mi-Ling would have been joyful with her beloved *Amma*. Could I ever be all that my daughter needed by myself?

Angus had been able to keep the horses at the station. He greeted Kitchi warmly, giving him a manly hug and slapping him on the back. "It is good to see you again. Thank you for helping us."

Kitchi raised his hand. "Peace, my brother."

Angus sent the horses rushing back to the castle. They had barely come to a stop when he directed me, "Drew, show Kitchi where we think *Sun in Her Hair* was last seen."

"I must speak with the woman Morag that Drew told me about," Kitchi told Angus. "She may know the way in the night if she meets her lover by the light of the moon."

It was common sense to catch up with Morag to see what she knew. Yet it also meant that the enemy would know that somebody was making enquiries. Bryant already knew who we were – or at least who I was and where I was.

Anton said, "Now that you have arrived here, I will go back to modern times. Then if you need me I can be like the Cossacks and come charging to the rescue." There was a pause. "That is, providing she lets me."

I looked at him. "Providing who lets you, my friend?"

Anton shrugged his shoulders. "Just think: somewhere in modern times there is a girl who is in for a treat – me!"

We laughed – apart from Kitchi. Kitchi's entire focus was on finding Meryl. Anton puffed up his chest importantly. "Well, what more could a girl ask for? You are all busy here. The station is not far away. Me, Anton, I will walk like a Cossack." He shook hands all around and trotted back down the drive. We heard him talking to himself along the way. "Tatyana, Natasha, Maria... I wonder what her name will be?" Then he was lost in darkness and his voice faded.

If Brown fully understood why we wanted to talk to Morag, he would go and persuade her to spill the beans. He seemed a 'hands on type' of guy when it came to the Queen's safety. We arrived at Morag's mother's cottage once we had found where she lived. Morag was there and we asked if we could come in and ask some questions about a young woman who was in the wood at the same time as she had been and on the same path.

Morag's eyes darted from one to the other of us. Kitchi seemed to frighten her, as he lacked a smile and made no attempt to act anything other than he was – angry. The threat to Meryl made him single-minded.

Kitchi stood in front of a nervous Morag and asked, "When you were in the forest did you hear someone behind you?"

"No, sir, no one." She didn't meet Kitchi's gaze.

Kitchi planted himself directly in front of her and willed her to look at him. "She who has been taken is to be my wife. If she is hurt I will be angrier than I am now. You do not want to see me angry. If you know where she is, and you tell me, then you will have my friendship. Those who have taken Sun in Her Hair mean to harm her. If they do not let her free, they will be subject to the white man's law. If they hurt her, they will face my law."

Morag considered him with something akin to horror on her face. "You-o-or law, sir? What does that mean?" Her voice had dropped to a whisper.

Kitchi slowly drew his knife from its sheath. It made a rasping sound. He pushed it back in again, just as slowly and noisily as he had pulled it out.

Morag gave way to the psychological warfare, as Kitchi had intended. She darted behind me. "Please, sir! I don't know who he is or what he is, but keep him away from me!"

"Tell what you know. If the lady is safe, this will go no further. I promise you. If she isn't, then we don't have enough men or strong enough men to keep you from her fiancé's anger."

"My brother," said Kitchi. "Maybe the memory of Morag needs to be encouraged."

Again the knife drew slowly out of the sheath with a deathly rasping sound. This time, Morag panicked. "Please, sir! Don't let him hurt me! There's a hut about two miles along the path. It has a grey roof and is made of wood. It has two chimneys, one at each end of the house. She's in there."

Kitchi began to slide the knife back into its sheath, and then quickly pulled it out again. "You have spoken wisely. How many guard her?" he demanded.

"Four of them. One can't move as quickly as the others. He has a bad limp."

"Bryant," I said, "from our meeting in Foochow, China, when he ran a sword through Meryl and I retaliated. I know Bryant. If we rush the hut, they will kill her."

Kitchi said, "That is why I am here, my brother. We must stalk like cougar and watch like the hawk."

"Four hours on and four off," I told Kitchi. "We need to keep being seen back at the palace. Morag, you're coming with us. We can't trust you. We can't have you telling anyone."

"What will happen to mother?" Morag cried. "My sister can't stay away from her job at the palace."

I dropped money on the table. "Leave a note for your sister. Tell her you've been called away and she'll have to take care of your mother for a few days. The money will help. I'll make sure her job at the palace will still be there when this is over."

A note was duly left. Morag said her sister would be there within an hour. Her mum was asleep. Morag packed a bag and followed us out of the cottage.

We returned to Balmoral. Morag was locked into one of the bedrooms. We explained to John Brown that Morag was there to help with enquiries about our female co-worker who was missing. "We believe she's been kidnapped."

"We need a search party to comb the woods," Brown immediately decided. "I will organize it."

I shook my head. "Thank you for your concern, sir, but I must ask you not to do that. We believe we know where she is. The men who have taken her will kill her if they suspect anything. It must be done by stealth."

"Why not just send the savage in with his tomahawk?" Brown asked sarcastically. "He would scare anyone." Kitchi flinched at the thoughtless insult as Brown added, "The Queen's safety comes first."

"Please, sir. Give us twenty-four hours. After that you can get your search party."

"I am sorry, but Miss Meryl's safety is second to the Queen's."

"Who is this who speaks without council?" a voice demanded from the open door. "Should we not be consulted on what concerns our safety?" There was what could accurately be termed a pregnant pause before the Queen continued. "What has happened to Miss Scott?"

Brown responded. "She has been kidnapped, Your Majesty, but Major Faulkner says he knows where she is. The information was gained by this savage." He gestured towards Kitchi.

"This is my friend, Kitchi," I told the Queen. "He helped us track Meryl. We believe we know where she is. But, if there's a big search, they'll kill her."

Kitchi addressed the Queen. "You are the chief of all the white men?"

Much to Brown's disgust, Queen Victoria smiled welcomingly at Kitchi. "When dealing with wolves, one has to be cunning."

"The Great Chief of all the white men has dealt with wolves?"

"Yes, Kitchi, I meet them every day, although their appearance may differ from the ones you know as wolves. Thank you for coming to help us."

Kitchi smiled at Queen Victoria and nodded his head in approval. "The Chief of all the white men has a warrior heart."

"We are gratified at what you say. To do what we do, a warrior's heart is necessary."

Brown suddenly found he had something stuck in his throat. "Ye can take all the time you need," he told me before slipping out of the room.

* * *

Craig and Angus made up one team and Kitchi and I the other. Because Kitchi would brook no waiting, we went first. Following Morag's directions, we found the hut – or at least Kitchi did. You haven't had a work out until you've attempted to keep up with Kitchi, dog trotting through the forest.

"We must watch," Kitchi said. "It may be that they, too, will have only two watching *Sun in Her Hair.*"

We crept as close as we could. I followed Kitchi, who was in his element.

Then I heard Bryant's voice. "Sam and me are gonna try and get a drink in this God-forsaken place. You two stay here and guard her. If you want fun one at a time, we've been good long enough. But don't get greedy! One of you remains on guard all the time – understand?"

Kitchi moved up as the two figures brought out a small wagon and two horses. The other two kidnappers were at the door. Bryant and Sam got up into the wagon and set off. "We'll be back soon, no, not that soon. Plenty time for you to have fun with her. Just don't kill her yet. We want our turn when we get back."

We waited until the wagon left. The two figures at the door produced a bottle. The bigger of the two said, "Me first with the woman." The other man began to complain. "Dougald , it's always you first…"

Kitchi produced his knife. I had mine ready. Kitchi counted down on his fingers three, two, one. He sprinted for the door. I followed. The two guys were stunned. The sight of an angry Kitchi even scared me.

Kitchi was behind Dougald in a second and drew his knife across the back of his leg. The man screamed in pain and fell. I hit the second guy hard. He groaned and hit the floor. "If woman is hurt," Kitchi told them both, "you die – slowly."

Kitchi raced to the back room with me on his heels.

Meryl was tied to the bed. My relief at seeing her alive and seemingly unharmed was so enormous that my legs went weak and I stumbled. Kitchi remained imperturbable. He cut the ropes away from Meryl in one fluid motion. Gently, he removed the gag from her mouth.

Neither Meryl nor Kitchi spoke. He held her and she buried her face in Kitchi's chest. Finally, through bruised lips she whispered, "Kitchi…you came for me."

Kitchi said, "Only death would have kept me away, Sun in Her Hair, and only death will keep us apart now."

Meryl had not even noticed me. I went out of the room and closed the door behind me. I had seen enough to know that I was not the one for Meryl. The flame she carried in her heart for Kitchi leaped brightly into life and passion. Only death could extinguish it again.

I was thrilled that Meryl was safe, but to be truthful, I didn't know what to feel.

During the dark night of the soul, Meryl had always been the light to guide me to safety. We had shared physical intimacy – joyful, passionate sex - but even after that, our hearts had not joined perfectly. Her path was different from mine.

The two thugs blocked the door. The one I had hit was still unconscious. Dougald was whining as he attempted to stop the flow of blood from the back of his leg. "Where's Bryant?" I demanded. "Who's with him?"

"Go to hell."

I dropped down beside him and produced the Bowie knife. "Listen, you worthless sack of excrement, when my friend comes out of the back room, he's going to cut you into little pieces. He'll do such a good job even your own mother wouldn't recognize you. The only person that might – and I say might – be able to stop him is me. So you better start answering my questions while you still can."

He looked at me with fear in his eyes. Good.

"So let's try this again. Where's Bryant and who was that in the wagon with him?"

He hesitated. "If I tell you, they will kill me."

"If you don't tell me," I pointed out, "he'll kill you. And we're here first. You have to deal with us now. You can worry about them later." I shook my head at him in mock sympathy. "It looks like you are having a bad day."

"Sam Pollock is the other man. He was to take care of things. There was someone to be put out of the road. Just injured, not killed. Bryant and Sam Pollock hired us to guard the woman after she was kidnapped."

"Was anyone else involved?" I asked. Even as I asked, it dawned on me that we didn't know when Bryant and Pollock would be back. The chances were that they were both armed. Pollock, if he got a gun out, would not miss. Professional assassins did not get paid for missing.

"Are there any others?"

Dougald thought. "Two others, they weren't normal. Spoke about power and taking control."

"Kidnap is bad enough," I told Dougald. "But you are up for regicide. You did know Bryant and Pollock are planning to kill the Queen?"

He looked at me with genuine surprise. "The Queen! Gaud man! We didna ken! We were only to take the girl."

The girl. My girl. Now Kitchi's girl. My stomach turned over sickly and I wanted to just drop down beside Dougald and stick a knife in him. But I had a job to do. "Will you turn Queen's evidence against Bryant?" I asked. "Stand up in court and say what you know? If you don't, Kitchi will kill you. I won't try to stop him."

The second thug began to stir. He saw me and leaped to his feet, running for the door. I tried to grab him, but missed. He got outside and started shouting. "Run! We've been found oot! Run!" There was a shot and he fell. By that time, my eyes had adjusted. The figure was aiming at me. I rolled to the one side. Then there was a crash of bushes, a shout, and silence.

Kitchi came back, wiping his knife. I hadn't even seen him exit the hut. "He's dead," Kitchi said with a certain amount of satisfaction. We went over to the body. His rifle lay beside him. It was topped with a scope. I searched through his pockets and found letters addressed to Sam Pollock.

Suddenly, we heard the sound of a carriage leaving at break-neck speed and a voice urging the horses. I knew not even Kitchi could catch Bryant in the dark.

I picked up the dead man's rifle and we went back to Meryl. She looked at me through swollen eyes. "I guess I've looked better."

"You always look good to me." I tried to smile, but the smile had died somewhere deep inside my gut. I turned away. "Kitchi," I said, pointing to Dougald. "We need to keep this one alive. He's going to give Queen's evidence against Bryant."

Kitchi eyed the man and nodded. "I will take this one to Brown."

"If you meet Angus and Craig on the way, tell them what happened."

He nodded. "Yes, my brother. You and Sun in Her Hair must speak. She has told me everything."

Meryl couldn't have told him everything. Not even she knew how sick and broken I was inside.

We found a stick for Dougald to use as a crutch. "If you try to escape," Kitchi warned, "you die."

After they left, Meryl and I were looked at each other. "How are you feeling?" I asked.

"Sore," she said. "In a lot of ways. I'm sorry I endangered things by going off like that."

"Yes. It was a stupid thing to do, a very stupid thing to do."

She looked at the floor. There was a long silence. "Drew…"

"Meryl…" I said at the same time. We smiled at each other – a tired, sad smile. "You first," I said.

She pointed to the other side of the table and I sat down. "Drew," she said in a rush. "I'm sorry. I didn't mean to do this, but I can't marry you. I love …"

"You love Kitchi. I think I knew that all along. We've both been pretending, Meryl. I should have been willing to face what I knew in my heart and let you go a long time ago. The fact that we got engaged, but never set a date. I guess I thought if I didn't think about it, reality would stay the way I wanted it instead of the way it was. Are you sure? No going back this time."

She took my hand, which of its own volition made no resistance. If it would have changed things, I would have swept her into my arms and crushed her to me and kissed her. Since meeting Jesus, we had withheld ourselves from sex, wanting to wait until we were married. But at that moment that I would have thrown her to the floor and taken her if in that taking I could have made her love me.

"I will always be your friend, Drew. Listen to me! I sound like a character in a romance novel. I disgust myself."

"At this point I'm supposed to get angry and start throwing things about," I replied sadly, "but real life is often unromantic." I tried to smile at Meryl as my "friend." The hurt and cold inside had frozen my lips. They couldn't respond. "I hate going to *SavaJava* on my own."

"There will be someone else," she said softly. "You're a real hero, Drew, inside and out." I felt more like a discarded moth-riddled coat. "You really are a good looking boy." Her cracked lips forced a smile, and she squeezed my hand.

"Suppose she doesn't like *SavaJava?*" It was the only response I could muster.

I couldn't spoil things for Meryl by telling her that a cold, empty, pointless feeling about life invaded my spirit. I shivered. This was literally the lowest point in my life. I'd been wounded in a knife fight. I'd been shot in a duel. Nothing I'd ever been through matched this for pain. And, yet, the pain was hidden inside where no one looking at me could see it. I was a walking wounded; a train wreck still overturned on the track. Then, like an imperceptible breeze that moves the flowers, the Lord's voice somehow found its way into my spirit. *Drew, my child. Look with your heart and not with your eyes.*

Without warning, Angus and Craig barged into the hut. "Well," Craig said, "it looks like we missed the fun." Then Angus saw Meryl's face and the banter fell like a dropped rock. "Oh, Meryl! What did they do...are you okay?"

"You want to see the other fellah," she quipped.

"Pollock is out there, about fifteen paces from the door," I told Angus and Craig. I'm going back to the castle." I stood up and headed for the door.

"Drew," Meryl said.

"Meryl, leave it. I just want to be on my own. I need to get used to it."

Little was I to know that the answer to my rapidly emptying heart was at the castle. So often God closes one door only to open another

I got back and found John Brown and Sir Charles Gray. "The Queen should be safe for a while. Bryant won't try anything on his own. He's wanted by the law, now even more so."

Sir Charles asked, "Is the young lady safe?"

"Yes, Sir Charles. I think I can say she is in safe hands."

"We thank you so much. I will pass onto her Majesty all that you have said. I have no doubt she will wish to convey her thanks to you personally."

I bowed and said, "I am gratified."

Kitchi had been the first back. He had already handed the kidnapper over to John Brown, and Brown had called the authorities and unlocked the bedroom to allow Morag to return home. Meryl had come back with Craig and Angus after I had left. Now she was with Kitchi, and he had his arm around her protectively. Seeing them together, I knew in my heart it was right, but it still didn't make it easy to accept.

"I want to wish you both all the happiness in the world and God's blessing," I told Meryl and Kitchi, managing not to choke on the words, which were true.

"Thank you," Kitchi replied. "You will always be our brother."

"If I had to choose people to watch my back, you two would be high on the list."

They looked so happy and so right together that it made me angry. Where was my happy and right? Didn't I deserve the joy and respect of love? I knew I was being selfish, but Meryl's words came floating back to me from the night before I left for China; *"I will always love you and if they were to kill me, they would find your name written on my heart."*

My name — Andrew — and Kitchi's names both had six letters. Even so, whoever said, *it's better to have loved and lost than never to have loved at all,* really didn't know much about love.

Craig and Angus were playing billiards when I found them. Angus' face spoke even more than his words. Sorrow was written into every line. "I'm so sorry, Drew. At least we got a result and got the assassin."

"Thanks, Angus. But Bryant got away again. Where is he? We've got to get after his ship. I wonder if the two goons from PATCH are still wandering about?" I paced the room, eager to complete the mission.

Truthfully, losing Meryl was crippling. It hurt far more than I realized was possible. What hurt even worse was knowing that she belonged with Kitchi, not me. All the things we had been through and all the love we had shared replayed through my memory like a repeating CD. After the passion we had shared at the hotel in Gettysburg — how could she have left me? Hadn't our lovemaking meant anything to her? How could she forget a tenderness and love so deep that it buried itself in the gut and reawakened at the slightest touch? A broken heart writes its own script.

I decided sleep would be a good panacea. This palace had so many doors. I found that three people can open a door, the person on the outside, the person on the inside and God.

What I didn't realize at the time was that God was about to open a door that would lead to a stellar performance.

PART 3

CHAPTER 8 - Marie, Two Hearts Seeking a Home

I was passing down one of the long corridors in the castle when I heard a piano playing. I recognized the music of Chopin, the *Fantasie Impromptu No 4*. It was my favorite piece of music. The keys were being played at lightning speed, and then the music broke into the dream-like central theme. I found the door and gently opened it. I slipped in and sat on a chair at the back. A girl was at the piano. I could only see her back. She wore a blue dress and her hair was as black as a raven's wings against the blue. As she swayed from side to side, the music seemed to become part of her. Her playing filled the room with musical notes like silver velvet. I lack the right words to describe beautiful, but it was like being carried away to a far off land on heavenly wings. I had never heard anything more enrapturing. Her music touched my spirit with the heart of God.

She stopped playing and applause sounded from the other side of the room. The clapper was an elderly lady who reminded me of an older version of Mrs. Jamieson, my former landlady in China.

"Marie," she said, "you have had an audience. Major Faulkner, if I'm not mistaken."

The girl did not turn around. I went to the piano after looking at the elderly lady, who nodded. "Your playing touched my spirit," I said, "*Chopin impromptu No 4*, my favorite piece of music."

The head turned towards me. "Thank you. You are very kind."

"Kind? Indeed not! It's a rarity to hear such lovely music. Where did you learn to play, if you don't mind my asking?"

"In Paris," she replied. "From age six to eleven, I was taught by a famous pianist."

Her accent was not thick and her voice had a soothing effect, enhanced by the slight accent.

"You play so well with such a gentle touch and…" My voice trailed away. I suddenly realized by her unblinking gaze that she was blind. Dear God, how did she play like that?

"You're visually impaired," I said, using the modern politically correct term. Only then I realized how awful it sounded as an added description of this talented and beautiful woman.

"I'm blind," she said. A look stole over her face as if by releasing that information she expected it would end the conversation and I would make an excuse to leave.

I didn't want to leave. "When you play, you and the piano become one. You live your music. He really must have been a good teacher."

She smiled and I found myself nearly drawn into her lovely face. "He was. His name was Chopin."

She must have heard my intake of breath. "No wonder you're so good!" Then I realized that my words might have unintentionally seemed rude and dismissive. "Even aside from such a teacher, you are gifted. I looked over at the lady in the corner and she nodded at me. She was smiling.

"Please tell me your name."

"Marie Waleska."

"Drew Faulkner. Miss Waleska, I sincerely hope I may hear you play again."

She held up her hands to my face. The old lady nodded and I remembered that some blind people feel a person's face and hands.

I closed my eyes and felt the touch of her fingers on my face. Her touch made me cry. Tears ran down my cheeks.

"You have a kind face, sir, and fresh breath." Marie said. She felt my hands. "You work with your mind, not with your hands. Do you play an instrument?"

I sighed. "No. I wish I did."

"Scales came before what you heard. Days, weeks and months and years of practice."

"My daughter is young enough and dedicated enough to play," I told her. "Someday, I hope she will be at least half as good as you are."

The look on her face changed slightly. "Does your wife play?"

"I'm a widower," I explained. "My wife was killed on our wedding day."

She gasped and covered her mouth with her hands. "Oh, how tragic and sad, I am so sorry."

"My daughter Mi-Ling is adopted. She's from China."

"Mi-Ling…what a beautiful name! Does she sing?"

"You embarrass me, Miss Waleska. Mi-Ling's been with me for a while now and I must confess – I don't know. But her heart sings and her smile sings. She is a joy to my life."

Marie was writing herself into my heart like a living musical score and I realized that I didn't mind.

"Does it hurt?" she asked gently and with real curiosity. "Losing someone you love and thinking you might spend the rest of your life…" Her voice trailed off and I knew intuitively that she had been going to say "alone."

I couldn't address Marie's fear over spending the rest of her life alone. I had only just met her. But I could answer the other question. "Lucy is with the Lord. That's my compensation." I hesitated. "If I see you out walking with your companion, may I walk with you?"

"To help a poor blind girl?" she asked

"No, Miss Waleska, so we can talk. I promise I will not try to help a poor blind girl if you promise not to try to help a poor widower."

Her face broke out into a smile that mirrored the loveliness in her heart. "Very well, monsieur, we have an agreement."

"Please call me Drew. How may I address you?"

"'The blind girl'. They soon forget my name."

"I will never forget your name, Marie. And blind? But you see so clearly with your heart. May we meet tomorrow? At what time do you go on your walk?"

"At two o'clock."

"Until then."

I bid her farewell and went over to the elderly lady to tell her goodbye. She said to me, "Major, you have found Marie. My name is Martha. I am Marie's chaperone, but a chaperone that also likes Chopin and sometimes has a hearing problem. In certain circumstances, I get bouts of deafness. A problem I must not try to cure too quickly." We grinned at one another like two conspirators. I left to the tune of the *Raindrop prelude* and to the sunshine that seemed to have burst forth in my spirit.

The following day was long. The Queen would give us an audience at five o'clock. "Weighty matters of state detain us or we would have expressed our gratitude sooner," was the message conveyed.

Why did it take two o'clock so long to come? Yet, what was I thinking? I had only just lost Meryl and would be saying goodbye to her yet again – only this time would be the last time. I was outside ready to meet Marie from one o'clock on. I paced in front of the castle. Ten minutes early, Marie and her chaperone appeared.

Why was I so excited? Why was my heart full of joy?

Martha saw me and said something to Marie. To my delight, a smile broke across Marie's face.

"You kept your promise," Marie said to me. "Thank you."

We made small talk. Martha suddenly stopped and drew her arm out of Marie's, then indicated to me that I could take her place. "I will walk behind," she said with a smile. She dropped as far back as decency dictated.

"Do you smell the roses," Marie asked, "and the scent of thyme?"

"The roses are red and yellow," I told her.

She frowned slightly. "I have forgotten color. Red and yellow are only names to me now."

"Yellow is like the touch of sunshine," I explained.

"And red?" she asked with a smile.

"Red? If you have ever cut your finger and felt blood and rubbed it between your fingers, red is like that. It is also the color of love."

A slight tinge of the color under conversation flushed her cheek. "You somehow seem different from other men."

"Yes, Miss Waleska. I fear so. You see, I have two heads and howl at the full moon."

Her laughter was like the music that was so much a part of her. "Where were you born?" she asked.

"Edinburgh, Scotland."

Her next question caught me on the hop. "When?"

Without thinking, I gave my birth date – in the modern century.

"Can you say that again, please?" she queried.

After a quick calculation, I started to say 1842. I couldn't. I knew in my heart I wanted to have relationship with this woman based on truth from day one. If she thought I was mentally insane and didn't want to have any further contact with me, I would understand. But I couldn't tell her an untruth that I would have to retract later.

"Miss Waleska, may we sit?"

Martha overheard my question. She nodded and indicated a sitting area. "You young people do your talking and I will sit and think of afternoon tea," she said.

Marie and I sat down, keeping a slight distance between us. "I must tell you my story," I told Marie. "It will be the truth. If you think me mad or eccentric after hearing it, then call your chaperone and leave. I won't trouble you again."

She nodded and said, "Say on."

So I did. I told her everything. She often used her imagination to see in her mind's eye what people described to her, so my story did not seem strange in the least. I included my rank as major. I covered Mi-Ling and Lucy and the tea clipper race. Then I told her about Gettysburg and General Lee and getting lost in 1755, and winding up with General Braddock. Finally, I brought her up to date. "We got word that the Queen's life was in danger. We came to stop PATCH. With God's help, we have succeeded."

There was a pause and she turned to face me, following the sound of my voice.

"I cannot see you with my eyes, yet you are the only man to whom I have spoken that I can see with my heart."

"I hope I am what you see," I replied "When I leave here, I will join Mi-Ling at our home, Bellefield. It's between Huntly and Aberdeen. The people here believe we have come from Pinkerton's Detective Agency. It was thought that because Bryant was American, an American agency could help. The important thing is that for now, the Queen is safe."

"I wonder if the American President Lincoln thought he was safe when the Civil War ended," Marie mused thoughtfully. She asked several more questions and then said gently, with empathetic perception, "I'm sorry, major, it must have hurt you inside to let Meryl go after you had been engaged to her."

Her words stabbed me in the heart and made my gut ache all over again. I steadied myself and gave her the answer that I knew was right, even if my body hadn't grasped it yet. "When you know something is right, it is easier to let go. She and Kitchi belong together."

"I see," she said, and then giggled at her words.

I didn't know how to react. "Come on, Major," she teased. "Laugh, you know you want to. Don't take things so seriously. One day I may see your face and it would be nice to see laughter lines."

So, to my great relief she had not thought me mad, had not called her chaperone, and had not left. "Can I ask why you are here? Does the Queen like your playing? That would be understandable. The Queen still has a sad heart. Your ministrations would help bring her peace." I paused, and then burst out before I could stop myself, "At the risk of sounding indelicate, is there someone in your life?"

She sighed. "No. Sadly, there is not."

It was out before I realized what I said, "The young men must be blind." I gulped. "I'm sorry! I didn't mean to offend you. Please forgive me. I would not wish to hurt you for all the world."

She laughed at me. "I'm neither hurt nor offended. A gentle and caring soldier and a blind pianist. We are a contradiction in terms, Major. Maybe we will be good for one another."

Martha had claimed she would be thinking, not listening. But at Maria's words, a broad smile spread across the chaperone's face.

"If you were to come with me when I left," I told her eagerly, "I could read to you. I have a library full of books. There's quite a good piano in the house, at least I was told it was good. There are lots of places for walking; if the Queen will let you and Martha leave here." I had not intended to make such an offer. It seemed to tumble out on its own accord. "I'd like you to get to meet Mi-Ling."

Passing us on the other side were Meryl and Kitchi, walking arm in arm. I tried not to look at them. It was easy when I kept my eyes focused on the soft, gentle beauty of Maria's face.

Soon, all too soon, our walk ended. It was time to meet the Queen. Angus, Craig, Meryl, Kitchi and I were taken to yet another room where the Queen sat behind a desk. John Brown and Sir Charles Gray stood by the desk. The Queen dismissed them. "We would see these on our own."

Brown and Sir Charles left. Brown shot me a brooding look as he passed, as if he blamed me for the Queen's decision. Queen Victoria rose and came round the desk to where we stood.

"You have our sincere thanks. We are indebted to your courage and bravery," and looking at Meryl, she added, "your valor.

"Kitchi," the Queen said, "your Chief Running Wolf will be proud of you." She returned to the desk and retrieved a medal on a green ribbon. "This is the Albert Medal given for acts of courage and bravery. Very, very few have won it," she said. Kitchi knelt and she put it round his neck.

Kitchi said, "Great Chief of all the white men, Kitchi will treasure this always and wear it over his heart." Meryl looked up at him with pride and love in her eyes.

"Our blessings to you both," the Queen said. "Please accept this." From behind her desk, she produced a beautiful Long Rifle.

Kitchi took it and said, "Thank you, a warrior's weapon."

Then she thanked Craig and Angus. "You have our thanks and gratitude."

We bowed and started to back away. You did not turn your back on the Queen.

"Major Faulkner, we would talk with you alone," She said.

The others left. Queen Victoria came to the point. "Marie Waleska. She has been hurt and rejected. We would not wish to see her heart hurt again. We are prepared to make a settlement on you if your intentions are honorable."

"Your Majesty, may I have permission to speak freely and candidly?"

"This is a time for candor."

"Ma'am, please keep your settlement. If there is any further relationship, it will be because of us, the people we are, and not because someone has offered money or land – no matter how well meant. One thing I am determined is that if we have a relationship, an honorable relationship, it will be based on truth – and if it happens – love."

The Queen smiled. "We had hoped that would be your answer. Please take good care of Marie. We will miss her playing. We will speak with her."

I met Angus later that day. He was cheerful. "Well, at least for now our work is done. We need to get Kitchi back…er and Meryl with him. She has promised to return to Vanguard if she is needed again." He clasped my shoulder. "Sorry Drew, son. I know this wasn't how you expected things to turn out."

I sighed and shook my head, sounding every bit as morose as I felt when I thought about the finality of losing Meryl out of my life. "Well, at least it's settled now. I never could get peace that she and I would work out, even though I really wanted it to."

"A blind girl," Angus said. "Does she know what you do? Does she believe it?"

"Yes and yes."

"Does it not seem strange to her? Unbelievable?"

"No. Maybe if you're blind you have a different way of looking at things."

"Are you going to get her to a modern day doctor? Maybe an eye surgeon?" he asked in a fatherly tone of voice.

"Yes."

"Suppose they can't help her?" Angus questioned. "Even modern surgery has limitations. Have you realized that if they can't cure Marie, you will have to spend the rest of your life with someone who's blind?"

Angus was right. I had to think it through. Was I ready to commit myself to someone who might remain blind? If not, now was the time to stop it.

"Craig and Kitchi have gone back," Angus added. "I'll take Meryl. Abigail is not far from Kitchi's camp, but what about you?"

"I'll have to get back and do a debrief with Colonel Carlisle. Then I can get back to Mi-Ling. It will be good to report success to the colonel. Not entire success with Bryant still on the loose. What else happens depends on Marie."

"And you," he added. "Keep in touch, son. I have my Abigail. Kitchi has his Sun in Her Hair. It's your time for love and happiness, Drew. You've suffered enough." He clasped me on the shoulder again.

"Thanks, Angus. How differently things have turned out from the way they started in Foochow."

Angus and I parted. When I got to the front door of the castle, I was completely shocked. Meryl and Marie were walking together arm-in-arm. Martha sat on a seat with a tea tray on a table beside her. "Oolong," she pronounced, ignoring my shock at seeing her charge with Meryl. "It is all the way from Foochow. It's rather good. Join me, Drew."

"Thank you, Martha. I'd love to join you, but I need to talk to Meryl if I can prize her away from Marie."

"It's a wonder your ears are not burning, Major," Martha said. "I rather suspect you may be high on the topics of conversation."

I caught up with the girls.

"Unless I am very much in error," Meryl said, "It is the cavalry coming."

"I am glad you two are deep in conversation."

Marie smiled and said, "When I hear your voice I feel happiness and peace, Drew — a calm haven in a turbulent world."

I was slightly taken aback. Meryl looked at me and smiled. "Is it me with whom you wish to converse?"

"May I?" I asked.

Marie said, "I will go and make sure Martha doesn't drink all the tea, until the next time, major."

I guided Marie back to Martha, and returned to Meryl. There was a moment of silence.

"Drew, Marie is a lovely girl. One thing I see that she can't is that you've never looked at me the way you look at her."

"Well, that is not intentional. Are you sure about Kitchi?" I asked to change the subject.

"Yes. I'm sorry, Drew. But when I saw him again, I realized how much I missed him. I don't want to be parted from him."

"Mmm…reckon you can exist without *SavaJava*?"

"I'll try. Maybe I can teach Kitchi's village how to make coffee. You are a kind, lovely man. Marie will be good for you."

"Yes," I agreed, "but will I be good for her?"

"Mi-Ling will love her, you wait and see," Meryl added. "They both see things through their hearts, not their eyes."

"The trouble is that I think I have become a kind of adrenalin junkie. I can't give up the rush of time travel."

"And when you're sixty? And there's no Marie? You were ready to give it up for Lucy."

I sighed. "You're right, Meryl. It's just that I hate it that the old gang is breaking up. Lucy, you, Angus."

"Did you really expect things to remain the same, '*we few, we happy few, we band of brothers?*' Besides, how do you know that what's to come is not going to be better?"

"True. The Lord is in control of time and eternity. I guess I have to trust Him."

"Same thing I'm doing going back to 1757, No *SavaJava,* remember?"

"One last thing," I said. "Can I get a hug?"

"Of course, my friend," Meryl said softly. As I held her, I inhaled the scent of coconut from her hair. "We may need to work together again," she said, her head resting against my shoulder. "But you have Mi-Ling, Marie and a new life to start, and a villain to catch. None of us are safe until Bryant is removed and Professor Reynolds is stopped – in whatever century that might be. God keep you." She kissed me on the cheek, pulled out of my arms and glided back toward the castle. *And Kitchi,* I thought bitterly. But what she had said was true. I had no right to hang on to my bitterness. Mi-Ling needed me and I did have a new life to start.

Meryl and I had shared so much. As I watched her walk away, I couldn't stop the "what ifs" that plagued me. Like the rainbow, she had come and now she was going. Reality was a much less colorful place. I was reminded of a song by Ella Fitzgerald that went, "*every time we say goodbye I die a little.*" Would I ever see Meryl again? I did not know at the time that the answer was yes, during a time of great joy.

Marie and Martha were still on the seat as I walked towards them. Martha shook her head at me and said, "Marie, Major Faulkner had to leave. We can get in touch with him later." She then walked her fingers over her open hand as if to say to me, "You need a walk and time to think." I took the hint and walked away, my glance drawn to the retreating figure of my dream girl Meryl.

Meryl turned as she reached the castle door. For a long moment, we stared at each other across the distance. Then she slipped inside to her new life and left me standing outside, cold, alone and empty.

CHAPTER 9 - Broken Hearts Mend -Eventually

I had never felt as dejected as I did that day after Meryl had slipped through that door into the castle. Anyone passing me would have seen tears running down my face. I could hear Ella in my head singing, '*every time we say goodbye I cry a little, every time we say goodbye I die a little…*' I envisioned Meryl running back out of the castle and throwing herself into my arms. It didn't happen. This was real life, not a romance novel.

As I walked, I saw in my mind's eye a vision of two doors, one open and one shut. As I approached the open door, it shut. As I approached the door that had been shut, it opened. Jesus' words, "*I am the way, the truth, and the life*" came floating into my mind.

"*Lord, what do I do? My heart is breaking. What do I do?*"

"*Trust Me,*" came the reply, "*be patient.*" I realized that even after meeting Jesus, I was still new to this God thing. Slowly, gently, peace returned. The more I thought about Jesus, the less pain I suffered. How did He do it?

* * *

Even the thought of royal fare did not end my aimless walking and return me to the castle until eight o'clock. Maybe Meryl had not gone! But she had, as had Angus. I was on my own. I suddenly missed Mi-Ling even more than usual. She was virtually all I had left.

Unbidden, a mean thought popped into my head…*a blind girl? Is that the best you can do? Remember the days when Meryl and Lucy were chasing after you? Now you are reduced to Marie. Give it up! You're an action man, not a nurse maid.*"

I knew an unkind thought like this didn't come from God. False criticism was not God's way of speaking to His children. I remembered the peace I had felt when I heard Marie play the piano. I could see her in my mind, first being serious, then giggling and breaking into a musical laugh. I had enjoyed that. I had enjoyed Marie's company.

Then I remembered Meryl's words and what she had seen. "You didn't look at me like you look at her." Marie didn't need a nurse maid. She was tough and had fought to get where she was.

The strange thing was that when I thought about Marie it reminded me of Mi-Ling. Mi-ling had been in a situation from hell and had come through. Somehow they seemed alike. I was suddenly sure they could benefit from friendship and encourage one another. Perhaps even like mother and daughter?

I imagined that if Marie were playing tonight, it would be in the same room as I had heard her before. Shifting a huge grand piano was a king-sized task – even for royalty.

Hearing piano music, I hurried down the hall. As quietly as possible, I opened the door, hoping the seated assemblage had their backs to my entry point. I timed my entry during a natural break in the music. One piece ended and there was a round of polite applause. I slipped into the seat closest to the door. The Queen was there, along with John Brown and various family members.

There was a pregnant pause, as the room awaited the delivery of a piece by Beethoven. When Marie started, a footman glided his way over to where I sat and whispered into my ear.

"Major, her Majesty requests that you take the empty chair behind her at your earliest opportunity."

It seemed rude to keep the queen waiting. At the end of the first movement, I headed for the royal party, bowing to the Queen. She beckoned me to the seat behind her. As her Majesty's fan came down, there was a smile on her lips.

I became lost in a forest of Beethoven's music. Too soon, it ended. There was a round of applause, mine probably being the most enthusiastic. The footman returned.

"Her Majesty wishes to converse with you, Major Faulkner."

I gathered from that that one did not speak to the monarch over her shoulder. I went before her and bowed.

"We are gratified by your presence, Major. Perhaps you would convey the fact that you are here to Miss Waleska? We are sure she would find such knowledge beneficial."

I bowed again and responded, "Of course, your Majesty."

Others were congratulating Marie and I slipped into the admiring crowd. "Your playing is as lovely as a rainbow over a waterfall in a forest glen," I said.

She smiled. "You came! Martha said you would, but I was not sure."

"Wild horses couldn't have kept me away."

"I am so glad you are here. Thank you."

"The joy is mine, "I replied sincerely.

"Sit near me, for my last piece. Please?" she responded

"I must ask the Queen's permission as I was in her party."

The queen had finished a small glass of punch. She beckoned me forward.

"Your Majesty, Miss Waleska requested that I sit near her for the final score."

The Queen smiled, then putting on a stern expression she replied, "Major, we would offer you this advice, that when your Queen makes a request it is better to comply, away with you."

I returned to a seat next to Martha, three feet away from the piano. A velvet hush fell down from heaven. Marie stood up and faced the crowd. "Your Majesty, my lords, ladies and gentlemen. There is a change in our final piece. I will now play Chopin's *Fantasie Impromptu No. 4* in C Sharp minor." When she picked up her fan, it fell from her hand. I jumped up and retrieved it from the floor and placed it in her hand. As I did so, she said softly, "This is for you, Drew."

I was sure the choirs of heaven stopped to listen. Her fingers flew over the keys, first with passion, then with tenderness. She plucked the notes of music out of the air and wove them into combination of sound like the beating of angels' wings. The Queen's expression wore a maternal smile as she looked at us – two of her children.

All too soon the piece ended. Marie stood up to a cannonade of applause. Marie held out her hand. Concerned, I went to Martha's chair. "Martha, I think Marie needs your help."

Martha laughed. "Silly boy! It's not my hand for which she is seeking."

The applause continued and I took Marie's hand.

All that, a gentle voice said in my spirit, *and that without sight – and you were worried about being a nurse maid.*

Marie was being thronged by congratulatory people. She squeezed my hand and then let it go so she could shake hands with other people.

Martha joined me. She was smiling broadly. "Her Majesty has given us permission to leave in three days and will provide transport to Bellefield."

I smiled back in obvious relief. "I must leave tomorrow morning, but I'll be at Bellefield when you arrive. I look forward to my daughter Mi-Ling getting to meet Marie. But just now, it's wonderful to see Marie get the praise her playing deserves. I hope you will like Bellefield, Martha."

"One day I will be surplus to requirements and I shall retire and buy a tea plantation in China. Then I can have all the tea I want, while in a coterie of neighbors and friends solve all the problems of western civilization there on my own verandah."

"Keep a weather eye open for a lovely new ship next year for the tea run," I prophesied.

"What would her name be?" she asked

"The Cutty Sark," I replied.

"Will she stand the journey?" Martha questioned.

"Oh yes," I said. "My sources tell me she will last."

I went back to Marie, who was gently coming down off cloud nine.

"I must leave tomorrow," I told Marie. "But I'll be home to meet you when you and Martha get to Bellefield. I hope you and Mi-Ling like each other."

"I am sure we shall, but are you sure you want me to come?"

"Do the flowers under the ground long for the end of the cold of winter and the chance to feel the earth warmed by the spring sunshine? I have been living in cold winter Marie and now my heart hears the voice of spring."

Marie held out her hand and I put mine into it. Then I kissed the top of her forehead and promised, "Until Bellefield."

"Be careful, Drew. God bless you," she said.

With the question about Marie settled, it seemed pointless to remain at the castle longer. I was too excited to sleep and I needed to get back and see Mi-Ling again and tell her about Marie. I asked John Brown for a lift to the station.

"Man, tha'll nae be trains at this time of the nicht."

"Humor me, please. I have a couple of loose ends to tie together."

Probably because we had never hit it off and he would be glad to see my back disappearing, he agreed. "Weeel, if you are sure, I will arrange it."

I went to my room and packed. It was only then that I realized that Meryl still had her engagement ring. She was normally precise. Why had she hung onto it? Maybe it was at HQ waiting with a *Dear John* letter, but what if it wasn't? I didn't mind her keeping it, but did it mean that she planned to keep me open as a future option? No, that was gone.

I still had the Bowie knife and the Webley. I kept them within easy reach. My assigned driver took me to the station and let me off. I gave him five shillings in appreciation.

"God bless you, Major. If you are sure there is nothing else I can do, I will be getting back to the castle."

I was left at the station alone with my thoughts. Things had changed, whether for the better or for the worse was still to be seen. I stood and breathed in the cold evening air, then summoned the time car.

Opposition from PATCH and Bryant I expected as I headed back. However, I was unknowingly heading back to face an opposition far more deadly and evil than anything PATCH or Bryant could have dreamed up, more deadly, because it sprang at me from a totally unexpected source.

* * *

"I'm sorry about Meryl," Colonel Carlisle said as I sat with Craig in his office. "I suppose it's better finding out now than later. When Meryl came through she seemed upset and sad, quite out of character for her."

I hesitated, and then asked, "Did she leave anything for me, sir?"

Colonel Carlisle thought. "No. Nothing that I'm aware of, I'm afraid. She said she hoped you would be happy and counted you as her dearest friend. *'Amigos no amores'?*"

I explained about Marie. "Maybe our doctors can help," he suggested. "Keep me posted."

He thanked Craig Carter for his help and told him he was free to rejoin his unit. "Yes, colonel, but how I am going to fit back into the chow hall with the guys again after dining with the Queen at her castle, still it was good experience.

The colonel laughed. "Don't be too disheartened, major. We'll call on you again – especially when we relocate Bryant. Thank you for being part of combined ops."

"My pleasure,sir." Craig replied. He left Colonel Carlisle's office and I started out in his footsteps.

"Wait, Major. Before you go, I'll be returning Dr. Lucy to you soon for Mi-Ling. Thanks for the help from Mike and she , Hera seems completely comfortable in modern times and is starting to speak English quite well. Mike's teaching her to drive." He paused. "But back to Dr. Lucy. When I told her of Meryl's departure with Kitchi, she seemed inordinately pleased. Strange, is it not?"

I nodded. "But that's good about Mike and Hera. So they're still a couple?"

"Getting on like the proverbial house on fire. She's an attractive woman and definitely Mike's type. Hera is teaching some of our operatives unarmed combat. How to use a sword and other weapons." The colonel laughed. "When the young men see Hera they think disarming her will be easy. She soon disillusions them!"

I caught up with Craig and we had coffee in the canteen.

"It's not *SavaJava*," he said.

"No," I replied, "but right now *SavaJava* holds hurtful memories for me." I paused. "I hope we can work together again. You're a great guy to have on the team."

"Thanks, Major. I hope we can, too."

For no reason I could name, a slightly uneasy silence seemed to fall over us.

"Major, I've got this kind of gut feeling that it's too quiet!"

"Strange you should say that, Craig. I was thinking the same thing!"

Sadly, we were both to be proven right.

* * *

Heading home, I had gone into Aberdeen to buy chocolate for Mi-Ling. Such was my nous for parenthood that I couldn't think of anything else to buy her. If Marie and I hit it off I would also need to spend more time with Mi-Ling.

Maybe we could take her on an educational trip, I thought then realized how boring that sounded.

I got back to Bellefield. Was it my imagination, or did the place have a bit of an echo now? To them, it would only have been a few days since I left. I was eager to find Mi-Ling and Caroline and explain the change to them. Suddenly it dawned on me that the house was going to be as busy as when Lucy was here.

Mi-Ling saw me as I came up from the basement. "Papa!" she cried, launching herself from three steps up. I caught her and spun her round. She giggled and wrapped and her arms around my neck. I carried her into the sitting room. She kept looking back as if she were looking for someone.

"Lost something?" I asked, kissing the top of her head and putting her down.

"Where's Miss Meryl?" she asked.

I sighed, time for a father-daughter talk. "Miss Meryl won't be coming to stay," I told Mi-Ling. "She realized she loved someone more than me."

She had that knowing look. "Was it Kitchi, Papa? She liked Kitchi. He is very handsome, but not as handsome as you, Papa."

I would have blessed her little cotton socks if she had been wearing any.

"Things like this happen," I added. "Sometimes we get it wrong." She nodded encouragement.

"I have a friend coming to stay." Carolyn glided into the room.

"Is your friend a lady, Papa?"

"Yes."

"Mi-Ling understands. Papa has a lonely heart. It needs filling up."

"Mi-Ling, Marie is blind."

Caroline didn't say anything, but she picked through the books on the shelf as she listened to me, taking one out she began to read, except it was upside down.

"She plays the piano beautifully," I added, as if trying to convince Mi-Ling that Marie coming would be a good thing.

Mi-Ling thought for a moment. "Maybe Mi-Ling can take Marie for walks in the garden. I show her the garden and all the lovely flowers, the ones that have nice scent. She can smell them and soon she think of it as…as…" I could see her mind working overtime, looking for the right phrase. "Soon she will think it is *The Scent of Home*.

Mi-Ling will think about how to make Marie feel welcome. Is she pretty?"

"She has long black hair and a lovely smile just like you."

"I can read to her, Papa," Mi-Ling said with enthusiasm. "Mi-Ling has learned to read gooder and gooder." She saw Carolyn then and flung herself across the room to repeat everything I had told her to Carolyn in an excited tone of voice. Carolyn smiled and nodded, not ruining the news for Mi-Ling by letting her know she had already heard it.

After Mi-Ling went outside to find Connie, Carolyn spoke. "Drew, this is quite an undertaking. A girl who's blind? It's none of my business, other than how it affects Mi-Ling. At the moment, she seems to be delighted. But, Drew, just be sure you're not clutching at straws."

"Marie is a lovely and talented woman and very independent. Her companion will be with her, as is proper. Meet her and you can judge for yourself. Her name is Marie Waleska and she was playing the piano for Queen Victoria."

"Drew, think about Mi-Ling. Is this really what is best for her?"

I felt hurt. "Don't you realize that I've thought this out, Carolyn? You're carrying the fruit and joy of your love. You can go to Myles for love and comfort. Sometimes I feel like my heart is a tennis ball, getting whopped from one side of the court to the other. The crowd sits and watches the ball go from side to side, waiting for the first break in serve.

Am I doing something wrong in loving or does it have to meet everyone else's approval? I lost Lucy to a callous murderer and Meryl to an honest man in Kitchi. Would you have me make a criminal suspect of my own feelings? You loved Myles from the first time you saw him. You trusted what you felt and it has proven right. Will you not allow me the same liberty of spirit? I want what God wants and I want who God wants."

Carolyn sighed and shook her head.

"Just give me a chance. Why should Marie not be the one?" I asked. "Surely that is for me to say. I hope with all my heart that she and Mi-Ling become friends. My gut tells me they will."

Carolyn smiled gently. "I'm sorry, Drew. I didn't intend to sound disapproving. I just don't want to see you hurt anymore."

"Marie comes in a couple of days. Suddenly I have a hope for a future that is not just work or nearly getting myself killed."

"And I'm very happy for you, Drew. Please forgive my misgivings."

The conversation turned then to the more comfortable topic of Carolyn's baby. Her tone of voice as she said, "I hope Myles will get back soon," made me realize that, like me, she was lonely.

"There is still the question of catching Bryant." I mused. "We will never be fully secure until he is stopped."

"Does he know about Marie?"

"No," I replied, "At least, I don't think so."

Carolyn took the book she had finally selected and left the room. I sat in a comfortable chair and thought. Marie already cared about Mi-Ling just from having met her in words, just as Mi-Ling seemed to have already accepted her. Surely part of Mi-Lings future would be wrapped up in Marie. I was keenly aware that Mi-Ling and Meryl had merely tolerated each other. Had that partly caused Meryl to turn to Kitchi?

* * *

I tried to get the house as ready as I could. How did one get a house ready for someone who is blind? Martha would help and so would Marie herself. We had a lot of learning to do and adjustments to make.

A telegram arrived the following day, a Monday, stating they would arrive at Bellefield by three o'clock Wednesday.

Seven o'clock Wednesday morning found me up. I went all over the house trying to get the servants to make it tidy, in spite of the fact that it was something they always did. I knew Marie couldn't see, but I wanted Bellefield to be perfect for her anyway. She couldn't smell dust on the floor, could she? I treated the house as though Marie could see everything in it before deciding whether she wanted to stay. Yet she would use different criteria from anything I could do. To her, the criteria she used for daily living would be applied at Bellefield, and I didn't know what it was. Maybe Mi-Ling's idea of *The Scent of Home* wasn't so far off track.

Rushing about, I bumped into Mrs. Fraser, who was busy. "Maister, calm doon. The lassie is nae comin' tae see the hoose, she's comin' for aye thing – tae see you. Ye need to shave. Fit will the lassie think if she gie's ye a hug and scrapes the bonnie skin off her face with yer bristles?"

She was right. I ran up stairs with Mrs. Fraser's voice following me, "I'll send up a jug o hot water."

Shaving with a cut throat razor was a slow business. I tried not to cut myself and managed fairly well. I had seen people who had been so quick shavers, but who had ended up with half the newspaper from the night before stuck over their face, the black print becoming stained with scarlet.

It was Mi-Ling who opened the door to Marie. I only caught snatches of laughter, and chatter. Trying to do up collar studs in a hurry is a fruitless task. They manage these things in the films, but real life is different.

By the time I finally got downstairs, Marie, Martha, Mi-Ling and Carolyn were in the living room. There was no mistaking the sparkle in my daughter's eyes – a sparkle that had been missing since Lucy's death.

"Papa said you were lovely and had hair like Mi-Ling," Mi-Ling said, taking Marie's hand. "Papa was right. You are beautiful, Miss Marie." Then suddenly being quite grown up, Mi-Ling added, "You must be tired after your journey. Please take a seat. Do you want to be near a window for fresh air, or near the fire to be warm?" Mi-Ling's eager words flooded out like a river tumbling over rocks and boulders.

Marie laughed, a golden sound that warmed my heart even as it sent a thrilling chill up my spine. "You speak as fast as I play the piano."

"Hello, Marie," I said. "Or should I say, Miss Waleska?" I walked over and took her outstretched hand.

She held out her arms for a hug. I was glad I had shaved. She said close to my ear,

"You wear *The Scent of Eternity*, or maybe it seems how long I have been waiting."

Then in a voice meant to carry, she said, "Marie will be fine. If you address me as Miss Waleska, I shall feel like an exhibit in an art gallery."

Mi-Ling said, "An art gallery is where they put pictures so people can go and see them."

"Yes," Maria agreed, "so people can go and…"

"In the pictures I saw at the art gallery," Mi-Ling interrupted. "Some of the ladies were smiling, but it was painted on. But when you smile, Miss Marie, you show your happy face. Real, not painted." She stopped. "Oh! Mi-Ling has just thought of something she must do. Excuse me, Papa, and Carol Lady, and Sunshine lady." Mi-Ling touched Marie's hand and ran out.

"Sunshine Lady?" Marie said out loud to herself "Yes Sunshine Lady."

I realized that God's gifts come in many shapes and sizes. Mine was in the form of my daughter.

I introduced Carolyn to Marie and Martha. Predictably, the conversational topic proved to be babies. I heard the door open. Mi-Ling must have returned, but she didn't enter the room.

Eventually Carolyn said to me, "Drew, perhaps Marie and Martha would like to get taken to their room to freshen up. Mi-Ling barged into the room, then, looking a little flushed. "I can take Sunshine Lady to her room."

"I will take your luggage," I offered, going into he-man mode and shouldering the cases and valises. Mi-Ling took Marie's hand and said, "There are fifteen steps to the top. Then we turn left and walk another five steps and it is your room."

I followed Marie and Mi-Ling, with Martha at my heels. When we got to the room, I placed the cases in a corner where Marie wasn't likely to trip over them.

"Thank you," Martha said, puffing slightly from the exertion of climbing the stairs. "I will show Marie about the room."

Marie inhaled deeply. "Oh," she said with a radiant smile, "How lovely! I smell lavender, my favorite bloom and perfume."

Looking around, I was briefly surprised to see a bouquet of lavender on Marie's bed. She was standing beside the bed. Her hands reached out to search and caught up the bouquet. "Thank you, Drew. That was very kind and thoughtful of you."

"Don't thank me, Marie. I didn't put them there, but I wish I had."

Mi-Ling slipped forward shyly. "I hope you like them. I wanted you to smell the scent of our welcome, Sunshine Lady."

Marie's smile was brighter than her words. "Thank you, Mi-Ling. I am deeply touched." Mi-Ling stood on her toes and kissed Marie's cheek, then ran out the room. I was standing close to Marie and wondered if I was the only one who saw the tears trickle down her cheeks like two silver calling cards of a too-long neglected heart."

Then the thought passed through my mind, *If she can shed tears, she might with help be able to see!*

Mi-Ling was right. With Marie in the house, sunshine flooded in again. Marie smelled the piano and headed to it. I was amazed. I had honestly forgotten it was there.

"Come, Major," Marie teased. "How could you not know it was there? Are you blind or something?"

The room went silent in shock. None of us knew how to respond.

Maria's laugh hit the musical scales in a light, soothing touch. "Come on, Major, you know you want to laugh! Don't be a sourpuss."

I felt my face slide into a lopsided smile. Mi-Ling had no such inhibitions. She pulled out the stool for Marie. Marie lifted the lid and ran her fingers up and down the keys. Then she sat down and began to play Chopin. It was as if someone had taken the roof off the house and poured in the very music of heaven. The brightness of the musical notes was lighter than air. Mi-Ling was transfixed. After the last notes died away, Mi-Ling asked, "Sunshine Lady, can you teach Mi-Ling to play the piano?"

Marie smiled at her eager pupil and nodded. "Let's start with you finding Middle C. But you must practice."

The two of them were lost in conversation. Carolyn said to me, "There goes my little helper. But I'm not jealous. Drew, I've never seen Mi- Ling so happy." She hesitated. "She loved her Amma Lucy. But I don't think she was ever this happy with Lucy. It's almost like Marie has plucked a wounded bird from the ground and is helping it heal so it can fly again, bringing her joy, peace, and inner strength."

Watching Mi-Ling and Marie, Carolyn and I had forgotten about Martha. Martha remarked softly, "Marie has lost the pain from her face. Like the child, she looks joyful. So do you, Major. There are good men in the world and honest ones. It may be that Marie has found her one. I feel that tea plantation coming a little closer." She winked at me.

Over the next couple of days, my heart warmed up and reawakened again as I watched Marie and Mi-Ling together. It was as if they had known each other for years - walks, laughter, games and piano practice. Did life get any better? Then, on Friday evening, the devil showed up in a silk dress and proceeded to make the Mohawk Indians of General Braddock's expedition look like Boy Scouts. Dr. Lucy appeared at the living room door.

"Oh, Drew darling, how wonderful! You're back. You must introduce me to your friends. Mi-Ling go upstairs please. Who are these people – more charity cases? Drew, you have such a kind heart, but there is no room in our house for everyone."

Words fail me to describe the look on everyone's faces, especially on Marie's. *Lord!* I thought. *Please help me!*

I came to my senses first. "Mi-Ling please stay here with us. Don't go upstairs."

Then trying to control the anger I felt, I addressed the devil in a dress. "These are my guests – in my house – Dr. Lucy. Please treat them as such."

Dr. Lucy crossed over to me. "Darling, don't be so touchy." She flashed a false smile at the astonished Martha. "He's got such a temper when he's roused, prone to outbursts of violence. The number of times I have rescued poor, dear Mi-Ling from his anger." She shook her head.

Mi-Ling was confused. She had loved Dr. Lucy and accepted her as a friend. Tears brimmed in her eyes and she shook her head helplessly, not sure what to say or do. She ran across the room and threw herself against me, burying her glossy dark head against my chest.

The evil woman directed, "Drew and I need to talk alone. So if all of you so-called house guests would leave us, please?"

I looked at the assembled company. They showed no signs of leaving, as if offering me silent support by their very presence. That made the mentally whacky woman angry. She spat, "You see, ladies, Mi-Ling has never been adopted by the major. One has to ask the question, why is she here? What goes on when the lights go out?"

Marie stood up and pushed the piano stool away. "Martha, can we go for a walk outside?" Martha looked at Dr. Lucy with open hostility. She knew Lucy was lying. I thought, *Bryant was evil but he was just a learner to this kid.*

Mi-Ling looked at Lucy with hurt and shock registered on her young face. Lucy tried to get Mi-Ling to stand beside her. Shaking her head angrily, Mi-Ling refused.

"Do you want me to stay, Drew?" Carolyn asked.

Lucy tried to mock her voice, "Do you wan' mee to stay, darling? Whose baby is that you're carrying?"

Anger that I had not seen since the *Night Arrow* days and our race back from Foochow to London flashed across Carolyn's face and sparked in her eyes. "Forgive me, Drew. If I don't leave this room right now, I'll get us both into trouble." Carolyn stomped out of the room and sparks seemed to fly even from the bottom of her delicate buttoned boots.

"One by one the rats desert the sinking ship," Lucy jeered.

Mi-Ling and I were alone now with the deranged woman. Even worse, on one stupid oversight, Lucy was right and the bisom knew it. I had no official documentation saying that I was Mi-Ling's father. I could have kicked myself for having been so neglectful. Lucy saw the look of defeat in my eyes. "Drew, darling ..."

"Stop calling me darling! I'm not your darling."

Lucy smiled like the sun glinting off the silver plate off a coffin before it gets lowered into a grave. "You'd better get used to it. Once we're married, things will change. And married we will be. If not, the local newspapers would be very interested in the story of a respected local landowner with a young whore in the house."

She breezed up to me and tried to hug me. Mi-Ling and I both evaded her. "Darling, we will have a wonderful life together. And when I adopt Mi-Ling as my daughter... Well, it's obvious that you are not Mi-Ling's father. It would be best for her, and you've said all along that you want what's best for Mi-Ling."

"I don't want you as my Amma," Mi-ling said bravely. "Papa will find me a real Amma."

"Be quiet, child! You're too young to know what is best for you."

"Drew, darling, we'll have a wonderful life together – a happy threesome."

Fighting back anger and sheltering Mi-Ling with my body, I stated as gently as possible. "Lucy, you're sick. You need help. You need to go back..."

"Tut tut. Just think of the newspapers. They will love the story. *Public interest*, I think is the phrase. But it doesn't have to get to the papers. It can stop right here, right now with us. Once we're married, darling, everything will be in order."

"I will never marry you, Lucy. You're lost in a dream world right now. You need to wake up."

She ignored my words. "Shall I contact the minister or shall you?"

Mi-Ling broke into hysterics. "I don't want you for a mother!" she screamed. Before I realized what was happening and could stop her, Lucy grabbed Mi-Ling's arm, jerked her away from the safety of my body, and smacked her across the face. Mi-Ling stumbled backwards and fell down on her bottom. "Shut up, you little whore!" the maniacal woman screeched. "And when daddy resigns from Vanguard and comes to work for PATCH, then you will be brought up properly to bear children for the new order. We might even let your father, father the first. Ha, ha, ha.

"You are weak, Drew. You rely on your morals. Morals are weak. Only strength will win in the end. Might is right."

I couldn't think straight. I ran to where Mi-Ling sat on the floor crying and scooped her into my arms. I hugged her and kissed her, then put her down on the couch. I had to find some way to appease Lucy until I could think of what to do or get help somehow. "If we were to ever get married …"

"If? If, darling? There's no *if* about it. Now, let's get the minister and the banns and make it nice and official. Then we can think of the place for a perfect honeymoon, love, passion, and no interruptions."

"Lucy, I can forgive you for trying to ruin my life. But for the hurt you've caused Mi-Ling, I almost feel like killing you…"

She laughed. "Now, darling, marriage, honeymoon. Then we can see about my adopting Mi-Ling properly. Shortly after that, you can say good bye to your little girl. We won't need her underfoot when we're working for PATCH."

My hands clenched and unclenched at my sides. I wanted to wrap them around her throat and squeeze until she quit moving, breathing. I took a step toward her and warned again, "I will kill you…"

She mocked, "You are weak, Drew, you and your morals and your God, PATCH is the new god. You haven't got it in you, to kill me. I on the other hand…"

I sank into the couch beside Mi-Ling and cradled my sobbing daughter.

Dr. Lucy smiled. "Poor baby, you're not having much luck with women. You lost Lucy and Meryl. Now it's Marie. And when I've finished with you, you will be glad to lose me. You are pathetic," she screamed. "Turning to Meryl when I was right there in front of you, loving you, and trying to make you see that I loved you. Me, even Chinese like your daughter, and you never gave me a chance -Pathetic!"

To my shame, I didn't know what to do. "Mi-Ling," I said gently into her hair. "Go on upstairs, sweetheart. You shouldn't be hurt like this. And your pathetic papa would hate you to see him cry."

Stubbornly, Mi-Ling shook her head and refused to leave.

The deranged woman was winding up tighter and tighter. "Remember the famous actress whose phrase was, *I want to be alone*," she taunted. "Well, you only have me now and only I can keep your reputation intact – which will be important because when you sign everything over to me, your reputation might be the only thing you have left."

"Oh, God!" I cried out into the room. "Where are you?"

The un-hospitalized mental patient laughed, mocking my voice. "Oh, God where are you? Where's your God now, *darling*?"

A familiar voice cut across Lucy's ranting. "I appreciate the elevation in status to divinity, but – no – it does not become me."

She was quick. "Anton, the sot, the womanizer…"

"The bringer of good news, for a foreigner you have amazingly bad command of the English language" he said cheerfully, seeming to take no offense at Lucy's rude words. Anton produced a couple of papers from behind his back and held them out to me. "Drew, you left Mi-Ling's adoption papers on the colonel's desk and he thought you should have them back. Hey, I've always wanted to be the U.S. Cavalry! Here they are signed, sealed and legal."

Lucy looked wild-eyed and dangerous. "Let me see!" she screamed.

"These are copies," Anton said, as Lucy leaped for the papers. "Judicial copies, the originals are in a nice safe place."

"Impossible!" Lucy snatched the papers from Anton and read them.

"Don't even think about it," he warned, and then added something in Russian.

Lucy gulped and produced a gun from the folds of her dress. She pointed it at me. "If I can't have you, no one can! Die!" Then she added a Russian word that I found out later cast aspersions on my parentage.

Mi-Ling leaped off the couch, tore across the room and hurtled herself into Lucy's back like a human torpedo. The gun went off and hit the floor. Lucy shot forward, falling heavily. Her head crashed against the piano. She slumped to the floor in a tangled, unmoving heap. A crimson gash on her head spurted crimson onto the carpet.

"Old Russian saying," Anton intoned. "When you think you have got rid of the wolf, watch out for the cubs."

Mi-Ling flung herself into my arms again. I kissed the top of her head. "Thank you, sweetheart, again"

"I don't want any other Papa but you. I love you, Papa."

"And I love you, angel. Next to Jesus, you're my best gift from God."

Carolyn, it turned out, had not left. She had hovered just outside the door in case I needed reinforcement. When Anton arrived, she had watched everything from the doorway. She told Anton about Marie and he went outside to look for her. When he returned, Marie and Martha were with him.

I felt Lucy's wrist for a pulse, and found one. We had to decide what to do. In 1868, Dr. Lucy might suffer an internal cranial hemorrhage and die. If we took her to modern times, back to Vanguard HQ, she might be persuaded to talk about why she had suddenly allied herself with PATCH and who had been behind that decision. I didn't think it was just because Meryl and I had been engaged – briefly. The danger with humans and time travel was that anger or desperation might tempt us to embrace the tactics of PATCH. We had to keep the difference between the two organizations. No matter how "weak" Dr. Lucy believed it to be, we must stick with doing right. We owed it to God. It was what set us apart from the enemy time travel organization. It would be the colonel's task to decide what to do about Dr. Lucy.

Holding Marie's hand, Anton approached. "Drew, my brother, there is something you need to know."

My heart froze in terror. *He's not going to tell me they were lovers at sometime and now they have met again.…*

"Marie and I grew up in the same area of Paris just for a couple of years. We were eight or nine. Our families, they were close. It's been years since we last met and it was purely plate on it, if that is how you say."

I couldn't hold back the laugh. "I think it's platonic, but I understand."

Marie held out her hand. "Drew, I'm sorry my mind doubted you, even though my heart never did. I didn't know what to think."

I took her hand. I was so relieved that I chuckled. "I didn't know what to think either, Marie! That was the whole idea. Because you couldn't see, you wouldn't be able to guess whether she was telling the truth or not. We're taking her back to HQ. They have good medical facilities."

"Will she live?"

"I don't know. I'm not a doctor, but I hope so. Sometimes people get sick in their heads. I think that's what happened to Dr. Lucy. Plus, she may have things to tell us about our enemies. The time we are gone will only seem about an hour to you."

"Drew," she asked softly, "can we try again? I will play for you. We can walk together and we can..." Then her voice fell away like broken flower petals and she shook her head, silver tears threading their way into sight - longing eyes.

"No, forgive me, Drew. It was a weak, selfish moment. What can a blind girl offer to someone as brave and strong as you?" Had she been able to see, she would have run from the room to hide the tears that chased each other down her lovely face and caught brightly on the raven locks.

I took her elbow to keep her from turning away from me. "Marie, without you I felt such despair and emptiness. When you smile, and play, and laugh, and make fun of me – my heart sings. All the pain, and loneliness, and emptiness vanishes. When I'm with you, I can't see anything else. Miss Waleska, you have enchanted me. If my Queen allows, I will joyfully enter into your world."

"Oh, Drew...my heart has taken flight and makes its way to you. Make her a home, please? But how unforgivably forward of me to speak like this to you. I should be ashamed of myself...but for some reason...I am not."

Okay, you may wonder about Dr. Lucy and PATCH. This time I was putting me first. I was not going to risk losing Marie again.

We had to get Lucy back to Vanguard and we had to hope none of the staff had seen her. We didn't want anyone arrested for "murder" like Anton had been when his girlfriend "Svetlana" disappeared. We hoped that no one would see us smuggling the injured woman out of the house.

Anton came up with the answer. "You have a time machine, Drew. Can we not go back and stop her before she comes into the room? I will still have the adoption papers. You know now that she is working for PATCH. Apart from you, nobody will know anything about it. It will be as if she never came here. Don't forget, Dr. Lucy is still alive. It was too late to save your Lucy when Bryant murdered her, because she had already died. I can go back with you and act as witness to tell Colonel Carlisle what happened."

Anton and I got her downstairs. If this didn't work, I could be in serious trouble.

The time car came. We bundled Dr. Lucy inside, timing the control as best we could. We got to HQ. When we opened the door and turned to get Lucy – she was gone. She had vanished.

Anton said something in Russian, which probably translated to, "oh bother," and we both headed as fast as we could for Colonel Carlisle's office.

Lucy met us halfway there.

"Drew, darling, I was on my way through to see you," she said breathlessly. "So sorry to hear about Meryl, but she wasn't really your type. Help me get my things and I'll join you, darling. Let's get married. Mi-Ling needs a mother, and I'm Chinese, like her." Lucy wore the same dress as she had worn at Bellefield just a short time ago.

Astonishment had robbed me of speech. I backed away from her, shaking my head.

Not expecting trouble, Anton said cheerfully, "I will go up and see the colonel." Thankfully, he changed his mind and stopped a short distance away.

With Anton's assurance that he was leaving, Lucy grabbed at my sleeve. "Drew, why have you been so cruel to me? You must know that I love you! Flaunting Meryl at me, and now I've heard a rumor about you and a blind girl. Blind! Instead of me! How can you spurn me like that? After all I've done for Mi-Ling! After all I wanted to do for you."

Lucy's hand reached into the pocket of her dress. She had the pistol pulled halfway out before I could grab her wrist. I was so busy grabbing for the gun that I didn't see her other hand coming toward me with a small, vicious stiletto.

Thankfully, Anton had. So here we were at Vanguard HQ, my hand on Lucy's pistol arm and Anton's hand on the dagger arm, with Lucy between us twisting, kicking, shouting and trying to bite us. She was so strong that she nearly broke free.

Like a spring welcome, Colonel Carlisle's voice rose above the din. "Dr Francis, stop fighting or I will fire." She saw the pistol secured in his steady hand and stopped.

"You are under arrest," he told the angry woman. Two men behind him stepped into sight, "take her to our guest quarters and make sure she doesn't get out," Colonel Carlisle told them.

"Thank you, sir," I said somewhat breathlessly from the exertion of having held one-half of a wild cougar. "You're not going to believe what happened."

"Try me!" he replied, re-pocketing his weapon. "Come to my office."

In the colonel's office, over coffee, Anton and I related the events that had taken place at Bellefield.

"That's useful to know about her disappearing from the time car and you meeting her here on the stairs," Colonel Carlisle said. "We've known for some time that someone had been feeding info to PATCH. After the A10 Investigation, we traced the leaks down to either you or Dr. Lucy."

"Me!" I exclaimed, trying to hide hurt feelings. "Why would I do that?"

"That was the question A10 asked, as well, and could find no answer. When the A10 Investigations unit can find no answer, there is no answer."

"That's a relief!" I said." She's working for PATCH."

"We know that...now."

"How did you get the adoption papers, sir?"

"I knew it was one thing you didn't have and I thought it was about time you did. Our Dr. Lucy seemed inordinately interested in whether or not you had actually adopted Mi-Ling. Rather suspicious behavior, I thought. She shed crocodile tears when she found out about Meryl, but when she heard about Miss Waleska, she really got upset.

"You can't let Drew throw away his life on a blind woman...or words to that effect. If she could gain control of Mi-Ling, she was betting she could gain control of you. When we realized she was working for PATCH, we suspected she would try to engage you to work for PATCH as a double agent."

"I owe my life to Mi-Ling again, sir. She body-charged Lucy when Lucy pulled her pistol on me."

The colonel smiled. "You know, that girl has the raw material even at her age to make a very good agent."

"Well, sir, in the future if I ever get stuck in time somewhere, you can send Mi-Ling to look for me. She seems to specialize in saving my hide."

"She is brave," Anton observed. "I am rolling through my mind for old Russian saying for that little one."

Carlisle added, "We will treat Lucy and question her. I want to find out what went wrong. You two better get back to Bellefield. Remember, this time Lucy was never there. Take the adoption papers with you, Drew. We will let you know what we find out from our patient, and Major, see if you can find Bryant in the area. I'm getting fed up with him. I want to detain him legally or illegally. When we get Bryant, we find Professor Reynolds. If we get Reynolds, it could drastically affect PATCH, might even stop them permanently. Right, dismissed, No — wait! Sebastian asked me to pass on a message to you — *Keep on truckin'*. That's not code, is it?"

"No, sir, it means keep going."

"Right, that is what I thought. Get going. Keep me informed."

"Sir, how is Meryl? Is she happy?"

"Seems to be, but says she misses *SavaJava*. Sounds like some exotic location. Or code. Is it?"

I shook my head. "No, sir, it's a chain of coffee houses."

Colonel Carlisle reflected, "When I was growing up, all the coffee houses had Italian names and sold expresso until someone realized there was no 'x' in Espresso. Wonder what Cavour or Garibaldi would have made out of that?"

Anton suggested, "One day we could go and ask them? Combine it with research about pretty girls."

The colonel's mention of *SavaJava* hit me in the gut. Meryl was gone. I guess I was at the *'wondering if things could have been different'* stage of recovery.

We stowed Anton's suitcase in the time car and climbed in after it. Anton sighed and remarked, "The shame of it all is that I cannot make a dramatic entrance like the last time. I know the ladies would be disappointed if they could remember. It's been a long day."

When we got back, I reintroduced Anton to Marie. The childhood friends were delighted to see one another and shared stories of their adventures. I think it helped Marie to have someone she had known and trusted at Bellefield.

Anton said to me later, "She has turned out very lovely. I think you will find there is a lot more to her than you have yet realized."

All through dinner, I couldn't stop looking at Marie. She was alive and animated, being around her woke up dead spots sheltering in my heart. After the meal, Marie played for us. Anton smoked a cheroot, and as Marie's music filled the air, smoke from the cheroot seemed to add character to the room, changing it from a dining room to a place where plans were made and deeds of daring do planned. Marie was going to play her fifth piece of music and I went over to the piano and put my hand on hers.

"Stop, because you need to rest and we have already been enchanted by your playing."

"Is that an order, Major?" she asked with a slight rebuke in her voice.

"No," I replied. "It's a request from a friend who will dream about you. The difference is that when dawn comes, I will see you, and hear your voice, and feel the touch of your hand."

She tilted her head toward me and said, "I wish I could see you."

"One day it could happen. For now, let's all get some rest. Mi-Ling has beaten the rest of us to bed."

Martha started toward us.

I bent down to kiss Marie's forehead. With a neat twist, she found my lips and her kiss thrilled me. "One day it may be that someone else will be taking me to bed."

She and Martha started out of the room together. Marie stopped suddenly and asked Martha, "Can you wait here? I need to ask the Major something."

"Marie, it has been a long day. Would it not keep until tomorrow?" With a sigh, Martha signaled to me.

"What's wrong?" I asked Marie. "That terrible woman who was here earlier today that you had to take to a doctor. What happened to her?"

I was speechless. Marie shouldn't have remembered that. With the time change, it hadn't happened.

Anton had excused himself to go to bed, but he returned to the room. "I hate to be a gooseberry, but Tam Shepherd is here to see you. He has some news about Bryant."

"Anton, Marie remembers about Dr. Lucy being here, but I don't know how. She should have forgotten with the rest of them. Marie asked what had happened to Lucy."

"Then perhaps my dramatic entrance, it was not wasted. But, Drew, my friend. How can she remember?"

"Is she working for PATCH? No, surely not," I said, answering my own question.

"If she thought she could pull the hair over the sheep's eyes, then she would have been silent as the tomb," Anton agreed. "Tam Shepherd is waiting to see you."

I hit my fist on the inside of my hand, "I forgot about that."

"Carolyn," I called over, "will you see if you can wake up Mi-Ling and take her into your room with you? Take a revolver with you."

"Déjà vu? Yes, I will do that," she replied. "We seem to get a lot of practice handling guns when we stay at Bellefield."

"I wish Angus or Meryl were here. I can smell a rat, but I can't see it."

"Old Russian saying…" Anton said cheerfully. "Sometimes it is easier to know where a rat has been than where she is."

"Go get Tam and stick around. I want you to hear this, as well."

Anton gave me a puzzled look. "Where am I to be stuck to? It could prove inconvenient."

"Just stay here with me. That's all it means."

"Phew," said Anton. "Russian, it is much easier to understand."

Anton left to fetch Tam. I thought, *I sure could use another friendly face. I paced up and down in front of the fire. Lord, I don't know what to do. You have got to help me."*

Anton came back with Tam Shepherd. "Tam, what's the word on Bryant and his ship?"

Tam said, "The ship's still at Crawton but Bryant's been comin' an gaun." I gave Tam more money for expenses and asked him to continue his surveillance.

"Tam, do you know how far it is from here to the Crawton?"

"About forty-eight miles as the crow flies if he's had a dram."

" Thanks, Tam. Go by the kitchen see if you can get a feed from Mrs. Fraser."

Tam left and Anton asked, "What are you going to do?"

"We've got to get a team onto that ship. Or, if necessary, get the crew off and blow the thing to bits. If we can't catch the wolf, we can ruin his den."

"Sounds like old Russian saying. I knew I was good influence on you." Anton replied

Then a voice floated in from the doorway, "Shore nuff is dark in here. Ain't they invented lights yet?"

"Sebastian!" Anton and I exclaimed together.

The big guy came into the room. "That's what I done said when I knew I was a' comin' through here. I looked in the mirror and said, 'Yep that be you.

I'd shore nuff know you anywheres.'"

Anton and I pounded him on the back in welcome.

"Man, we thought you had emigrated. I guess the colonel was working you too hard?"

He beamed. "Well, I reckon it's like this. I gotta do something to earn my corn. So the colonel, he done sent me through to help you guys."

"We're going to organize a raid on Bryant's ship," I explained, "and blow it up. Though in 1868, it will look accidental. We have to stop PATCH from using it as a relay station. We've got to start raining on PATCH's parade."

Anton looked thoughtful. "What makes me think is that PATCH may have put something on board Bryant's ship to go *boom* when we go on board? They must realize we might try something like that. That may be why the ship isn't moving."

"What that means," Sebastian said, "is they wants you to come on board and they are willin' to boom the ship if they can get some of us. Is that not called nutrition?"

"I think you mean attrition," I told him.

Sebastian smiled. "Yup, that's just what I was thinking 'cept I spelled it different."

"Right, Anton, if you would be so good as to return to HQ and suggest to Colonel Carlisle that now would be a good time to put in his plan about attacking *The Allegheny* into action. Suggest to him it might be booby trapped. We need speed and silence. Say we would appreciate being there for the action."

"Booby trapped? What's that?"

"What you suggested, Anton. Covered in devices that might make it go *boom*. We may need an IED boffin."

"I wish I had studied harder in my colloquial English class," Anton grumbled. "Still, as the Crimean War was on, we hoped you would all be learning Russian by the end of it."

"One other thing," I added. "See if the colonel has any idea of Professor Reynolds whereabouts. We've got to get him, as well."

"Now, I don't want to dump creek water on no one," Sebastian said, "But ain't there a law against just goin' in an blowin'something up?"

"Seb, we're dealing with a ruthless organization that will use anything including the law to gain their ends. They don't care who they hurt, kill or maim. Bryant is in that up to his miserable neck. They're after power and control. They want to enslave and take away freedom and have everybody bend the knee to their sick propaganda. They want to change history so they win. So it's easy for them to succeed. Bryant murdered Lucy in cold blood and PATCH helped him and helped him escape. If we don't stop them, they will do something to change history that we can't undo."

"Yea, I guess they kind of upset you," Sebastian said.

"Now," Anton put in, "you're thinking like a Russian! I knew I was a good influence on you."

After Anton left, Sebastian scratched his head. "Major, I don't want to tell you your business, but this place can't be defended."

"How do you mean?" I asked.

"Well, suppose PATCH organizes a raid on this place. How are we going to defend it? We got you and me. Then we got us a blind girl, a pregnant lady, an elderly woman and a young girl. We don't stand a chance. We've got to get them out and to somewhere safe like HQ. If PATCH's eight men or whatever they are come here, or if Bryant and his gang turn up, we's gonna be outgunned."

Sebastian was right. We were planning to strike them first, but suppose they returned the compliment. If the SEALS had been here, it would be different. We needed to abandon the house. We had never time travelled a pregnant woman before. *Lord I sure could use some help here. What do I do?* They always knew what to do in the films, but this was real life.

I ran to Mrs. Fraser's room and told her of the danger. She got her stuff and left with the help of two of the estate workers. I promised her questions would be answered later. I gave her the £30 I had on me. She was going to ask something, but then saw my face and just left with a hug.

"Sebastian, go waken Carolyn and Mi-ling. Be sure to knock and try and be calm. Tell Carolyn there is a danger of a raid from PATCH and the house can't be defended so we have to go through to modern times and Vanguard HQ. I will get Martha and Marie. Quick! We need to move! I've got that gut feeling that they're coming tonight. We'll meet downstairs."

I raced to Marie's room and knocked. A sleepy voice answered. "Who is there?" Martha asked.

"Major Faulkner. Miss Martha, I must ask you to get dressed and pack a few things you and Marie need. We must leave tonight. We're in danger. Please, hurry! Put on your least bulky dresses. We'll meet downstairs."

I went to the gun room and grabbed a couple of revolvers including my Webley, a Mauser, and a .22 handgun for one of the ladies. Carolyn had a pistol, and knew how to use it. Fear crept alongside me. *You're not going to make it,* fear lied. *They will get here too soon. Or else, they won't come at all and you'll look like stupid a coward. You thought you could be a hero overcoming the odds for the woman you love. Instead, you're going to lose number three — well done, Romeo.*

I was scared, and scared by the responsibility. Sebastian had Caroline and a very sleepy Mi-Ling ready. I kissed the top of my daughter's head and smiled at her.

"Right, get to the basement and wait for the rest of us. Sebastian, if you hear anything happening, get into the time car and get them out of here. Understood?"

"It sounds as if there is something hammering at the door it — might just be my heart beating too fast and scared like."

I ran to get Marie and Martha. "I don't understand what all the panic is about," Martha complained.

"Trust me, Martha. Bryant already killed my wife. He will kill you, as well. Please, hurry, for God's sake, you will have to leave your things. We'll come back here as soon as it's safe."

I carried a lamp in one hand and a pistol in the other. Marie moved well on the dark stairs. I wasn't sure whether it was Marie helping Martha, or Martha helping Marie.

We got downstairs to the hall and were heading for the basement, when something hit the big front door.

"Break it down," a voice from outside commanded. It was Bryant and he sounded like a bad extra from a movie. The door shivered from the hammering on the other side even while the voice issued another command. "Curse you! Put your backs into it!"

"Hurry," I whispered to Marie and Martha urgently. "These men will kill you."

We made it safely to the basement. Everyone else was already there. The time car came roaring to a stop and Sebastian and I looked at each other in horror. It was a smaller version. There wasn't enough room for all of us.

"Sebastian," I said, "Get the girls inside and get going, I will hold them off. That's an order. Carolyn, Martha, Mi-Ling and Sebastian climbed inside. The banging from upstairs grew louder

"Papa!" Mi-Ling cried in alarm.

"It's okay, sweetheart. Go! I'll be right behind you."

Marie got it, but the door wouldn't close. She jumped out to stay with me. "Go!" I yelled at Sebastian and the car shot off.

I guessed we would need a couple of minutes before we could summon the car again. Marie clung to my arm. "Give me a gun, Drew," she said.

"But, darling, you can't..." I stammered.

"Blow out the light, Drew. Don't ask why, just do." So I did. We were in the dark like rats in a trap.

"Down here!" approaching voices shouted. "Let's look down here." Then the steps down began to creek. I couldn't see a thing and realized they must be wearing night glasses.

Marie whispered in my ear, "There are two of them. Turn me in the direction of the stairs and press the button for that thing to come back."

I have found with women there are times when it's not wise to argue. This was one of them.

I heard Marie whisper, "Closer, closer, closer." I knew she didn't mean me.

They were talking as they approached. "Blast! It's a woman! She can see us."

Four shots were fired in rapid succession, followed by two loud thumps – the sound of two bodies falling. The time car burst in on us as lights were heading down the stairs. I pushed Marie in, jumped in, slammed the door, and pushed the button. The time car shot off.

CHAPTER 10 - The Fight Back

Marie's brave action gave the phrase 'a shot in the dark' a new meaning for me. Marie and I got to HQ. The others were still standing at the terminal. Mi-Ling threw herself into my arms in relief, and then ran to hug Marie, too. It had been a close call — a very close call.

Colonel Carlisle came to see us. I tried to explain our sudden appearance and Carlisle said, "Good thinking Major, I'm…"

"Sir, it wasn't me. It was Sebastian's idea. He realized the place couldn't be defended and that once the wolves broke in, we sheep we wouldn't stand a chance."

Colonel Carlisle clasped Sebastian on the shoulder. "Good thinking, Sergeant-Major."

Sebastian smiled and shrugged, "Just another quiet day at the ranch, sir."

Martha was totally bewildered. "Where am I?" she asked.

"Where you were before," I answered, "but about one-hundred-and-fifty years later."

"Get Victoria Conroy down here," the colonel said into a microphone. Then he smiled at Martha. "I've sent for someone who will explain everything to you, dear lady.

She curtsied. "You are in charge, I assume?"

"Your assumption is correct."

Marie asked, "Am I really in twenty something?"

"Yes, you are, Miss Waleska. I'm glad you're here."

"She shot two of the villains in the dark," I told Carlisle. The colonel looked impressed. He put his hand on her shoulder. "Indeed, Miss Waleska, that's unusual"

Marie smiled and shook her head. "My hearing is attuned to the slightest variation in music and it was a closed space. Their voices funneled. The rest was not hard."

"Miss Waleska, medical science has moved on in the past one-hundred-fifty years. We might be able to return your vision. Would you be willing to be examined by our medics?"

"Medics?" she asked.

"Doctors," he explained.

"Well, yes. But others have put my hopes up before." She said slowly. "And I don't have a lot of money."

"There would be no charge to you, Miss Waleska. Vanguard would cover any expense."

Mi-Ling had run back to me. She slipped her arms round my waist and hugged me. Sometimes words were not enough.

"Right," said the colonel. "Now that everybody has breathed several sighs of relief, we can get you some accommodation."

As if on cue, Victoria swept over to us and we introduced her to Marie and Martha. We also introduced her to Mi-Ling. "Mi-Ling," I said gently, "this is Amma's mother."

Victoria bent down to Mi-Ling's eye level. "Amma loved you, Mi-Ling. She was proud of you."

"I miss her," Mi-Ling said, brushing tears away. "If she was your daughter, you must miss her even more."

Victoria kissed the top of Mi-Ling's glossy head. "You are right, brave one. I do miss my Lucy."

Mi-Ling thought out loud. "If Amma was still here, you would be Mi-Ling's grandmother. Your smile makes my heart joyful. Amma is where Jesus is. Jesus will take good care of her for both of us."

"Let's be extra special friends," Victoria suggested.

"Maybe you will tell Mi-Ling about Amma when she was the same age as Mi-Ling, Grandmother."

Victoria laughed and hugged Mi-Ling. "That will be fun! And I have pictures to show you."

Victoria asked Martha and Marie to follow her. "We'll get you settled, then I can explain everything to you. At least – as much of everything as I know, myself."

"You are dressed so differently from us," Martha observed, looking at Victoria's colorful knee-length dress.

"Things have changed, dear," Victoria said. "One very good change – no whalebone."

"No corsets?" Marie marveled. "That sounds like bliss."

The colonel cleared his throat. "Well, ladies, I'm sure you have a lot to discuss. Goodbye for now."

"Colonel," Martha said with a twinkle, "I do believe you are blushing."

Sebastian noted, "That's one advantage for me. Can't nobody tell if I'm blushing."

"Right," the colonel said briskly. "People, get some rest. Meeting Staff Room 1, nine o'clock,tomorrow morning. Meanwhile, I'll see if I can galvanize our American cousins. We're going to need their help."

Victoria took the ladies and Mi-Ling with her. Mi-Ling gave me a quick goodnight hug and kiss before following the others. Sebastian, Anton, and I went off to our rooms. It gave us time to think. The scary thoughts were about what tragedy would have struck if we had stayed at Bellefield. When we went back we would have to time it about ten minutes after we left. We didn't want the place burned down. If Bryant was there, would his ship have some way of contacting him if they were under attack?

Certainly if the SEALS could take care of the ship, we might be able to get the house back.

Perhaps Mike and Hera could help. If the attack on the *Allegheny* was timed properly, then we might – just might get Bryant to leave Bellefield to save his ship. Would PATCH tell Bryant to leave his men to face the music and get Bryant out where he could be useful? Ach, it was late and I was tired. Tomorrow would be another day. I went to bed and set my alarm and put the light out. One question did nag at me though. How had Marie remembered about Dr. Lucy?

* * *

When I woke up, it took me a while to figure where I was. Perhaps I was suffering from time travel lag, instead of jet lag. Breakfast at the canteen was bacon in a roll. The others joined me, including Victoria. I don't know what Victoria had done, but Marie looked gorgeous. It looked strange to see Martha and Marie dressed in modern clothes.

"Good morning Marie," I said, and took her hand.

"Drew," she said with a certain sense of relief. "Did yesterday really happen? It feels strange being dressed like this. Do I look acceptable?"

"You look lovely." I decided not to tell her she had gorgeous legs. That had better keep for a more appropriate time.

Martha sampled the tea. "Is this what passes for tea in this time?" She paused. "Dear me, sea water must have entered the clipper's hold. As a chaperone appears to be redundant in these modern times, I was hoping for good tea. One makes the assumption that if one has been brought here, one can also go back. I will be a fearsome tea plantation owner, supplying the empire with the drink that fortifies and edifies."

I informed everyone where the meeting with the colonel would be held. "You're all invited to join us there once you've finished breakfast if you like."

"Marie and I will be here a while, I fear, Major," Martha said. "Trying to get used to this hot beverage that's being passed off on us as tea."

Carolyn and baby were getting checked over by a doctor. Mi-Ling was with her.

So just before nine, Anton, Sebastian, and I headed for the meeting room to see what hot chestnuts the colonel had been able to pull out of the fire. We entered the room. I recognized the American naval uniforms as SEALS. I counted eight, along with Mike and Hera. Mike and Hera sat at a separate table and Sebastian, Anton and I headed for them. There were two other soldiers at that table and their sand-colored berets identified them as SAS. I tell you, this was heady stuff. These guys were the top of the range. The presence of the SEALS didn't seem to faze the SAS boys one bit. Then I remembered that Angus McTurk had helped train some of them.

Colonel Carlisle entered the room along with an American major who proved to be the SEALS commander. Hera was wearing a British army uniform. Her hair was up. Some of the SEALS looked appreciatively at her legs.

"I am Colonel Carlisle. This is Major Buchanan, commander of the SEALS detachment."

Buchanan looked around. The two SAS men looked back at him and he surveyed the others, taking in my rank as the second ranking British officer, even though I knew the SAS men were so far ahead of me as to be stellar.

Buchanan caught sight of Hera. "Colonel, with all due respect, the SEALS work best on their own. Fast in and fast out. No place for a woman who looks as if she belongs in the typing pool." There was a laugh from the other SEALS and much nodding.

Colonel Carlisle said, "Major Buchanan, Lieutenant Hera is part of my organization, with specialist training, and this is a joint venture."

Buchanan sneered. "Even so, colonel, the field missions we do are no place for a woman."

Hera decanted herself from her chair. The muscles on her legs rippled under tanned skin. She produced a knife from the band of her skirt. One minute her hand was empty, the next the blade flashed. The number of SEALS who were laughing was reduced in half.

"Maybee you would like to – how you say - take this knife from me," she purred.

"Yes, sir," a couple of men said. "Go on! It can't be hard."

"I don't want to hurt the lady."

"It is okayee, Major," Hera responded. "I will kill you gently."

Anton whispered to me, "My roubles are on Hera. This is going to be interesting."

The major put a sheepish smile on his face – a kind of apologetic look, and put his hand on the desk.

The knife flashed and the blade pinned Buchanan's sleeve to the wood. "Or are you with much afraid?" Hera asked. The laughter stopped.

Buchanan pulled the knife out the wood and tried to grab Hera. She sidestepped He missed. She grabbed him and the knife was at his throat.

"See! Told you!" Anton said gleefully.

"Man," one of the SEALS said, "she can come in my boat anytime."

"The room fell silent. When Hera let the major go, she was careful not to turn her back on him. "Is there anyone else who wants not a woman in thees fight?" Hera asked. There was no one else. My two SAS colleagues shot a glance at each other and nodded. They had been impressed. Hera glided back to her seat next to Mike, who patted her arm.

Buchanan said, "My apologies, ma'am, I was wrong. You never underestimate your opponent." Hera gave a slight nod but apart from that her face was impassive. How many people, I wondered, had she killed in the arena? Probably more than some of the others. As a gladiator, it had been kill or be killed. Hera had survived.

The rest of the introductions were made without further ado. Then Colonel Carlisle said, "This is a joint operation to seize and if necessary destroy a ship being used as relay station for time travel by an organization called PATCH. All this was mentioned in your briefing. The basic problem is that the ship may be booby trapped with IED's, triggered by lasers or pressure devices. We would like to see the time travel technology PATCH is using, but we'll not put lives unnecessarily at risk. We either capture or kill the crew unless they surrender. We would like Captain Caleb Bryant alive.

"The other thing is…you may get there and find just a sailing ship and crew. We tried to scan the inside but something was blocking our technology and we got no pictures." A projector was switched on showing the *Allegheny* from four sides. "The place where the *Allegheny* is anchored faces open sea. There is one road into Crawton, and one road out. The people there know more about the sea and what it can do than you do. It might be 1868, but do not underestimate their knowledge. I have explained on your briefing how PATCH can transport its operatives, but they can and do use conventional means. The other thing is, there is a large sea bird colony there. If they are disturbed, the noise they make will be enough to warn anyone on board ship."

Carlisle looked around. "Are there any questions so far?"

There were none.

Major Buchanan took over. "We're going to hit the ship at 3:00 a.m. their time. That's the time when people are most sleepy and most liable to be off guard. There should be no moon and our night glasses should give us all the light we need. We go in quietly, staying in the shadows until the last minute, and then we rush them. Any control for devices is liable to be in the wheelhouse or the captain's cabin. We'll be there and have them hogtied before they know what's hit them."

Anton looked at me. "Old Russian saying, *never count the wolf dead until he has stopped breathing.*"

Sebastian added, "Never count a rattlesnake dead till you done stomped on his head."

Despite our misgivings, there was a positive vibration in the room. "So, gentlemen," the colonel added, "get your gear together and we can go and get things sorted out."

"What the colonel means, guys, is we can go kick some butt," Buchanan corrected.

The door to the briefing room flung open. A white-faced Carolyn staggered into the room with Victoria, who had her arm around her. "Carolyn! What's wrong?" I asked, running to her.

She turned a tear-streaked face to me. "Drew..." she croaked. "I'm so sorry! It's Mi-Ling."

"Mi-Ling! Carolyn, where's Mi-Ling? What's happened to her?"

"Drew, Bryant and PATCH grabbed her and took her into one of their tunnels, she's gone."

Carolyn handed me a crumpled sheet of paper. It was a terse note from Bryant. *We will have the little whore on board my ship. Any attempt to interfere and she will be killed. So back off, boy. You can't stop my friends. You are way out of your league.*

To say I felt sick to my stomach was an understatement. I ran to where the colonel was standing.

"Sir, Mi-Ling has been kidnapped again." I showed him the note.

Carlisle hammered the table with his fist. "Lady and gentlemen, there will be a change of plan. We have a hostage situation. Major Faulkner's daughter has been kidnapped and is being held by the terrorists. We need to review the plan."

"Sir," said Major Buchanan. "We need to stop this man and this group before they do any more damage." He looked at me. "I'm sorry, Major, but you can't make an omelet without breaking eggs."

I looked at him incredulously. "We're talking about my daughter! Not broken eggs!"

"Stay calm, Major Faulkner. Shouting won't get us anywhere. We can go in and move as fast as we can and get the girl and destroy the ship."

"And if you don't get her in time?" I asked.

He held me in a steady gaze. "Everything in life is risky, but there is no other way. We must stop him."

"*Oh, Lord,*" I said. "*You said if anyone lacks wisdom let him ask. Lord, I'm asking, begging.*" A glimmer of hope came to me. "Sir," I said to Colonel Carlisle. "A four-man team, one boat."

"Okay, Drew. You've got it. Who will be on the team?"

I thought fast. "I would, along with Angus McTurk and Lt. Hera."

"That's three. Who's the fourth?"

Okay, in for a penny, in for a pound. "Kitchi."

"Kitchi?" asked Major Buchanan. "Who's Kitchi?"

"A Native American from 1757," I replied.

His eyes opened wide. "Major, you have eight top professional seals and your two SAS men to choose from and you want a Native American? That is the stupidest thing…"

"Major Buchanan," cut in Colonel Carlisle, "I support Major Faulkner's choice. Kitchi could find a drugged black cat at the bottom of a coal mine with all the lights fused."

"That good, huh?" Buchanan muttered.

"Yes, that good."

Carlisle turned to me. "Once you've set out, we'll give you four hours. You'd better take this Kairon detector. It could be useful."

I took the device the colonel held out to me, a gadget that didn't seem to have an off switch. It hummed gently. I slipped it in my pocket. I had volunteered Hera. I guessed it was only right to go and tell her, though I suspected I would put it more as a favor than a command.

"Lieutenant," I said to Hera, "may I have a word with you?"

"Greek or Eeenglish?" she asked, flashing even white teeth at me.

"English, please. I'm proud of you. You have learned English very quickly." The smile widened. "When you are gladiator, you learn pieces of many tongues."

"Hera, my daughter has been kidnapped by Captain Bryant and is on board that ship." I waved in the general direction of the picture of the *Alleghany*.

The expression on Hera's face changed. "When I catch him do I kill him queekly or slowly?" She savored the word *slowly* as if it were a morsel of steak.

"You will help?" I asked

"Yes, Hera help get your child back! She veery good to help."

"There are two other people coming with us. They are both in 1757, so I have to go and get them."

"Can they fight?" Hera asked. "Veery good fighting like gladiator?"

I smiled at her and nodded. "You will like them both. Angus taught me to fight. Kitchi is a brave warrior."

We headed out after Mike and Hera kissed one another and said their goodbyes.

Marie and Martha were sitting on seats outside. When I approached Marie, the Kairon detector beeped. Two security guards rushed up.

"What was that?" Marie asked.

"You have Kairon on you somewhere," I said, trying not to panic as I wondered where on earth Marie had got Kairon and why she had it. I passed the detector over her and when it came to the amulet she wore around her neck it gave a high reading.

"Marie, your amulet is either made of Kairon or has Kairon in it. That must be how you remembered about Dr. Lucy and her attempt to kill me. Anton and I traveled back before she turned up at Bellefield and stopped her from coming. She tried the same thing again. She's alive and well, under arrest and being questioned. How did you get the amulet? How long have you had it?"

There was a silence. I was aware of the two security guards standing by ready to arrest Marie. Fortunately, while Marie knew they were there, she didn't understand the reason.

"As far as I remember," Marie said, "it was a gift from a friend of my father's. I was ten at the time. My father was keen that I should wear it. The funny thing is that after he gave me the amulet, I never heard from him again. Is there something wrong?" Fear found a pocket in her lovely face as she suddenly found herself unwittingly involved in something she didn't understand. "I have done nothing wrong, have I?" she asked anxiously.

I took her hand. "No, Marie. You've done nothing wrong, but our people will want to look at the amulet, if you don't mind. By wearing it and remembering the events of a past occasion that you should have forgotten, you've shown us a property Kairon has that we didn't know about."

She took the amulet off and held it out to me. I handed it to the colonel and he made a call. A short while later, a figure in a white coat came and took it for examination.

The colonel drew me aside. "How did that come about?" he asked.

"Well, sir, from what Marie just told me, it must have been that PATCH sent an operative with the full knowledge of not only who Marie was, but the part she would play. They must have laid the ground years before. Yet, in saying years before, all the PATCH operative had to do was to be kind and pretend to befriend the family. Perhaps give three or four-hundred francs to a needy family, maybe enough for piano lessons."

"Unbelievable, Major, although that would solve the mystery."

"Sometimes, sir, the devil appears as an angel of light."

Carlisle thought for a moment. "We have to catch Reynolds and try and figure their command structure and find out who is bankrolling these people. Bryant, first. He's been a pain in our side long enough."

"Amen to that."

Hera and I sped back to 1757, and Kitchi's camp. As we headed towards it, I wondered if Meryl would be there and if they were married yet. But it was merely a passing thought. My mind and heart were ruled by the need to get Mi-Ling back – literally before the cavalry charged to the rescue.

Hera had a presence about her, confidence and beauty. At no time was it more obvious than when she looked at Mike and love flooded into her eyes. Years in the bloodbath of the arena had not hardened her heart to the point where she could not feel attraction. She was also an expert fighter and it brought great comfort to know she was watching my back. She carried a large axe as weapon of preference, as well as a rifle. Firearms caught her attention because she said that after shooting someone there was less mess and you didn't have to wash blood from your arms. She wore buckskins. In case any guys reading this wonder if she looked good in them – figure it out for yourselves!

Kitchi's chief, Running Wolf greeted me. "Every time you come to our council fire, Kitchi go on a far journey. He has many tales to tell for long winter nights." He looked at Hera appreciatively. "Is this your woman now?"

"Err, no, she fights with us," I said.

He eyed the axe Hera carried, as well as the short carbine and the knife at her belt.

"A man would feel his back well guarded." To my surprise he stood up and produced a tomahawk, and handed it to Hera. She weighed it up appreciatively and nodded her thanks.

"Sun in Her Hair is out hunting," the chief said. "She and Kitchi are not married yet, but the day comes close."

Meryl's words floated back to me, *I will always love you.'* Oh, hang it all! That was a long time ago. This was her home; this was where she belonged. I knew if I told myself that often enough I would someday believe it. At the moment, it still had a little part of the journey to make.

Running Wolf looked into my spirit. He put his hand on my shoulder. "For a warrior like you, the hardest fight is not with any enemy who seeks your life. It is the battle within your own heart and the courage to sacrifice your own joy for that of another. Yet this you have done. Where did you learn this?"

"From the greatest teacher of all," I said.

"Was he a paleface?"

"No," I said. "His skin was much like yours. He is called Jesus."

Running Wolf pondered my words, "I will think on what you have said." There was a pause. He didn't move away. Somehow he knew the conversation was unfinished.

"Running Wolf, you know Angus McTurk?"

"Kitchi speaks highly of his courage and bravery." He smiled. "Kitchi says that the only thing that makes him afraid is his woman, yet still he stays with her. This I do not understand."

"If he tried to leave Abigail, she'd kill him."

"If this is truth, then it is a good to consider other paths. Could she do such a thing, this woman called Abigail?" Running Wolf asked.

I smiled. "Yes," I've seen her fight."

"Then McTurk is wise to have such warrior woman. I have much to learn about the white man's ways, and even more to learn of white woman's ways."

I nodded agreement sagely.

Running Wolf sent a runner to McTurk's cabin with a message I had written previously.

"Since the killing of the General Braddock, *les français* have become bold," Chief Running Wolf said, "they send raiding bands. If they saw you they might kill you, while one of my people would go unnoticed. They have killed many *anglais.* They and their Mohawk dogs have caused much harm."

A rifle ball slammed into the side of the lodge close to where Running Wolf stood. A visual check disclosed a mixed war band of French Infantry, voyageurs and Mohawk. They stormed out of the woods, shooting and shouting. Replies from the Powhatan camp dropped one of the French infantry. Blood stained his white uniform where the ball had slammed into his chest. Running Wolf fired. I aimed at the voyageurs. Hera stood like some Wagnarian heroine and fired her carbine from the hip, hitting a Mohawk.

None of the Powhatan had been hit. They had been taught to fire from a prone position, which made them a smaller target. Wind blew in our faces. Hera took off her cap and let her hair fall. That stopped two of *Les français*, a deadly mistake for the other weapon the Powhatan had, the fast shooting bow and arrow. There were individual combats, but the French were more grouped and began to push through, expecting victory. Two went for Hera. The axe swung from her shoulder. The surprised look was still on one face as his head bounced along the ground.

Bit by bit, the Powhatan warriors started to gather round Running Wolf.

Mohawks killed two of the children. The mother started to wail and was hit over the head. Her remaining child screamed at his mother's inert form. With some of the Powhatan warriors gone in hunting parties, the Powhatan were at a disadvantage. Hera fell when one of the French rammed her in the back. One of the Mohawks wrapped his hand round her hair pulled her head back, but got no further. I ran over and rammed my Bowie knife in his back. The blade came out through his chest.

Gunfire increased. The French looked behind them to find a line of Scarlet coats. The disciplined British Infantry fired a volley into the backs of the French, then charged with fixed bayonets. Just to the left of the scarlet line, I recognized Angus. The French had attacked, not realizing British troops were in the area. The French surrendered. Some of the Mohawks escaped.

Kitchi had followed *Les anglais* to see where they were going and had fought his way through the line of the French. I noticed Hera eyeing him appreciatively – I guess it must have been his aftershave!

Kitchi and Angus joined us. Hera had gained an appreciative audience after her prowess with the axe and knife.

I told Kitchi, "I need your help again, my brother. "Mi-Ling has been kidnapped by the same man who took her last time and I need your help to get her back. This time we know where she is. We need a quick raid to recover her. She's on Bryant's ship."

"This Bryant, the one who took her before? It is a pity he was not killed."

"A pity," I agreed grimly. "This will be a night raid. We must board the ship and get to Mi-Ling before they harm her. As long as they think we won't attack with her there, she will live. If we are discovered, she will die. There are four of us. I will be one," Kitchi nodded. "Angus is another," again Kitchi nodded his approval. "Our fourth member is Hera, the woman with the axe."

"This too is good," Kitchi said, as he and Hera measured one another. "A ship, it is big," Kitchi noted. "Do you know where the little one is on the ship?"

"No," I replied. "I only know that she's there."

Angus slammed his fist into the palm of his hand. "This time we stop Bryant for good," he announced. "He has cost us dear, especially you, Drew. The first thing is to get Mi-Ling back safely."

Kitchi spoke to Running Wolf in his own tongue. The Chief put his hand on Kitchi's shoulder. Kitchi picked up his kit and we headed out. Hera shouldered her axe and unslung her carbine. Then she stopped and walked over to Running Wolf and gave him her axe. He weighed it up and nodded approvingly. If this team couldn't recover Mi-Ling safely, then nobody could.

The British officer in charge of the troops who had saved our bacon stopped.

"Captain Carpenter, 62nd Foot. Thank you for the opportunity to capture these prisoners."

"What about the Mohawks you caught?" I asked him.

"We hang them, mutinous dogs."

"The French officer and what's left of his staff, will they be paroled?"

"Of course. Monsieur le Marquis de Plombal said he wanted field experience."

It struck me that I was to meet a direct descendent of the Marquis in Foochow about a century later.

"You can't run with the fox and hunt with the hounds. Thank you again. God bless Good King George. Good day to you."

He saluted and turned away. It had been a brisk reminder that his was a war, which historically would soon end, but how long would it take the scars to heal? Time to head back to Headquarters

Three hours had passed in modern times since we left and the colonel greeted Kitchi like an old friend. Kitchi got a crash course in how to use a pistol and silencer. He was a quick learner. The four of us could fit into an inflatable rubber dinghy with room for Mi-Ling on the return trip. The colonel was optimistic and his optimism was infectious.

"Right, gentlemen: four hours from the time you begin your travel, we will bring you out as near as we can to the bay at Crawton where the *Allegheny* is anchored. After that, the cavalry arrives. We can't let Bryant escape again. Oh, one other thing; I am sending Mike Argo through just after you. He will guard your exit point and warn you of any danger that might be waiting for you on the way back."

Mmm back up, I thought, *at least if the ship blows up, somebody will know what happened.*

"How are the people at Crawton going to write this one in the history books, sir?" I asked.

Carlisle smiled, "Maybe we will find out, perhaps the journal the account is in is in an attic somewhere. Just get Mi-Ling out of there. Good luck."

We had our choice of equipment. Shipboard fighting required a different technique. As well as close-quarter weapons, we took tear gas which is fine if the wind doesn't change. Caution was required for the gas. We took stun grenades, which had worked admirably in the amphitheatre when we got Mike out. Night vision glasses were a must. They would allow us to see, providing nobody shone bright light at them. The last time we had boarded the *Allegheny,* we had blown the rudder and main mast, but had not gone below decks. We would need to be search fast and deal with whoever was there. Some of the crew would be ashore unless Bryant had recalled them. We needed to come out away from the ship and work our way round, then inflate the dinghy and paddle out to the ship. We would stick to the darkest patches of water and tie cloth round the paddles. We collected our gear and had a look again at the model of the terrain where we were going.

CHAPTER 11 - The Road to Dunnottar Castle

Scotland, 1868

When we came out in 1868, at Crawton Village, we smelt fish, seaweed and heard the sound of seabirds. Several of the windows from the stone houses had lamps in them, but at 3 a.m. local time, the majority of the residents were asleep. The houses were built to survive a buffeting from wind and rain and looked cozy inside.

It was cold and Hera was not adjusted to cooler temperatures. Still, she rose to the challenge. One day in the arena, the next on the Scottish sea coast. I wondered what she thought

Angus inflated the dinghy and Kitchi kept watch, fading into the shadows. We lowered the empty gas canister into the deep water. We hoped it wouldn't be found until it could no longer be recognized. Salt water works wonders on metal.

Kitchi with night glasses would have been enough to scare anyone. Hera had plaited her hair and had it under a woolly hat. We got into the dingy and pushed off, trying to use hand signals as much as possible. The night glasses made communication easy. Voices carried further over water. We moved slowly, trying not to let the paddles drip. The wind stirred the surface of the water.

Angus pointed to the stern of the *Allegheny*. We knew there were good handholds there. The stern of the ship was also in darkness. Anyone peering over the stern would see nothing. To us, it was as bright as day. Angus wanted to go up first. Kitchi would go just slightly further up so that the two would then be on the deck simultaneously. Hera and I would follow. Hera put a dagger between her teeth and I realized that maybe in the subtle nuances of combat, I would not like to have met her.

Kitchi seemed to have the climbing ability of *Spiderman* without the webs.

He and Angus disappeared over the top. Hera and I were about to follow when a couple of guys came to the rear of the ship, unbuttoned their fly's and started doing an impression of water fountains over the stern. Hera and I pushed quietly away from the stern. If the two guys did not hear the sound of water meeting water they might realize something was wrong and raise an alarm. When the peering, peeing pirates had finished, they vanished. Hera and I climbed up the stern, fading into the shadows once we got over the top. The Allegheny wasn't moving so there was nobody at the wheel.

My mind attempted functioning. Would Bryant have put Mi-Ling in with the crew? If he had, he would know that when I saw him again it would be shoot first and ask questions later. Perhaps he didn't care. Could he have stowed Mi-Ling in his cabin for his personal use? No, if he had wanted that, he could have got someone else who wouldn't have a father ready to kill him on sight if he found out. He must have kidnapped Mi-Ling to get at me; to worry me. If that was the aim, he had succeeded. I was so worried for my daughter's sake that bile rose chokingly into my throat and I had to force back a gag.

I looked at my chronometer; fifty-five minutes left before the cavalry showed up. We had to make a choice. Should we go down either side of the below decks passages, which linked together, and listen for evidence of Mi-Ling's presence? She might be asleep and therefore totally quiet. It was a shot in the dark, but shots in the dark sometimes hit targets, as Marie's shooting had proved.

Snoring met us as we ventured softly down into the ship. We ran into two crew members, cold cocked them, and tied them up with plastic biodegradable tags. Who would know what plastic was 150 years before its time? We didn't know how many more we would encounter. I didn't believe in luck, but I did believe in God.

Again, it was Kitchi who found Mi-Ling. He ran up to me on silent feet and indicated that I should follow him. We disabled two more of the crew on the way back around. Mi-Ling lay on the bed in the cabin. She looked up when I came in. Her face broke into an incredible smile that broke my heart with joy. She started to leap up and hug me, then stopped and put her fingers across her lips. She pointed. I saw the second girl; a mass of curly black hair and wide frightened eyes. I guessed she must be a couple of years older than Mi-Ling.

Kitchi drew his knife. "Someone come," he said. We hid behind the door.

151

Bryant flung the door open. Kitchi grabbed him and held a knife to his throat. "One word, you die."

The thin trickle of blood wending it's way down Bryant's neck got the point home. I looked in the eyes of the evil, callous man from hell who had destroyed my life time and again. "Why did you murder Lucy?"

Even with Kitchi's knife at his throat, he smiled cruelly. "To make you pay. To let you feel what it was like to see someone you love die."

"What are you talking about, Bryant? Who did I kill, that was part of your family?"

"Think back to China, boy. The night of the British Ambassador's Ball. You did some real fancy shootin.' You got in the way of my plan, and murdered my son, Michael."

Even from Bryant, I couldn't believe it. "You set up your own son up as an assassin to kill British Ambassador Sir Charles Gray?"

"Gray was getting in the road of my smuggling. Money in opium trade, boy. Big money, more than you'll ever get in your lifetime." I thought of the ruined lives and broken homes.

"Gray tried to stop me." He continued, "He had to go. Lancaster got him after you killed my boy. So I was going to spoil your big day. Besides, Lucy could have got me. I wanted her. So she wasn't going to get nobody else, least of all a runt like you." The blade went a little deeper as Kitchi reacted.

"Are you going to kill my Papa?" the frightened girl on the bed with Mi-Ling demanded. Kitchi and I stared at the girl.

Mi-Ling said, "Papa, this is Mi-Ling's friend Libby. Libby Bryant. She has been kind to Mi-Ling, Papa, to keep Mi-Ling from being so much afraid."

Libby's tragic dark eyes stared at me from below a mass of black curls.

How long had we looked for Bryant? How long and how many times had he escaped justice? Now before us, was a golden opportunity for retribution? Hand him over to justice or take revenge? Why not save the paperwork of a trial and end it all now?

Then I saw the stricken look in my daughter's eyes. She had been hurt so many times, endured so much. How could I add to her young grief?

"Libby," I said, "Your father has to stand trial for what he's done. They will hold a trial for him in an American court."

She nodded her head. Angus and Hera burst into the room. "Good," Angus noted. "You've got Mi-Ling, Kitchi's got Bryant. Let's go."

I pointed to Libby. "We have an extra, a friend of Mi-Ling's. It will take us two trips to ferry everyone from the ship to land."

We warned Mi-Ling and Libby that they must be quiet. We told Libby any noise could endanger her Papa's life.

"Angus, Hera," I directed, "you go first. Take the girls and get them to shore. Hera, once you land, stay with the girls. Angus, you row back out if it's safe and get the rest of us, including Bryant.

"Hera, once you get over, watch for Mike. Get the girls back to HQ quickly. When the cavalry gets here there could be a fire fight. I don't want the girls hurt. Understood?" They both nodded.

Hera sighed. "I was looking for some action." Angus and Hera went quietly on deck with the girls and we heard no noise, no shouting.

Kitchi asked, "How much time do we give them to get off the boat?"

Bryant snickered, his cockiness restored by seeing his daughter was safe. "My friends in PATCH fixed me up good. I don't limp no more. When I get away, I can run like the wind. I still owe you for my leg injury. If I was to shout out now, you'd get me – but you'd never see your little girl again."

I tore off a bit of sheet and bound it round Bryant's mouth so all he could do was curse incoherently. "Just in case you get any ideas."

Kitchi said, "For him to get down the side of boat, he will need his hands and feet." It was an obvious statement, but something that had escaped me. A look of triumph gleamed in Bryant's eyes.

"Where is the cavalry when you need them?" I muttered. "Let's get him up on deck. Keep that knife at his throat. It would be a terrible tragedy if it slipped."

We left the cabin, but with his knife at Bryant's throat, Kitchi was vulnerable to attack from behind. We worked our way along the passageway and I wished that Sebastian with his photographic memory had been with us. Still, so far so good. Then our quiet breathing space ran out of air. The door leading into the deck from the opposite side burst open and a canister of tear gas was tossed, followed by two guys in camo and gas mask. That stuff stung like blazes. Within seconds, Kitchi and I spouted fountains of tears and jagged, nearly incapacitating coughs. One of the guys hit Kitchi. It was only then that I realized they were part of the rescue team. Bryant dived into one of the cabins with great presence of mind. Two or three of the crew came out and started coughing.

I shouted to our should-have-been rescuers, "It's Major Faulkner and Kitchi! Get us out of here."

"Sorry, sir, we didn't know." They helped us on deck. "Where's Bryant?" I shouted at them, "Kitchi had him. He was here with us."

"Bryant?" the soldier asked.

"Bryant! The captain of the ship," I yelled. " Man he's the one we're after!"

They looked at each other. "Well, sir, the truth is we were told to take the ship. We don't know what the captain looks like."

"Where are your transports?" I asked.

We heard the sound of an outboard motor coming from under the bow of the ship and ran to the edge just in time to catch a glimpse of Bryant and another crew member leaving in one of the launches.

"You two with me," I ordered the two guys.

"Major Faulkner, we can't leave."

This is a joint op. I'm a major. Now move!"

Kitchi and I pulled down our night goggles and the four of us got into the boat and churned across the water after the fleeing Bryant. We seemed to have been left the slowest boat. Bryant knew how to get the best out of an outboard motor. He was quickly outdistancing us.

Bryant's boat crossed over to the shore. He and his passenger leaped out and ran down the beach. By the time we landed, they were no longer in sight.

Tam Shepherd and Sandy Hammond found us. How, God alone knows. Angus located us and assured us that Hera had taken the girls back to HQ.

Tam Shepherd knew where there were horses, but we didn't know where Bryant had gone.

Tam said, "Sir I would think he would ging till Dunnottar Castle. It's a great place to hide out. Nobody is going to come looking for him there. He may have tackle stored there already just in case something like this happened."

I asked Angus if the boat we had gone out to the Allegheny in was still intact.

Angus said it was fine and still usable. I sent the two soldiers whose boat I had borrowed back to the ship.

"When you guys get back, locate Major Buchanan and tell him what's happened. Tell him we're going to try to locate Bryant in Dunnottar Castle. Have you got me?"

"Yes, sir," they replied. "Please, sir," one of them said. "My name's Hank. I've had night fighting experience in Afghanistan. I'd like to stay, and I think I can help."

"Thank you, Hank. That's a good plan. It will give us two teams of two."

There are only two gates into Dunnottar Castle and you have to go up some long stone steps. Two guys with rifles could stop a lot of people. I wondered how well Bryant knew the castle. The only other way to enter or leave would be over the walls – a dangerous climb up any of the sides and absolute suicide in the dark. It's about 160 feet up the walls. There is a small postern gate to the north, but even with the night goggles it would be hard to find. The night goggles gave images a green hue, transforming everything into a mystery, surreal landscape.

We procured a wagon, lamps and two horses. Local knowledge and support was vital. Bryant had not made himself popular with the locals. We headed off the two miles to Dunnottar. Even by moonlight it was formidable looking. This is the closest we had been to grabbing Bryant and bringing him to justice. I had to remember that he was not just evil – he was also wily and cunning.

When we got to the castle entrance, we went slowly up both sides of the stepped entry tunnel. There was evidence on the steps that a horse had not been long passed and it must be inside. We couldn't take our wagon and horses in, so we left them behind bushes, hoping the snorting would not be heard.

"I was trying to think," I said to Kitchi. "Why would Bryant come in here? Wouldn't it be easier just to build up speed and keep going?"

"He must look for something or maybe someone." Kitchi replied.

Who? I wondered. *It can't be one of the PATCH men or they would open a time portal and leave. Maybe the attack on Bryant's ship has damaged something and now transportation is not so easy for them until they get to their next booster place for their travel signal. That would mean that help from PATCH command center could not get through to their men, either.*

I said to Angus, "You and Hank go to the right when we get to the top of the stairs. Kitchi and I will go left. We'll both work towards the Keep in the middle of the castle. Any questions?"

"If he's in our sights, do we fire?" Angus asked.

"Try to wound him. If that's not possible, shoot to kill." It was the first time I had issued that order and when I heard myself saying it, it kind of shook me to hear my own voice.

It's a long climb up the steps of Dunnottar. They are flat and slope up gently, and there was plenty of time for someone to aim and fire. It was cold, but as we moved

I could feel perspiration run down my back. I could feel my throat tighten and any noise was magnified in my mind. Kitchi was silent; you could not even hear him breathe. Halfway and you feel your body prepare itself for the thud and kick of a bullet. Thankfully, none came.

Hank and Angus, at the other side of the steps, kept pace with us. We communicated by hand signals, which we could see with our night vision kit. What we didn't know was if anyone was watching us, and if they were, what they could see of us.

We had to be careful not to slip on the moss and green algae. Crouch, look listen. It was amazing how noisy the night was. Suddenly we reached the entrance. *"Thank You, Lord,"* I said. Kitchi and I moved to the left. Hank and Angus went right. Kitchi whispered to me, "Bryant will put himself near a place where he can escape. If any other man is with him, he too, will wish to escape from danger."

In the Keep, Bryant could be cut off. All an enemy had to do would be to watch the entrance and the walls of the Keep in case he tried to abseil down. The Keep was too obvious a place not to go.

"Focus, come on," I ordered myself. What if I didn't make home it this time? Poor Mi-Ling. I didn't want to add to her misery. I was cold and tired. Marie danced through my mind. I saw her smile and heard her laughter, inexorably woven into strains of Chopin. I stopped and so did Kitchi, thinking I had heard something he had missed. I realized suddenly that I wanted to kiss Marie and hold her hand and laugh with her. I wanted to live with her and be with her when the sun came up in the morning and when it went down again in the evening. The scent of the sea came over the castle walls and reminded me I was far from home. Yet, where was home? Home was not a place – it was a

person – Marie Waleska. I couldn't give ten reasons why I loved her, yet I knew because I knew, because I knew. The certainty of my love for Marie mirrored my certainty that God was real. Now God had given me someone to love. That love filled me with thoughts of home and my future with Mi-Ling and Marie.

I shook myself. I couldn't afford to be caught off guard. I had the safety of everyone else to think about. I had got them into this, now I had to get them out. We got to the Keep and it was empty, but we spent a nervous ten minutes going through it just in case my surmise had been wrong. In the team, each of us carried what could be called a portable homing device built into our watches. Pressing a button on our watches delivered a small light. When that light came on it meant *center in on my position* as I was in charge. When everyone crowded together in the Keep, I said, "Okay, we've looked up here. Now where to? What about looking down into the vaults?" I asked. "Only, I don't know where the *Whig's Vault* is."

"I know," Angus said. "It's in the newer part of the castle below the King's bedroom."

I remembered the history behind the Whig's Vault. In 1685, there were one-hundred-sixty-seven people crammed into a vault about fifteen feet wide and fifty-two feet long in the castle. There were 122 men and 45 women. They could not sit or lay, only stand. They were Covenanters, and had been imprisoned for their refusal to take the Oath of Allegiance stating that the King was head of the church. They said there was only one head, Jesus Christ.

They were crammed into terrible conditions for about two months. Two fell to their deaths trying to escape. Others died of disease (portable toilets had not been invented). Thirty-seven took the oath in the end and were released. Twenty-two escaped but, fifteen of them were recaptured. The rest suffered transportation to Perth Amboy in New Jersey, USA, where many of them died of disease. Even when you go into the vault today it is claustrophobic and oppressive.

Angus led the way to the vault. We knew were searching for at least two people, Bryant and one other. It was possible that PATCH had other operatives planted in the castle. I hoped not, and I hoped that Bryant was in the vault, for by bringing everyone together I had given Bryant a way out. The easy exit was unguarded.

Kitchi offered, "I will stay outside. When you hunt the bear, all eyes are on the front. He who watches his back is wise. I will watch your backs. My senses tell me to be prepared, the trap is too easy."

My lips and moth began to dry up. I trusted Kitchi's instinct. I had seen where he hunted – a dangerous land where death or an enemy could wait behind the next tree. Kitchi was no coward. He was not avoiding a fight if it came to that.

Angus went to the top half of the vault and Hank and I went to the bottom half. Anyone inside should be trapped. There was a humming noise like some kind of generator. The noise was only audible close to the vault. I hoped I had given Angus enough time to get to the top half of the vault. I found out later there had been a guard at the top part of the vault and Angus had quieted him.

I looked at Hank and indicated that we should go in at the count of three. Hank tapped his night goggles and I did not pick up what he meant. I counted three and we dashed inside, shouting at them to surrender. Then I found out what Hank was trying to tell me. Night goggles are good for night vision; your eyes are adjusted and you can see in the dark. But if you're wearing them and someone shines strong light in your face, you're blinded. There were three figures in the vault. While I was stupidly congratulating myself for being right, one of the figures picked up one of these million-candle power lamps and shone it directly at us. We were totally blinded. It was only after we heard gunfire that we knew Angus had reached his objective. It was Angus who told me afterwards that we nearly got shot. We assumed the third figure was Reynolds. The guy who had been with Bryant, held Angus at bay. Bryant and Reynolds opened up a time portal and began to push the equipment into it. Then apparently Reynolds said to Bryant,

"Be a good boy and deal with them. They are blind at the moment. This time try and make a good job of it."

"You promised me I could go with you to safety," Bryant whined.

"Sorry, old boy, but you've become a bit of a liability. PATCH doesn't like liabilities. Good luck." And Reynolds was gone. At the same time, the man who had been holding Angus at bay was shot. Bryant pushed past us. I tried to grab him, but I was still half-blinded and his pistol barrel glanced off my head. Everything went dark. I groped about for the night goggles and found them unbroken. Once I put them on again, things began to make sense.

"Come on," I urged the others, "let's get him." The exertion of speech made my head throb. I don't know what made me look down, but I saw something on the ground and swooped to pick it up, swaying on unsteady legs as pain thundered through my head. The object proved to be a flash drive and I pocketed it. Hearing gunfire outside, we sprinted for Kitchi.

Thankfully, Kitchi seemed unhurt. "Where's Bryant?" I gasped. Kitchi pointed to one of the castle battlements along the wall. Remembering the plan of many trips to Dunnottar, there were two ways off the wall and a third way over it to a long, long drop. We split up again.

"Bryant," I called. "You might as well give up. Your so-called friends have left you."

From out of the darkness came Bryant's answer, "Go to hell, boy."

If his hubris hadn't caused him to taunt me, we might not have spotted him. His voice directed our attention to a place halfway along the wall. A figure stood on the top of the battlements.

"Bryant," I cried. "Get down! You'll get killed if you fall." The moonlight outlined him, making him an easy target. He had ruined and shattered my life. I could end it right now – one shot and no one would ever blame me. Jesus wouldn't let me fire that shot. What was it I had been reading in my Bible since meeting Jesus? Something like, *vengeance is Mine, I will replay, says the LORD*. And if I fired that shot, I would have to face the eyes of my daughter as I explained to her and her new friend how Bryant had died. I sighed. If we took Bryant alive, maybe we could get intelligence on Reynolds.

Suddenly, splitting the quiet moonlight, Bryant fired on us from the castle battlement. He must have lacked sufficient footing to compensate for the recoil. He went over. One minute he was there outlined in brightness and the next minute he was gone. We raced over to where we had last seen him. We trained a lamp on the side of the castle walls and spotted Bryant. He lay on a ledge some fifteen feet below. The ledge plunged into darkness. We could hear waves crashing against rocks.

I shouted down to him, "Bryant, we're going to lower a rope to you…"

He cut me off, "You'll have to come down here and get me, boy, my leg is busted."

I hate heights, but I was the ranking officer. I had to take the risk. *Oh, Lord, help me. Give me courage*, I breathed.

"Drew be careful!" Angus said. "Let me go."

"No, Angus. I got us into this mess. I need to get us out."

We threw a rope over the wall. It was tricky – and scary. There was no way to anchor the rope at the top and with the guys holding it, the pressure was uneven. I was about eight feet down when Bryant suddenly stood up and jerked the rope. The others weren't expecting that. My heart stopped beating as the rope swung out over nothingness and twirled around with me clinging to it like a tiny piece of lint on the edge of eternity.

"See you in hell, boy," Bryant snarled, jerking and thrashing the rope again. Bryant had incredible strength. That maneuver sent me flying into darkness with the words, *Jesus! Jesus!* pounding through my heart with my blood. Miraculously, my clothes caught on a bush, breaking my fall. There was a strangled cry from Bryant. Lights flashed from the top of the castle wall. With a look of hatred morphing into disbelief, Bryant slipped off the ledge. His scream of terror faded as he tumbled into darkness. Fear and pain immobilized me, running up and down the back of my legs and biting into my groin as Bryant's falling body plunged out of sight. He was gone. It was over and I had tried to save him.

Angus came down and got me. Someone had to. I couldn't move. When I reached the top of the wall and was safe again, I threw up. I was so relieved to be standing on safe ground that vomiting in front of the team didn't even embarrass me. My legs still shook and trembled. It took all my effort just to stand. "Down there," I gasped, an involuntary shiver passing through me, "How far?"

"Two-hundred feet easily," Angus replied.

"No chance he survived?"

"Not a hope in hell," Angus said cheerfully. "Bryant's one nightmare you can quit having. Come on, son, let's get you home. Although she can't see you, there's a young lady waiting there for you who will work wonders for you. The sound of your voice will do her a lot of good as well. And unless I'm very much mistaken, you've just added a family member with Mi-Ling's friend. Her daddy's just been killed and no matter how evil and no account he was, he's probably all that poor youngster had."

We met up with Mike Argo and got everything back to HQ. What would happen to the Allegheny I neither knew nor cared. When I got back to HQ, I was ordered bed rest by the medics. I tried to argue. I wanted to see Mi-Ling and talk to Libby. I wanted to see Marie. The medics won the argument unfairly, giving me something that knocked me out. I woke up two days later. Colonel Carlisle came to see me. "You got Bryant. Well done."

"Sir, in all truthfulness, he got himself. If he hadn't been so eaten up with hatred for me, he would still be alive. He wanted me to pay for the death of his son. Yet he was willing to turn his son into a murderer and to get Sir Charles Gray out of the road."

Colonel Carlisle walked over to the window of my rest room.

"A pro would have fired through the slats. Not pushed the rifle through them so it could be seen by anyone," he said.

"Maybe if things had turned out differently Lucy would be still alive," I thought aloud.

He turned from the window. "Major, we can't live on ifs or buts. As always, you've handled your job with excellence. The flash drive we found on you outlined Reynolds schedule; a very methodical man, Professor Reynolds, and clever."

"What about Libby Bryant? Does she know her father is dead and how he died?"

"The colonel took a deep breath. "Poor girl, yes, she does. Will you talk to her?"

I tried to look at things from Libby's viewpoint. She was alone in the world now. How much did she know of what her father did? How much did she need to know? I remembered Mi-Ling in that hellhole of a place in China. My stomach still did a queer walkover when I thought of the torture and suffering inflicted on my lovely daughter by scumbags. Human trafficking still stinks. I hadn't a clue about what Libby might have suffered under Bryant's nefarious care.

"Okay, sir. I will do my best."

Before I talked to Libby, Dunnottar Castle was checked for Bryant's body. We couldn't find it. During the darkness of that fateful night, Bryant's body must have washed out to sea. Bryant was dead. In the daylight, it was clear that no one could have survived a fall like the plunge he took. At least I could tell Libby that none of us had killed her father.

He is dead, isn't he? I kept asking myself. "N*obody could survive a fall like that − could they?*

CHAPTER 12 - The Blossoming Heart

That evening Mi-Ling and Marie came to see me, with Mi-Ling functioning as Marie's eyes in Martha's place. We were talking when Mi-Ling decided that maybe things needed a little help. Our adult conversation must have sounded a bit strained to my perspicacious daughter, since I felt I had no right to tell Marie my feelings: how that when I was hanging off the rock at Dunnottar, I had seen her face and experienced a horrifying fear that I would never see her again.

Mi-Ling took my hand and then took Marie's hand. She placed one on top of the other. "Papa will be your eyes while Mi-Ling go and find chocolate; Chocolate very good for growing girls, Uncle Sebastian say, and Mi-Ling is hungry."

Before either of us could respond, Mi-Ling had run out of the room.

Marie left her hand in mine. "How did you feel on the rocks?" she asked.

"Scared, cold and tired Marie…I'm ashamed, but I was scared to death. But what I was most scared of is that I'd never see you again. That I would die and you would never find out what I looked like. That I would never hear you play Chopin again or hear you laugh, that I would never be able to kiss you again. Your voice is my music. When I hear you speak, my troubles fall away. I see a future and a hope – lovely gifts from God."

"What if my sight does not return?" she asked.

"Love is blind," I told her, "blind to outer things. If I could define love then it would be like buying a painting or a lovely vase. Love is the desire to be with one person more than anyone else – to invest time in them and to give to them the keeping of your heart. Giving them the power to cherish it or break it with a few words thoughtlessly spoken. Marie, I don't love a vase or a painting. I don't want to spend the rest of my life with a picture. I love the woman who is Marie Waleska, I have found the woman I cannot live without. When I hung between this life and eternity on that ledge, what held me there was hope that we could be together. One day I might need you to be my legs or hands or feet while I can be your eyes. Each day, each day..." I hesitated. "Each day my darling for the rest of our lives. I love you, Marie. As I live and breathe, I love you, a love that can hold nothing back."

Rivulets of tears ran down her cheeks.

"Marie, please be my wife and make my life complete, and make my eyes – even if they do double service – the happiest eyes in God's creation."

"Drew, I have something to tell you." she said.

My heart sank. *Please, Lord, not another 'Dear John' speech. I can't take anymore.*

I swallowed hard. "Go on," I said, not knowing what to expect but still holding her hand.

"Colonel Carlisle took me to see Dr. Frazier. An eye surgeon. Dr. Frazier examined my eyes. He said they would need to do some tests, but he thought they might be able to help me recover at least partial sight."

"Darling, that's wonderful news."

"*Mon amour*, please listen. He said that it would be a very delicate operation and there would only be one chance. If it didn't take there would be no second chance."

"But it will! I know it will!" I said. "You just wait and see."

Marie put her hands around my face. "My love, ask me to marry you again – after we know the results of the surgery. When we know what the real picture will be like."

It was at this point that Mi-Ling returned, but with a nurse. "Come on, Major," the nurse said briskly. "You must rest. Mrs. Faulkner, you can come back for him in the morning. Then he is all yours."

Marie kissed me. I heard her repeat *Mrs. Faulkner* softly to herself. She smiled.

Mi-Ling bounced up and hugged me.

"Did you like the chocolate?" I asked her?

"Chocolate, what chocolate?" she asked.

The following day I thanked the medical staff for their hospitality and told them I felt 125 percent better.

"Hmm," said Dr. Bartholomew, "We must be slacking. We usually go for improvements of 150-plus percent. Still, if you will go suspending yourself over eternity, then I think we will have to make do. Perhaps congratulations are in order?"

"Congratulations?"

"You and Miss Waleska of course. "

I suddenly remembered what Lucy had said to me when we had gone to ask Jesus to heal Mi-Ling. '*You will see her before she sees you.*' Was that prophetic that Marie was the one? That we would be married? That Marie would see?

"Dr. Bartholomew, you must have talked to Dr. Frazier. What are the possibilities that Miss Waleska will see again?" I asked.

He smiled and patted me on the arm. "Oh, I can't really discuss a patient. Patient confidentiality, you know, but what about the phrase '*quietly confident?*' We reckon surgery in about ten days, then keeping the bandages on for four days, then everything should be fine."

I returned his smile. "Okay, doc, I won't report you to the General Medical Council."

"Ah. I'm gratified. That reassurance will do my blood pressure no end of good."

"Jolly good," I continued. "Doc, could I remove the bandages myself?"

"Yes. Don't know why not. Take her to some romantic spot and give her something wonderful to look at."

I sighed. "Well that rules me out. I can't compete with Morar beach."

"Yes," Bartholomew agreed. "Good idea. Take her some place where she can glimpse eternity when the bandages come off the eyes."

We parted company. I was hugely excited and joyful to have been discharged from medical care. I began contemplating visually romantic spots.

Next was an overdue visit to Libby Bryant. I would need Mi-Ling's help. Much to my surprise, Mi-Ling and I found her with Victoria.

"Miss Libby," I told her sincerely, "I am so sorry about your father. We tried to save him but..." My voice drifted off into a maze of uncertainty.

"I know," she said sadly. "The others said you risked your life trying to save him."

I started to say something else, but I felt Mi-Ling's hand on my arm. She shook her head.

In a moment, I found out what Mi-Ling had known that I hadn't. Libby needed to talk. "Pa was an enemy to himself," Libby remembered through quiet tears. "He was always a fightin' and could never settle anywhere. He wanted a wife to take care of me, but wouldn't anybody have him. Michael got killed and Pa shouldn't have done what he done. Pa promised Michael the world. Said in China there was a man who would spoil everything and he needed to be stopped. One of the people saw Michael trying to shoot the man and shot him. All Pa could think of after that was violence."

Libby's tears ran faster and freer and she choked back a sob. "I could get anything I wanted from Pa. He would buy me anything I asked him for. The one thing that I wanted the worst he couldn't give because he didn't know how. I just wanted him to…"

"Hug you," Mi-Ling guessed.

"Was that too much to ask him for?" Libby demanded with hurt and anger echoing in the young voice. "Just for him to tell me that he loved me. But he couldn't. He never did. He never could." Tears that sat in the green eyes released and splashed over Libby's hands. Mi-Ling threw her arms around her friend's shoulder and hugged her. She began singing gently, *Living without knowing you were loved. I had been living without knowing I was loved, then God touched my heart.*

"Libby," I said dropping to my knees in front of her, "will you hug me?"

Libby looked at Mi-Ling, who nodded. Shyly, Libby slipped her arms around my neck and began to cry. I started to cry too. Mi-Ling, like a Chinese Lucy, put her arms around us both. I felt the first tentative tendrils of trust reach out to me from Libby and I was not going to break them.

"Libby, you are with people now who love you. I don't know where it is yet, but your home is with us, if you want it to be."

From Libby's own account, Bryant had given her tons of material things. Yet, she would have swapped them all just to hear her father say that he loved her. I wondered how many other children longed to hear these words from the lips of mum and dad.

A knock sounded on the door. When I opened the door, I recognized the man outside as one of Colonel Carlisle's aide de camps. He saluted. "Major Faulkner, the Colonel would like to see you in his office at your earliest convenience, sir."

"Thank you, Sergeant. Tell the Colonel I will be along at once."

"Yes sir." He saluted and left.

"I have to go" I said to Victoria and the girls. I turned to Libby and said, "A promise is a promise."

She smiled and nodded. Black ringlets bobbed up and down like a nest of young blackbirds. Suddenly life had begun to take on meaning again.

* * *

Angus McTurk and Anton were in the colonel's office by the time I got there. Three heads turned as I entered the room. I saluted and the colonel indicated I should take a seat.

"Good. Now that we're all here, I can tell you why I summoned you." Then looking to me he said, "Major, that flash drive you found at Dunnottar. Seems it belonged to Reynolds, or at least was issued by Reynolds – maybe to the late Mr. Bryant. It contained Reynolds's itinerary for the next couple of weeks. Where he was planning to go on his merry jaunts and an indication as to what mischief he planned. If he gave it to Bryant, because they did not have the sweetest of goodbyes, he may not know of Bryant's demise yet. Or if he does and know how Bryant died, he may assume that when Bryant fell down the cliff at Dunnottar, it all went with him out to sea. If we move to intercept Reynolds and we mess it up, Reynolds will change everything and we won't know where he is until the next time he surfaces along with all the havoc that he may create. He is a cunning character, but he's not infallible."

"Where is he, and probably more importantly, when?" Angus asked.

"Well, it looks like he's in Rome," the colonel replied.

Anton said, "I often wanted a trip to Rome...Trastevere, via Venito, Fontana di Trevi, and other cultural spots...and the beautiful women...but this is work."

"Yes," said Colonel Carlisle, "and in 1940, a couple of days before war is declared."

We looked at him. "Why would Reynolds want to go there, sir?" I asked.

"I think I will let your Uncle Adrian answer that," he replied.

Adrian Conroy joined us ten minutes later, dressed in a much-worn white coat and finishing off a piece of crispy bacon. "Sorry. Got here quick as poss. How can I help?"

The colonel looked at him with bemused tolerance, possibly with the realization that in Adrian's line of work eccentricity was a definite asset rather than a liability. Genius and ordinariness did not seem to go hand in hand. "Can you explain to our people why on earth Professor Reynolds would want to go to Rome in 1940, and don't say to visit the shops along the Via Venito."

"Do you mind if I smoke? It helps the thought processes." Without giving the colonel a chance to object – which he surely would have done – the pipe came out, was duly filled and lit. My uncle certainly looked cognitive. The smell of pipe tobacco took me back to childhood when he used to come to the house, where his pipe smoke would blend with the scent of the three or four leather-bound volumes he always carried with him. When he sat in the big rocking chair reading, the scene looked as if it belonged on a cameo from 1880.

After thinking and a warning cough from Colonel Carlisle, Adrian said, "Jean Le Croix, that's why he's gone there."

"Who?" I asked the question I could see on everyone else's faces.

"Le Croix, the physicist. Didn't they teach you anything at school?" My uncle seemed somewhat disappointed that the name had not automatically rung a bell with me. "Look…" he explained, "Time travel to break it down to its simplest terms is the agitation of space to produce a rift in time to crack open the fourth dimension. Kairon provides the power for us to time travel, but before Kairon can be used, a rift in time has to take place. Kairon can't cut a rift, but once the rift is cut, Kairon can navigate through the rift increasing it in size until virtually a usable tunnel is created. Le Croix invented the time laser cutter, well, agitator really.

"Look, put it this way: if you have heart disease and one of your arteries decides it is not playing the game anymore and blocks itself off, then the blood is on either side of the blockage. If you put in a stent into the artery the blood can flow again and the stent stops it from blocking again for quite a bit. So it is with time. You are in present day. You want to get to 1700. You know both times are there."

"But surely," Anton said, "everybody in 1700 is dead?"

"Yes," said Adrian, "they are dead in 2013, but they are still alive in 1700. The time cutter that Le Croix invents enables you to do that, to get from present day back to 1700. It cuts the channel like the stent allows the blood to flow again from one part of the artery to the other. The cutter cuts the rift through the blockage, allowing us to get back to what year we want. Simple."

Quizzical glances bounced around the room, and yet Adrian had given it to us in the simplest possible terms.

"There is another cutter type device," Adrian added, "invented by the Russian Ulitzov. It's not as efficient as the one designed by Le Croix, but it's what PATCH have built into their systems. If they can kill Le Croix, then we don't get to time travel. PATCH will have the monopoly on the technology."

More puzzled glances, followed by the shuffling of feet.

"So what happens if the cutter goes too far?" I asked.

Another column of blue smoke went up round the room and Adrian seemed oblivious to the colonel's deliberate cough. "Well," he said, "laying aside the physics and formulae which I won't bore you with. Basically, without the cutter and the failsafe devices on it, you could start off and the Kairon would power it right through non-stop to heavens knows where. So basically you could aim to get to 1815 to cheer the Duke of Wellington on at Waterloo and end up in a nest of Velociraptors in a real life Jurassic times."

"They wouldn't be able to tell the difference between French and British," Angus observed.

"Perhaps they were neutral," Anton said, "like the Swedes."

"Gentlemen, let us at least retain a modicum of keeping to the point!" the colonel interrupted.

"Sorry, sir," I apologized.

"So you see," continued Adrian looking a little non-plussed at our banter, "anything happens to young Le Croix and we're stuck."

The colonel took out a folder. "Le Croix has to get the last train to Geneva before the Germans move in and he becomes a hostile alien. I think it was June 14."

Anton thought and said, "What is to stop Reynolds from trying to kill him another time in Geneva?"

The colonel scratched his head. "Basically nothing, except the fact that we know he's going to be in Rome just before Le Croix gets away. You might not be dealing with just Reynolds, but also the Abwehr, the German Military intelligence."

"Fine, sir," I said, "but how are we going to get anyone to trust us and even begin to understand what we are trying to say?"

Anton said, "As a well as being brought up to speak Russian, French and

Alan T. McKean

Italian are my second languages. My charm and personality will do the rest."

"With the help of some gold," the colonel added.

"Gold, how unromantic...but useful," Anton admitted.

"Gold, is that not kind of risky?" I queried. Angus nodded in agreement.

"You pay him to go to Geneva and set up there," the colonel said. "It's amazing how many doors gold opens."

"What is our reason for being there that will convince Le Croix that we are there as sheep dogs and not wolves?" Anton wanted to know.

"You are aware of his views on time travel and you are sponsoring him to develop them. Our documentation department has been working overtime and several operatives risked their lives to get you these documents." The colonel looked at us.

"This is serious. The Nazis took some of these quirky things seriously. Historical objects that they thought would give them power. Time travel is just up their street."

"China, sir," I said. "Could it be through Le Croix that the Nazis got to 1867 China to mine for silver to buy opium? I'm not liable to forget that and the fact that Angus saved me from Major Van Haas of the Abwehr. I would have been on the way to Berlin thanks to that Arian oaf. God alone knows what kind of reception I would have got there. It still makes my blood run cold thinking about it." Then I added out loud, "Thank You, Jesus for Your protection."

"Even so, Major, it was lucky that Angus was there to save your life."

"With all due respect, sir, while I am very thankful for what Angus did, luck had nothing to do with it. It was God's timing."

There was a silence. Anton said, "We had better make sure that Monsieur Le Croix does not leave any information behind for the Nazis to find."

The colonel added, "I'm bringing Mike Argo in on this. He speaks Italian. That means you can split up into two teams. In fact, you'd better go find him. He's still infatuated with Hera and it's time he got back to work. We'll wait here until you get him. We'll put Hera on standby."

I found Hera and Mike. With a face-splitting smile, she displayed the engagement ring on the third finger of her left hand.

"Congratulations, people!" I told them. "It's nice to hear some happy news. Sorry, Mike, but the boss wants you. You're going to Rome."

They laughed and as I looked at them, I thought what a well-matched couple. Amazing since they had to go back 2,000 years to meet and forward 2,000 years to marry! Well, that's time travel for you, never a dull moment, even if you do spend half the time trying to avoid getting stabbed, shot, scalped or otherwise disposed of.

Then Mike's face changed. "Rome? when?"

"As soon as," I replied.

"No, but what year?" he asked.

"It will be 1940. The colonel wants you both. Hera is backup."

Hera looked puzzled. "Back up to where?" she asked. "We have just come from canteeeen. Not more could I eat."

I laughed. "No, no more food," I explained, "you get prepared for the mission in case something happens to one of us. If it does, then you get to go."

Her face lit up. "To Rome to fight in the arena?"

"No, to help us, let's get to the colonel's office." We did and congratulations were offered all around. Seeing the ring on Hera's finger brought back thoughts of Meryl. Meryl was gone and hopefully happy with Kitchi. My future – if it ever got started – would be with Marie.

"Right," said the colonel, when we were all assembled. "You spilt up into two teams. Anton and Angus can make the initial contact. Major, you and Mike wait nearby in case anything goes wrong. Anton has persuasive powers. Anton, if anyone will make Le Croix believe that he can set up in Geneva it's you."

Anton bowed in acknowledgement, "I will give it my very best attentions." Then his face brightened. "Does that mean I get to carry the gold? I am not used to carrying gold. I need a little practice."

Colonel Carlisle in response shook his head. "You get some gold the rest will be for a bank draught for a bank in Geneva."

Anton thought and said, "You would think they could do repairs on their bank with all that gold and not have a draft in it."

"The draught the colonel means is a way of getting money," Mike explained.

"In Russia, if you get a draught you get sneezes. I think you call it *cold*," Anton said, still following his own path thought.

The colonel cleared his throat and finished explaining the mission. "Get

Le Croix to the station and get him on the train. Then get out of it. I don't want Reynolds to catch you, nor do I want you to get caught by the Abwehr."

"Sir," I asked. "Can I see Marie and Mi-Ling before I go?"

He nodded. "Certainly, good idea. You go at ten o'clock tomorrow morning."

* * *

I found Marie playing the piano. The notes filled the room with the sadness of tears running down a cheek as her fingers touched the keys. She stopped playing when she detected my presence.

"You bring peace to my heart and joy to my eyes," I said after I kissed her. I touched her cheek with the back of my hand.

She frowned, "Your touch has the touch of sadness about it. I think you may be sent to somewhere I cannot come." She conjectured further, "And there is danger."

I took her hand. "When we are married, we can go on honeymoon to where I am going – to Rome. Or should I say *we* are going to Rome. Mike, Angus and Anton are going with me."

I explained to her what the mission was as carefully as I could, including the dangers. It was only fair that she know.

Marie's grip on my hand tightened. She began to cry, her sobs erupting from somewhere deep within. She reached up and touched my face. "I want to see, to see what you look like. I'm tired of walking in the shadows and in the dark. I love you and I want to see you. I know what you're like inside – that's the part I love. But sometimes I want just to feast my eyes on you and drink you in and just have the joy, the breathtaking joy of looking at you."

I hugged her and promised, "You will. I will come back, come back to you."

For long minutes we just held each other. Then she drew away and said something that showed how deeply she had been thinking. "Darling, you can't fail. If time travel is based on his work – then if he is killed before he starts – all this will disappear. If he is killed it will be like time travel has never been. We will never meet and all the missions you have been on will never have happened. You and I will be separated forever!"

The import of Marie's words began to sink in. If Le Croix was killed, there would be no Lucy, no Mi-Ling, and the German plot in China might succeed. All that had happened would be as if it had never taken place, except for what PATCH attempted. With no opposition, they would succeed.

My mind filled with pictures of Washington killed back in 1755, of General Lee being replaced and Britain being drawn into a hopeless war, of Queen Victoria being assassinated or replaced with a 'doppelganger.' Bryant and Lucy would still be alive and he would still be determined to have her on his own terms.

"Dear Lord," I said to Marie, "you are right. Let's get my uncle's opinion on it. Come with me, darling. By the way, you look fantastic."

She smiled, but underneath I could feel her frustration. She longed to speak with her eyes as well as her voice. She wanted to see if I understood.

Adrian opened the door to my knock. "Drew, Marie, what can I do for you? Come in, come in, coffee?" He led us through the hall into the living room. Victoria was there and rose to welcome us.

"Marie has a couple of things to ask you," I explained. "I know they've probably been thought of, but for peace of mind."

"Ask away, Miss Waleska – or can I call you Marie, as you may be part of the family soon?"

I flashed a glance at Victoria, who seemed to be reading. I had learned that women have a knack of seeming to do one thing while actually contemplating another.

"If Drew and the others fail," Marie asked, "or if something happens to Monsieur Le Croix, will things suddenly change as if time travel had never been? I mean, will Bryant and Lucy be alive again?"

Out came the pipe.

"It's alright, Drew," Marie assured me before I could speak to my uncle. "I can smell the pipe tobacco. I don't mind it."

"Well done, Marie," Adrian said, "for spotting the flaw in the plan. We didn't mention it to Drew and the others because we didn't want to put pressure on them. Yes, Bryant would still be alive. You would still be back in Balmoral with the Queen. Lucy would still be in China at the school. God alone knows what PATCH would do with a free hand until- or if we ever – caught up. The only thing is that Drew and the others would be stuck in Rome at the start of World War Two. It would be the technology that would be affected more than the people. Oh, blast it! We don't know. I know it's a risk, Drew, but you have been successful up to now."

"Only by God's help," I told my uncle, then gasped. "Oh dear Lord that means Mi-Ling would be back in that hell hole in China." I suddenly felt overwhelmed. Talk about getting in over your head. I felt I had just been catapulted from the shore to the bottom of the Challenger Deep in the Marianas Trench – seven miles straight down…with just about as much pressure.

Marie said, "Drew, my beloved, failure is simply not an option." She squeezed my hand.

"So," I said to Adrian, "Reynolds would not be affected by Le Croix's demise because the technology he uses is different from ours?"

"Yup, is the short answer."

"Make that coffee strong," I told Victoria, "very strong."

* * *

The following day, Colonel Carlisle called us in. Mike and Hera were there already.

Without preamble, Carlisle said, "I was talking with Professor Conroy about the flaw in our plan that Miss Walenska pointed out. I have decided to make this a six-person team. We must stop both Reynolds and the Abwehr from getting to Le Croix. Historically, he did get to Switzerland, but what we have now is a situation where Reynolds is the unknown factor. The Abwehr did not get Le Croix historically. It's your job to make sure Reynolds doesn't get him either. So we are talking about covering him for approximately ten minutes to get from his flat in the Via Cavour to the station."

Mike said, "Sir, it depends whether Reynolds wants to use Le Croix's knowledge or just get him out the road. If you know someone has designed something more efficient than the machine you have, wouldn't you want to incorporate that into your plan?"

The colonel's brows came together thoughtfully. "It's going to be up to the six of you to use your initiative. I'm going to have Team Beta on standby in case there's a problem. If we have too many agents flying about it is going to look like Piccadilly Circus."

Hera was very pensive, "I have a bad feeling about this in my heart." She took Mike's hand."

"Darling," Mike said, "we're a team. When we get back, it will be a time for singing and celebration and a wedding. Angus can be best man."

"Glad to," Angus agreed. "It's time you two were married."

Mike looked into Hera's eyes. "Nothing will separate us, dear one, not even death."

All of felt encouraged by the loving exchange between Mike and Hera – that is until amid the laughter Angus came to me and said quietly, "I remember the last wedding I attended as best man."

He meant when Lucy and I married and celebrated joyful ten minutes before she was gunned down and died in my arms, her white wedding dress dripping crimson amid scattered orange blossoms. I tried to steady myself in the wake of that visceral memory. "Come on Angus, this is different. Bryant's dead."

"He is. Reynolds isn't."

I turned away from Angus, slightly angry at my friend for the first time I could ever remember because by directing my attention back through time to Lucy, Angus had reminded me of too much pain, too much loss, too much heartbreak. To hide the anger, I asked the colonel, "Sir, who is the sixth person in the team?"

The colonel flicked a switch and directed, "You can come in now."

Sebastian came through the door wearing a huge smile. "What you guys need is the services of a lean mean fighting machine and I'm your man."

Our new plan would send Anton and Angus to get Le Croix. James. Hera, Sebastian, and I would watch the street. One team would watch one direction, and the second team would cover the road in the direction of Il Termini station. We decided to go for the last train out at midnight. There would be fewer people about. If there was a firefight, fewer people would be in danger of getting hurt – or at least that was how it worked on paper. We would wear black leather coats and fedora-style hats that could be pulled down over our eyes. Sebastian said he was looking forward to real spaghetti, since he heard about it. He was slightly disappointed when we told him there might not be time for a snack. Once Le Croix was safely out of harm's way, we were to get back to HQ 'tout suite'. I also remembered that Sebastian had a photographic memory. He had got us down the right streets at *Beit She'an* to the amphitheatre and back again. At night in Rome we would need to know the way to the train station and back to the time car. We wouldn't have time for mistakes. If we engaged in a firefight with the bad guys and had to dodge up streets, we couldn't afford to get lost. Compared to Le Croix, none of us were under any illusions that we were indispensable.

We had been targeted to land in the basement of a house at the junction of the Via Cavour and the Via Santa Maria Maggiore. Le Croix lived in the upstairs flat. Anton and Angus would go upstairs to the flat and get Le Croix, who to our understanding had been warned about the Abwher interest. Sebastian and I would watch down the Via Cavour. Hera and Mike would eyeball the Via Santa Maria Maggiore. Then it would be a case of going down the Via Cavour until we came to the Piazza Santa Maria Maggiore and the church, then across the Piazza, down the via Manin, and to the station. Once there, Anton and Angus would get Le Croix on the train using the papers we would supply him. Once the train left, for us it was back to the basement and home. Technically, it would be by far our shortest journey. Little did we know then that the shortest journey was nearly our last.

On the journey in the time car Sebastian sang *Dixie*. I stupidly wondered what the Italian for *Dixie* was. Hera and Mike held hands. Hera rested her head on Mike's broad shoulder. As I was to find out, their love was stronger than death.

When we arrived, we took our places and Anton and Angus went upstairs. It was quiet, except for one drunk man who sang to himself in Latin and drank from a green wine bottle. The only words I understood were *In vino veritas*, in wine there is truth. It took Anton and Angus about forty minutes to get Le Croix out. Mike and Hera walked with them. Hera hooked her arm through Le Croix, which seemed to please him. Mike was just a step ahead of them. Sebastian and I followed behind, trying to check the road each step of the way, along with first floor windows. Angus and Anton followed a bit further behind. To say it was nerve wracking would be an understatement. Hera threw in the occasional girlie giggle for effect. Mike was professional enough to know she was acting. Then as we passed through the Piazza, being careful to cross at the rear of the church, a black Fiat limousine purred slowly along the road. Whether or not anyone in it saw us, we couldn't tell. It was best to assume they did. Whether they understood what they saw, that was something else.

Le Croix had been to Switzerland before. He knew the drill at the station. Gold is a great pacifier. Then on our way down the via Gioberti, Le Croix suddenly stopped and said something to Anton, gesturing with obvious expressions of annoyance. Anton translated; he had left a time travel file back in his room.

When you're the boss, you have to make decisions. If that was the Abwehr prowling about, we knew from history that they found the file and developed it. Otherwise, Van Haase would never have turned up in China. If Reynolds found Le Croix, then that was worse. We decided to get him on the train with the gold so that he could develop his ideas, because historically he would come up with the *time cutter*. Anton and Hera went into the station booking office and showed their passes to the guards. Hera became a focused point of interest to the Italian guards who knew a pretty girl when they saw one. We watched Anton, Hera, and Le Croix get onto the platform. Anton looked the other way while Le Croix and Hera kissed passionately. Poor Mike kept his cool and I heard him muttering to himself, "She's just acting."

It was good that we were outside the barrier. We saw three figures heading towards the platform. One turned to look at the station clock. Angus recognized Reynolds, who was trying to get the other two up to the barrier.

Angus said to Sebastian and me, "That's Reynolds trying to get his operatives on the train. We must stop them. The train goes in three-and-a-half minutes. No doubt they know what Le Croix looks like."

At the same time, Anton and Hera came out of the platform. Hera pretended to be the broken-hearted sweetheart. One bullet spent on Reynolds could save a lot of trouble, but we would never get back in one piece after that and our brief was to get Le Croix on the train.

I took off my hat and wiped my brow. When Hera saw me, I gestured to the two guys coming towards her. Anton had not seen me and wondered why Hera was suddenly stopping. She began to act in the finest line of Greek tragedy, and because she was tall, managed to stall the two men for about two minutes before the train left.

The barrier closed. Anton had just twigged what was needed. He had been slightly behind Hera. One of the men pulled a gun and shot Hera. She grabbed the closest man on the way down. She held on fiercely as the other man fired again. That gave Anton time to pull a knife. He stabbed the gunman. The crowd began milling around and the train left without either of the two goons getting on it.

Meanwhile, Sebastian had vanished into the crowd with his hat pulled down. Hidden in the shadows in the station, it was not obvious he was black. Sebastian's life had taught him to look for as many 'way outs' as possible; you never knew when a side door was going to be handy. The man who had been stabbed was weaving from side to side and the two guards caught up with him.

We got through the barrier and onto the train platform. Anton shouted "dottori." Mike rushed in and picked up Hera, holding her close to him. The panic allowed us to get back out of the crowd. We had to get Hera back to the time car in the basement of Le Croix's old flat. Since was a ten-minute walk, we split up and aimed for the taxis.

Sebastian had located a side door that lead to the furthest away rank of taxis, whose drivers had not yet noticed the activity inside the station. It was then that the second tragedy struck. The guy who had escaped had followed us. With all our attention centered on the wounded Hera, none of us had noticed him. A gun blasted at short range and Mike fell to the pavement, rolling to keep from falling on top of Hera. Angus turned and saw the would-be assassin aiming for the kill. Angus fired back and the guy fell. Mike struggled to his feet, ignoring the blood gushing out of his side. He must have been in fantastic physical condition. We somehow made it to the taxis. Anton poured spirits, which I assumed to be his emergency stash of vodka, over Hera and Mike. The stench would make the taxi drivers think his passengers were drunk and wobbly, rather than wounded.

We got to the first taxi. With the help of some gold, no questions were asked. The second taxi followed suit. We headed for the basement. Hera groaned. Her eyes rolled back in her head. Mike cradled her head in his arms, dropping light kisses on her face. Anton joked with the taxi driver to keep him from noticing the wounded passengers.

We saw the big limousine outside Le Croix's house. We pulled the taxis in about 200 yards down from the big, empty limousine and paid the drivers. No questions asked. We disappeared into the shadows. It had to have been Mike and Hera's superb physical conditions that had brought them this far. They needed immediate medical care, but we had to wait till the strangers came back out of the flat.

One of them came down to the car for a briefcase. He looked up at the light and I recognized him as Van Haase of the Abwher, the guy who had nearly killed me in China. The fact that he was going to the car showed he was not in charge and probably at this time not a major. He returned to the flat and we assumed they had found the file Le Croix had left. We were too badly shot up to start another fight. After Van Haase went back in, we slipped in behind him and managed to get to the basement and back into the time car. Mike held Hera and spoke Greek to her. It seemed an age till we got back. We had achieved our aim. Le Croix was safe and Reynolds had been stopped. But the cost had been high, too high.

Colonel Carlisle came straight down and both Mike and Hera were rushed to Aberdeen Royal. I was worried about Hera. She was seriously wounded.

"Debriefing can wait," the colonel said, as we crowded around and waited for news about Hera and Mike. I prayed for Hera. She had been my responsibility. When the phone rang the colonel said, "I see. Yes, I understand. Thank you."

Anton, Angus, Sebastian, and I looked at him fearfully. I think we actually quit breathing. I know I did.

"Lt. Hera is going to be okay," the colonel said. "Her superb physical condition helped her pull through. She will need rest, but she'll be fine."

"And Mike, sir?" I asked. "How is he?"

The usually impassive Colonel Carlisle raked his hands through his hair and released a deep breath. "I am sorry, major, but Lt. Argo is on a life support machine. He's in a coma. The strain of carrying Lt. Hera on the way back created the start of an embolism. He's in a very bad way."

"What!" I couldn't believe it.

"He risked his life helping his fiancée get back safely from the mission. You all did well in hellish circumstances."

"Does Hera know?"

"No, Major," the colonel replied, "maybe you should tell her."

Angus got up and wandered over to the window. There were tears in his eyes. "I'll come with you if you want, Drew," he said. "This won't be easy."

I nodded. "Thanks, Angus. But let it wait until morning. She needs her sleep."

The colonel paced the room, pounding his fist into the palm of his hand. Finally, he spoke. "*Freedom is the sure possession of those alone who have the courage to defend it,* said at the funeral of the Greek statesman Pericles. Mike did that and lived it."

"I wish it had been me," I said glumly. "I should have been in that hospital bed and Mike should be alive." That was me echoing the cry that had arisen from nearly every battlefield in history. When the medals had been handed out and the speeches made, it was the battle comrades and families who had to carry the pain. *Why does the cost of freedom have to be so hellishly high?* I wondered.

Sebastian said, "Major, the good Lord had His own reason for letting you live, else you'd be dead, You is needed for somethin' and three someones needs you, and they is waitn' here in this building somewheres. You got you a good woman in Marie and two little girls that need a daddy in their lives."

Angus and I agreed to meet in the morning. Right now we all needed sleep. I went along to Marie's quarters. When she opened the door, she threw herself into my arms. Just as suddenly, she pushed herself away from me, looked up and with clarity of vision from sightless eyes said, "Someone was killed, weren't they?"

"No," I said, "but as good as."

Marie led me over to the couch and sat down. She pulled me down next to her and cradled my head in her lap. "I'm here for you, Drew. My eyes might not work, but my ears do. Tell me about it, darling."

I told her everything. The last thing I remember was her gentle voice singing as I fell asleep.

CHAPTER 13 - The Scent of Hope

I spent the night on Marie's couch. What joy it was to see her in the morning when I opened my eyes. Then I remembered about Mike and joy fled.

"Go and tell Hera," Marie encouraged, "but gently. Maybe there is something belonging to Mike that you could give her to keep, even a picture. Don't be surprised if she gets angry and says things that she may regret saying later. She might be a fighter, darling, but she is also a woman in love.

"Get a shower and get going. Colonel Carlisle is right that it's better coming from you. I'll be here when you get back. And Mi-Ling and Libby should be up by then. They will want to see you, too." Her soft voice and Polish accent seemed to be a healing combination.

"Remember, Drew, you have been where she is. You know what it's like. And Mike's not dead yet."

I met Angus, who looked unusually nervous – or was it sadness? Mike's critical condition had affected all of us.

We found a photo of Mike and Hera on his locker. His katana hung on the wall in a replacement scabbard. It was a piece of living history to us. *We few we happy few we band of brothers.* I got his beret. It was a long walk to Hera's room at the medical center.

Hera was asleep when we got there, either from exhaustion or medication. I didn't know which.

How do you waken someone to give them bad news? Neither Angus nor I knew. In the end she opened her eyes, scanned the room, and asked, "Where's Mike?" Then she read out faces. The gladiatorial courage could not stop tears.

"Are you here to give me bad news? To say he's dead?" At that moment I would have given anything to say the opposite; to reassure Hera that the one man she had adored and trusted was good, and well, and would be in to see her soon. I had Mike's picture to give her, but the trouble is you can't hug a memory.

"No, he is on a life support. He's in a coma. He wanted to do this for you, Hera. There was no way he was going to let you go or leave you."

Angus had read her thoughts. "If you harm yourself out of pain or grief, then his sacrifice will count for nothing. And there's a chance he may come round. You never can tell."

A strand of black hair fell over her face. "He risked his life that you might live. He said that several times about his friend."

"Friend?" I asked. "Mike had a lot of friends."

"This one was called Jesus," Hera replied. "Mike would talk about Him as if they had grown up together." The sun filtered through the blind in her room and glinted off her engagement ring. Then it suddenly dawned on me that the colonel had not given me any effects of Mike's to give to Hera - no ring or watch. I shot out of the room with a stupid seed of an idea. I couldn't stand the idea of this lovely girl breaking her heart into slivers that would never heal over her lost fiancé. I sprinted to the colonel's office and knocked at the door.

"Don't beat a hole in it," a familiar voice said, "come in, Major."

I literally ran into the room, issued a sloppy salute and asked, "Sir, does Lt. Argo have any personal effects like a ring or watch?"

The colonel nodded. "Yes, he's still wearing them. He's on life support machine, as you know. But his condition looks hopeless. The machine may be switched off soon. His family will be here to see him, mainly his sister Anna. Mike's effects will, of course, be given to Hera. I gather she has been told?"

"Yes, just now. But, colonel, please bear with me. Keep them from switching Mike's life support off. I must go and see my uncle. I want to talk my idea over with him and then I will get back to you."

The colonel nodded. "If this revelation works then, let me know. And Drew, son…with all my heart, I hope it will."

"Thank you, sir. With all my heart, I hope it will, too."

A sleepy uncle opened the door of his flat as I hammered on it. "Drew, if it's a tiger chasing you, don't let it in."

I pushed past.

"Uncle, I have an idea. It may be stupid, but tell me what you think."

He nodded. "Certainly, come take a seat. We are always in favor of ideas. How else did we discover that the earth was flat?"

I ignored his attempt at humor. "Uncle, you said that once a person had died in time travel they couldn't be bought back to life. That's why I lost Lucy. She had died."

He nodded sagely "Yes, old son, sorry. That's true. We can't get you back to Lucy now. It's too late."

"No, I'm not thinking about Lucy at the moment. Uncle, suppose the person was on a life support machine – I mean with a heart that's still beating and blood that's still circulating. Would it be possible to go back in time to where that person was alive and change things?"

Even this early in the morning he reached for his pipe and baccy. The blue fug began to circulate round the room, a bit like his mind circulating. "I'm assuming you mean Lt. Argo?"

"Yes. Hera is breaking her heart over him. The rest of us aren't much happier."

"What exactly is your idea, Drew, my boy?"

"This is surmise," I said. "Mike's on life support, incommunicado to the outside world, but still functioning at a low level – I mean, all his bits and pieces are still going. Suppose Hera went back in time to Rome and to 1940, to the moment before Mike was shot and stopped it from happening. Shot the guy who shot him before Mike was shot." I thought over what I had said to see if it sounded possible. "The killer was shot anyway. What would happen if the killer was shot five minutes before he shot Mike? Then it would be as if Mike had never been shot. Then they could both come back. Mike would not have been here, so therefore, his body on life support would vanish."

Adrian nodded and I could see his mind thinking it over.

"What I don't know is what would happen if Hera saw Hera?" I mused. "If they were in close proximity to one another ? Is there an optimum range where two people who are the same person can be in the same space in time?"

"If you could solve that, my boy, you would be wanted by every physics department in every university in Christendom and then a few."

"Remember, in my case, Lucy was dead. Mike is still alive, even if it's in the loosest sense of the word."

The bowl of the pipe by this time glowed red. "It could work, but it would be terrible risk. Hera could be injured in the journey. She's just getting over her own bullet wound. She's still weak. Then, let's suppose it didn't work; that either you or she were killed or…"

"Uncle, do you remember when I was going to China? We were here and you said to me, '*where is your sense of romance and adventure*'? Well, it's here. Why should Hera be left to hug a memory if she can go back and hug Mike and be a very, very happy girl again? The colonel won't buy it unless you back the idea. We would have to go back to Rome from now. If we relive everything else except Mike's getting shot, then nothing should change except Hera's memories. To her, going back the second time would be forgotten about, but she would have to get back here first. When she comes back, Mike should be waiting for her. To him, it will be just like they came back and Hera had been the wounded one. He or she would never know and the only proof the mission to save Mike ever took place would be on file here."

A smile began to play round Adrian's lips. "Your mother would be proud of you, son. But Hera would have to agree and know the risks. It would be dangerous."

I laughed. "To get back with Mike, that girl would go through anything, you watch."

Victoria's voice came from behind me. "You could call it Operation Lucy. At least there would be two people who would be reunited."

I went over and hugged Lucy's mom. "I'm so sorry about Lucy," I told her as I had before. "I loved her. I really loved her. And I miss her like crazy,- so does Mi-Ling."

She kissed me. "I know that, Drew. And for the short time you and Lucy had together, you made her the happiest woman in the world. Thank you for that. That's what I remember to help hold the hurt away, that and the fact that my baby is in Heaven with Jesus."

Victoria and I held each other for long, warm moments. I relaxed and felt love and admiration for this brave woman flow out of me and around her. She seemed to feel it, too. She drew me closer. "Please," I asked her, "Please join with me in prayer about the safety and success of this mission."

"Lord," I prayed, "Your friend Mike needs your help. He trusted you and kept talking about you. Lord, You can make this happen. Jesus, you showed me Lucy again. That was a miracle and I thank You and praise you for it. Lord, I guess what we're asking for is another miracle,-a different kind of miracle. What joy and rejoicing there will be when Mike and Hera are reunited. Lord, we can throw the switches of the time car, but only You can make it happen.

Please, Lord. Please help Your friend Mike who loves you."

I got the okay from the colonel and hurried to Hera's room. Thankfully, her gunshot wound had been superficial, although painful. She was still bandaged, but she had been unplugged from the machines and was scheduled for discharge. She had been given Mike's things. Tears ran from the gray eyes and she was sobbing inside.

"Hello, again," she said. "Where did you go? One minute of time you were there and the next minute – woooshes, gone."

I pulled up a chair and sat by her bed. "Hera, please listen and try to understand. Mike is on life support. His body is still working, but only because the machine helps it. I have spoken to Professor Conroy. Try to grasp this."

The tears had stopped and she looked at me intently.

"Hera, if we take you back to Rome in 1940, before Mike was shot and the other man is killed before Mike is shot, then it will be like you both got back safely."

Her eyes opened wide. "Mike would be alive again? Really alive without the machine?" Her long legs shot out of the bed and her feet hit the floor. She staggered a bit, but recovered quickly.

"Come on, Drew, why be you waiting all slow?"

"Hera, you may still be shot and come back here wounded and have to go through the surgery again. You have to get back here before you and Mike get back – then you will be the real you recovering from your wounds and Mike will be well."

"What be with a little pain? Mikey will be there to put it away – wooooosh." She spun round and round like a six-year-old. Her grey eyes sparkled like dark diamonds taking a direct hit from an errant sunbeam.

A nurse came in to help Hera dress. It took both the nurse and me to convince Hera not to tear her bandages off. I left the room with Hera's voice following me, singing a cheerful Greek song. Hope is wonderful, but not so wonderful as the love that crosses time.

I found Marie and told her about our plans. She smiled a most lovely smile and her eyes crinkled. "Her heart will be like a Chopin prelude," she said. "You are the cause of that."

"The Lord gave me the idea. That was His part; now we must go and do our part."

There was a silence. "Darling," Marie said, "I have a date for eye surgery."

"That's wonderful, when?" I exclaimed. I took her hand.

"A week today in Aberdeen. Dr Frazier's doing the surgery."

"Then we can get married, as soon as the bandages come off?" I asked.

"It depends. But we will think about it," she laughed.

"I want to marry you, Marie. I want you to be my wife. I don't care whether you can see or not. I want to be with you for the rest of our lives."

"My Major, darling, when we are married I want two things."She kissed and licked my ear. "You and a bed. And if I can't see, you will just have to carry me there."

By the time we finished our conversation, I could hear my heart pounding in my ears and my mouth had dried up. Marie laughed at me. "You better go and get Hera back with her beloved," she said. Then she put her hands on my face. "Why, major, your cheeks are on fire. I do believe *you* are blushing."

Well it was getting warm in the room – wasn't it?

* * *

Hera and I were at the time car and Adrian was calculating the setting. The colonel had joined us. "Right, you two. We've never done this before. We're going to get you to the basement of the flat next to Le Croix's flat at the same time as you were there before. You'll have fifteen minutes until you find yourselves coming out of the station towards the taxis. Watch for the second assassin. When he identifies himself by pulling his gun, shoot! Just make sure he doesn't hit Mike once he's down and that Angus fires as he did in the original scenario. You two get out of it as fast as you can go. You need to get back here before the rest of the group and before your memories of events change.

"The Abwher will be buzzing about Le Croix's flat. You two get out of it 'tout suite'. Use smoke grenades and remember – you only have to get back into the flat. You don't have to get out again. This is a risky op. We only think we know what will happen. There's been no dry run. If this works, it may save the lives of other Vanguard operatives as well as your own one day. Try and not be seen by your other selves, it could cause confusion."

"Sebastian said one time in a joke, sir, that he wanted to leave before he met himself coming back. At the time, I didn't realize the possibility that he might be right."

The colonel smiled. "Yes, he was right, but there is still an awful lot we don't know. Let's hope our knowledge increases at a faster rate than PATCH's."

We shot off in the time car to view a real '*déjà vu.*' My stomach churned. Hera and I held hands for mutual support. Once we got to the other end, it would look more convincing if we acted like a couple. We were doing this for Mike. We had to act convincingly. We had to focus on the mission, which was to get Mike back alive. That was what counted.

Once we got there, we had to look out for Reynolds, the Abwehr, and us. We knew the original team would come out of the station towards the taxi rank. We had to watch out for the assassin. We had a job remembering what he looked like. The last time we had seen him he had been put out of action by Angus. I had not remembered as many people from the last trip, but this was Rome. Who noticed another pair of lovers disappearing into a doorway? We got a clear view of where we had left the station that night, the Il Termini exit nearest the taxi rank, and waited. It seemed like hours. We undid our coats and wrapped our arms round each other, for there were two *carabinieri* working their way up looking into the nooks and crannies. Hera said, "Kiss me like you mean it."

I began to groan and return the kiss, trying not to feel guilty about Marie. I was focusing on the mission, but kissing Hera even in pretense was distracting. It was only when the two *carabinieri* were level with us that it dawned on me that neither of us could speak Italian.

The *carabinieri's* head came round the corner, "S'*cusi,*" he said, with a smile playing across his broad lips. Then their attention was distracted by something else and they headed back for the station. We fell into each other's arms with relief. "Ouch," Hera said as the closeness pulled on her bandaged wound. Then I saw myself and Mike with the wounded Hera, followed by Anton and Sebastian.

Hera must have allowed the 21st Century to influence her. "My hair is a mess," she complained.

My eyes were trained on the approaching crowd. Where was the other assassin? There were too many people milling about. I had to get closer. I said to Hera, "You stay here, out of sight. I'm going to get closer." Then, before I ran into myself, I saw the assassin. He pulled out a Mauser pistol and was about to fire. I fired first and he went down. Mike continued carrying Hera to what turned out to be safety. I headed back up at a run to where I hoped Hera was. We had to get out fast and get back to the time car. Hera stood at the place where I had left her, but seemed unusually agitated. Then I saw a figure come out from behind her and point a gun to her head.

"You Vanguard operatives have interfered in my plans too often. Now you are going to die because you are weak and pitiful." I stopped. He had me cold.

"Drop your pistol and kick it away from you – NOW," Reynolds ordered. I had no choice but to obey. The pistol in his hand was still pointed to Hera's head.

Reynolds muttered to himself in delight, "Do I kill you myself? Or turn you over to Van Haase, whose acquaintance you made before that gorilla McTurk interfered." He nodded to himself. "I will kill you myself and save the paper work."

People with brains can be stupid. Reynolds made the mistake of underestimating a woman. He turned the gun away from Hera's head to point it at me. It was mere seconds, but for an ex-gladiator like Hera whose life expectancy was often measured in fractions of a second – it was enough. Her high heel came down on Reynold's shin and the pistol dropped from his hand. I dove for my Glock. Before I could use it, the place was covered in smoke. Reynolds had set off a smoke bomb and disappeared.

We had to get Hera back to the time car. Dear God, it was a long way! After what seemed hours, we got back to the basement of the flat. Heaven alone knew what a mess we were in. I went inside and bolted the door on the inside. As we headed to the basement, there was hammering on the door followed by gunfire on the door. The time car came. I put Hera inside and hit the forward button and we were away.

After about five minutes, neither of us could remember what we were doing. Then it didn't matter. When the time car opened at HQ, Mike was waiting for Hera. She fell into his arms. "I tried to visit you at the hospital," he said, "but was told you were too sick even for a fiancé. Thank God! You look fine! Wonderful…but what were you and the major doing?"

She shook her head groggily. "I don't know. I can't remember, Mikey."

I ushered Mike and Hera back to the colonel's office to explain what had happened to him. Anton, Angus and Sebastian were already there, eagerly waiting to see if the mission had been successful. When Mike heard the story, the color drained from his face. "You mean I was brain dead? You two went back to change the events? You could have both been killed – and you did this for me?" There was a silence in the colonel's office.

"Well, what is wrong with playing cupid?" the colonel asked. "Just so everyone knew of the danger and agreed to it. Otherwise, Hera would have had a face like a wet weekend and the rest of us would have been none too happy, either."

The crisp, sparkling joy on Hera's face made the risk seem more than worthwhile. We shared hugs, slaps on the back, and congratulations all around. Mike was a popular guy. Then we started filing out of the colonel's office for some well-deserved rest.

"Major, a minute if you please," Carlisle said after the others left. "You kept that recorder on you running. We picked up Reynolds' voice. He could just have killed Hera, but for some reason he wanted you. He may know something you will do or some action you will take in the future that spoil his plans. Adrian believes that Reynolds traveled back to the past to try and stop something happening that will happen in the future. Something that will make a difference to his plans and something he wants to stop."

"The only thing that I know of in my future is getting married to Marie. Angus and Abigail are getting married, and so are Mike and Hera. Oh! And Marie's getting her eye surgery."

* * *

My next stop was Mi-Ling. She and Libby Bryant had become good friends. Thankfully, Libby seemed totally the opposite of her father, Caleb Bryant.

Mi-Ling was her usual bouncy self and threw herself joyfully into my arms. "Mi-Ling has missed you, Papa," she told me, planting a kiss on my cheek.

Libby was coming out of her shell. She stood and waited for a hug, then following Mi-Ling's example, gave me a quick kiss on the cheek.

"Papa," Mi-Ling said after both girls had welcomed me, "Do you think it will make a difference to Marie when she can see that I am Chinese? I look different from you. Will she still want to be my Amma?"

The fact that Mi-Ling used the same name for Marie as she had used for Lucy touched me. A current of thrill ran through me. If I had ever had doubts about getting married to Marie before, they evaporated in the warmth of my daughter's question. I smiled and hugged Mi-Ling so tightly that she laughed and wiggled free.

"You, my daughter," I told her in mock severity that made Libby giggle, "are a beautiful young lady inside and out. When Marie can see you, she will love you even more. The Mi-Ling she loves she has already seen from the heart. You have been helping her when she was blind. You can keep helping each other once she can see. She will teach you to play the piano and one day you will play duets together. One other thing you can do for her is to teach her how to laugh and smile. But the greatest thing you can do for her if you find it in your heart is simply to love her."

Mi-Ling nodded and her trademark big smile flooded over her face. "Yes, Papa. I can do that. She can be my new Amma."

Libby sat on her bed hugging a doll, the black forest of curls bobbing up and down. Sudden tears rushed down her cheeks. *Your family is not yet complete,* Jesus had said to me. Virtually, all Libby had were the clothes she wore and her doll. She was totally alone in the world with no family to call her own – and the closeness between Mi-Ling and I must have brought that home to her.

I knew what I had to do. This was the child of my enemy, the man who had stalked, then killed, my wife of ten minutes. This was the child of a man who had kidnapped Mi-Ling and run a sword through Meryl. Could I adopt her after her father had murdered the woman I loved in cold blood and released every terror, evil and sorrow into my life? How could I forget the horrible beyond description fiend from hell? What if Libby turned out like her father? No, for the sake of Mi-Ling and Marie, as well as myself, I couldn't take the risk. I had to be strong. I had to find another home for her, other people to love her.

Then I heard the Lord's voice, *"Now abide these three, faith, hope, and love – but the greatest of these is love."*

Mi-Ling saw me looking at Libby and read my face. "Libby friend," she said, slipping an arm around the shoulders of the quietly sobbing girl. "My papa has big heart. It make room for Mi-Ling, but Mi-Ling does not take up all the room. My Papa has a big heart with room for Libby friend in it."

God had made room for me in His heart – and at what a cost? His very own beloved Son, Jesus, had died in my place so I could be forgiven of my sins – which were many and varied, I'm ashamed to admit.

Libby sat on the bed with her head down on her doll's head, hiding from the rejection she so clearly expected. I dropped to my knees in front of her. "Libby…I…Libby, can I be your…Will you let me adopt you and be my daughter?"

Dear God, if I live to be 150, I swear I will never see a face like hers again after I said these words. From tears to bright radiance in the space of a heartbeat. She jumped off the bed, threw her arms around me and buried her face in my shoulder. I heard God's voice in my heart, *She who was once the child of your enemy is now your child –son, I am proud of you.*

Over Libby's shoulder, I saw Mi-Ling. Tears of joy sparkled in her sable eyes.

Suddenly Libby pulled away from me. The face that had been radiant and joyful a moment before cast a seriousness way beyond her years. "Please, major. You must be careful! I have another brother. His name is Joshua. I don't know where he is. He hardly ever came to see us on the ship. He's so mean and angry that Pa threw him out."

That was just what I needed to hear. Bryant's death had left behind another psychotic family member who might have a grudge and I didn't even know what he looked like.

When Libby let me go, Mi-Ling patted a space on the bed beside her and said, "Libby sister." The girls hugged one another, breaking into giggles and laughter. I wondered if they could hear the voice that spoke into my heart again, *'and the greatest of these is love.'*

CHAPTER 14 - Libby's Courage

I found Marie to tell her the news that if she married me there would be another daughter to bring up. "Are you sure, darling?" she asked. "You know so little about her."

"What about the little Polish girl who got taught to play the piano by Chopin and hasn't looked back since all because someone helped her? Just because Libby had a creep for a father, why should she be condemned or punished? She didn't have a choice. It's not like she asked to be born as Bryant's daughter."

Marie laughed like the sound of music you catch on the breeze. "Part of the reason I want to marry you, Drew, is that you are teaching me what it is to have a heart. Libby needs a heart right now. She needs love and to experience the feeling of being accepted for who she is. If we get to have a home together, it's going to be a very interesting house."

She could not see the alarm on my face from her use of the word *if*. "If we have a home together? I'd rather you had said *when* we have a home together. Marie, I want to marry you and love you for the rest of our lives. We can be good parents – even should the Lord give us a child of our own."

She looked so pensive that I tried to make her smile. With as much hubris as I could muster and put into my voice, I told her, "When your eyes are fixed you'll see how dashingly handsome I am! You'll be swept away. I'll take you to my castle in the mountains and we will make mad passionate love."

It worked. She smiled and the musical laugh returned. "Watch out, Major! I will hold you to your promises! When we go on honeymoon you won't need to keep your journal up to date. You won't have time for one thing, and for another, you won't want to write about it for public viewing. Perhaps you should give your journal to Mi-Ling after the wedding and let her keep it for you until we get back."

"Eyes first, all the better for you to see me with once you get your operation," I joked. Perhaps it was in both our minds that the operation might not work. Then we would just have to settle for the status quo. As I had tried to explain to Mi-Ling, you love someone for what's inside and not what's outside because the outside changes. Where we would live and when we could sort out later with the girls having an input. I started to laugh and Marie squeezed my hand

"Come on; don't keep the secret to yourself!"

"I'm laughing at God's sense of humor. I speak English with a Scottish accent and you speak English with a French-Polish accent and Mi-Ling speaks with a Chinese accent. Libby is definitely American. I have a family that is a walking United Nations."

Marie chuckled. "Can the girls move in here with me? We can at least get to know more about each other, as I am going to have to adapt to instant motherhood."

I readily agreed. My heart was overwhelmed with gratitude for the gift of this lovely woman that God was giving me to be my wife, and the daughter of our children. Life just didn't get any better than this.

"Will you go to the infirmary with me," Marie asked anxiously. "I get sick with chloroform."

I smiled at her, which she could not see. "Yes, darling! I will most certainly come with you. But don't worry. It will just be an injection in the back of your hand. When you wake up, it will all be over."

At that point, I heard a click on Marie's window. I eased silently across the room to the window and was shocked to discover someone standing by the window with a listening device. He saw me and ran. I pressed the intruder alert button and gave a quick description before I headed out after him. The two guards stood in front of the door after I left and Marie said she would stay inside. I ran as fast as I could and saw the tail end of the intruder running through the car park.

Sometimes you think you have cracked some problem, then suddenly you realize you were wrong. Even from the distance, I could see that the hands of the guy who was running were empty. That meant he had dropped his device. Yet, as I had followed him, I had seen him discard nothing. Then it dawned on me, *Oh, my Lord! It's a bomb, triggered by motion! Please, Lord God — help!*

I skidded to a stop, spun around, and ran the other way. I looked quickly over my shoulder. The guy I had been chasing had also stopped. I tore back toward Marie's room, wishing I had spent more time in the gym. I got there just in time to see Libby go in ahead of me. The guards must have let her in.

I slowly opened the door and said, "Libby, stand still. Marie, stand still." Libby was at the open window, looking out. She froze when she saw the box. She was visibly shaking.

I spoke into my communicator, "Bomb disposal, Room Seven, come quietly. I think this device is triggered by movement."

A soft voice at the other end said, "Roger, understood."

"Drew...what's happening?" Marie asked.

"Darling, there is what I think is a bomb outside the window. It may explode if we move."

Libby said, "I remember this. The blue top tells how long it will be before it goes boom."

"Libby," I said, attempting to keep my voice calm, "can you remember how long before it goes boom?" She was mere feet away from it. I thought there might be a chance that I could grab it and get it safely away before it exploded.

The bomb guys arrived outside and the door opened a crack. "Leave this to us, sir," they instructed.

"Don't come in," I said. "Any movement could trigger it." I looked over at Libby.

Her face was screwed up in an attempt to remember. "I think it's seven minutes," she said.

Colonel Carlisle's voice came through the door, "Status report, Major?"

Outside, a distance away from the window was the guy I'd been chasing. Why had he come back?

"Sir, Libby thinks there may be a delay of seven minutes."

"You can tell when it's going to go boom," Libby said in a dull, flat voice. "Lights start to flash."

It was like being frozen in time, and the man who had planted the bomb was outside drawing closer. None of us dared move from our positions to go after him.

"Drew, darling," Marie said breathlessly, "do something!" It tumbled in and out of my mind quickly that as a non-sighted person in the middle of things she didn't understand, Marie was at the greatest disadvantage.

The window was half-open on the ground floor level. I suddenly realized with shock that Libby was inching imperceptibly towards the bomb. Why would she do that? Then my blood ran cold. *Dear Lord, she's going to grab the bomb and run to save the rest of us!*

"No, Libby! Don't do it! Just stay still!"

"Major Drew, I'm sorry for the bad my father did to you. If I die, it will make amends. I hope you and Miss Marie will be very happy together. Tell my sister Mi-Ling that I love her very much."

To say she moved fast was an understatement. She grabbed the bomb and was through the window and out onto the grass. Within seconds, the bomb activated. I saw the lights flashing. "Libby," I screamed, running for the window. "Throw it away from you! Please, Libby, get rid of it!"

I scrambled out of the window and leaped after her. She heard me thundering up behind her and threw the bomb as far as she could. I tackled her and fell on top of her, covering her ears with my hands. There was an-ear splitting explosion. We were momentarily deafened by the roar, but seemed to be otherwise okay. What Libby had not seen when she hurtled the bomb was the guy who had planted it. He was not as fortunate as we were.

Libby was crying and I took her in my arms. "Libby, you are brave and wonderful. You risked your life to save us. You are the bravest person I have ever met, sweetheart. Your life is precious and very important. We love you."

The others came running out except for Marie. Colonel Carlisle said, "Nicely done, Libby Bryant. Or perhaps I should say 'nicely done, Libby Faulkner.' We are in your debt, young lady."

There is never a dull day in time travel. Danger gets close sometimes; bombs, bullets, snakes, hostile forces, sharks, nearly getting blown up or scalped. I wondered what exactly the pension prospects in this job were.

The Royal Infirmary, also known as Foresterhill, is in Aberdeen. It's a big hospital, covering a catchment area of some 600,000 people. Marie was to get her surgery there and Dr. Frazier explained to her that she would not be able to see straight away and the bandages would need to remain over her eyes for four days. He warned her against bending and lifting heavy objects. He added a warning about not straining when passing bowel movements.

After four days we could take the bandages off and hope that everything had worked. Marie asked him if he was wearing frocked coat for the surgery. She seemed puzzled that he wasn't and asked permission to feel the fabric of his surgery gown, declaring it to undoubtedly be more comfortable than a frocked coat.

Dr. Frazier left Marie with Sister Szfraneck, a cheery, ample, and smiling lady who spoke to Marie in Polish. I decided that this would be a good point to go for coffee while they ran a couple more tests that Dr. Frazier had ordered. It also gave me a chance to think of some nice romantic spot where Marie could be reintroduced to the joys of sight and see her fiancée for the first time. She said that she had wanted to open her eyes to something beautiful. "What?" I had demanded jokingly, "apart from me?" Well, she was my fiancée after all.

In the days prior to the operation, there were two guards outside her room. Only certain people got to go in or out, which included Libby and Mi-Ling, of course, who had moved in with her since Martha had left to visit a sick relative. Martha had planned to return before Marie's surgery, but hadn't been able to leave.

Sometimes with input from Mi-Ling and Libby, and sometimes without it, Marie and I had dreamed, and planned, and talked where we would live and when. She supported my decision to continue my career in Vanguard. She wanted to become a concert pianist. In modern times, she would be up against stiff competition when it came to booking engagements.

"What about Rome for a honeymoon, or maybe we could do a Chopin tour, or go and see Beethoven." I tried to rattle off as many places as I could think of.

"Seeing you, she had said, "is the thing I look forward to most. Just to see if you are as good to look at as you taste."

"You make me feel like an ice cream."

"Ice cream, what is ice cream?" she replied.

"Like seeing me – an experience yet to come and it tastes delicious."

"Mmmm like you?" she had queried.

Now finally, the day of her operation had arrived. After the early morning tests ordered by Dr. Frazier, it was time for Marie to be wheeled into the theatre for the operation. We prayed together and commended each other into the Lord's hands. Before we got to the theatre door I told Marie, "Darling, I love you. Trust the Lord. He will go right into the theatre with you."

A half-sleepy voice responded with assurance of forever love, then the theatre doors closed behind her. All I could do was wait.

They said they would call me once the surgery was over and I had to leave it to them. One of our security guards from Vanguard, in appropriate hospital greens, was allowed into the theatre. He had been in Afghanistan with the medical section and could be trusted not to get in the road He had been sworn to preserve life. In his book, that included stopping the bad guys from taking it.

CHAPTER 15 - Joshua Bryant

My way of coping with the wait was to go back to HQ and to the gym and brush up on my fencing and shooting. I got Mike Argo to give me a few pointers on Kendo, but it became obvious it took years of study to become anywhere near proficient. I guess that I was glad that none of our travelling jaunts had landed us in the Mikado's Japan. I didn't really fancy my chances of survival against a fully fledged Ninja or Summari knight.

I had just showered and dressed when I got word that Marie was out of the theatre. I related the news to Mi-Ling and Libby, promising them they could visit at the hospital after Marie had recovered. Then I headed to Foresterhill.

Marie lay quietly as I crept into the recovery room. Her black hair had been tied back and she still wore a theatre cap to help restrain it. The guard nodded recognition and said, "It was ruddy hot in there, sir, but everything seemed to be okay. I think I will spare you the details of what took place." He smiled (something security people don't that often, thinking it's bad for the overall image).

Marie stirred. "Drew, darling, is that you?" I took her hand.

"You look as if you have been playing blind man's bluff," I said.

She smiled. "We used to play it at Balmoral. They liked me to play because there was no need to blindfold me. '*Oh, Miss Waleska,*' they would say, '*if only you could see!*' Then there would be a silence, so filled with sadness that it made me feel sorry for them, even the Queen." Marie's hand reached up to touch the bandages that covered her eyes and she continued, "Just a few more days, darling, a few more days. I never dreamed I would be able to see again. Drew, promise me I will be able to see."

I took a deep breath. Dr. Frazier had said things had gone well. I had no reason to believe that Marie would not be able to see. "I promise you will be able to see again," I said, smiling.

The next day Mi-Ling and Libby went with me to visit Marie. Libby declared, "I'm going to be a doctor when I finish my education." Whether it was a real desire or whether it was the presence and preponderance of young male doctors, I wasn't sure. Libby, at fourteen, was not immune to the charms of young male medical men.

Ages and birthdays went unrecognized and celebrated at the Chinese brothel where I had rescued Mi-Ling, so we weren't sure of Mi-Ling's age. We had thought her to be twelve at the time of the rescue, and she had since celebrated a birthday on the date she chose as her birthday. Incredible sadness stole over me. My daughter had only been with me for such a short time. Too soon, she would be a grown woman out on her own. That was depressing. I would miss her so much, but that was fatherhood; we only have our children on loan.

But for now, I was the most blessed of men. I had both Marie and Mi-Ling and Libby. The girls seemed to adore Marie. They asked her if she felt as if she would be able to see when the bandages came off.

At her advanced age, Mi-Ling seemed to think she was capable of offering medical advice. She explained to Marie, "You have to want to see, then it will happen. You will see what Papa looks like."

Mi-Ling looked at me, her huge smile spreading and lights bouncing around in her eyes as she declared to Marie, "Papa has long white beard and wrinklies all over face and nearly all of his teeth, mostly ..."

"Mi-Ling! You will scare Marie! Marie, don't listen to her."

Marie laughed. "Darling, you only joke with people you love. Don't worry. I won't mind a few wrinklies and white hair probably suits you. Is not white the color of snow, as I've been told?"

As the days grew closer to the bandages coming off, Marie got more and more excited. Her mind was filled with all sorts of things. She had been living in the dark. Now she would see sunlight and beauty and the whole of creation. I tried to put myself in her place and found it was impossible to imagine – rather like believing someone dead and then finding them alive again.

The day before the big event was due; Colonel Carlisle called me to his office.

"Come in, major, sit down. That's good news about your fiancée, but I want you to take someone else with you when you take Miss Waleska to have her bandages removed – a body guard, so to speak. Just in case. We don't want a possible repeat of what happened before. They can stay out of sight. I'm sure what is said should be between you two, but if any PATCH heavies turn up, you might need help. Once it's established that Marie's sight has come back again, and then she can act as an extra pair of eyes, so to speak. Because of her attachment to you, we want to give her basic training. Until Reynolds is caught and PATCH dismantled, you're going to be a target." He paused, ran fingers through his hair and drummed his fingers on his desk.

As for me, it was time to collect my beloved and head out to Morar beach which I had chosen to take the bandages off. Marie had recovered quickly from the surgery and Dr. Frazier had just called me a few minutes ago to inform me that I could come pick her up at my convenience. I was excited, but apprehensive. I told Hera about the change in plans and asked her to meet me outside when she and Jayne had finished talking.

Hera must have been nearly as excited as I was, because she ran gleefully out to meet me just a short while later. We drove toward the hospital to collect Marie. Hera said, "I feel like a strawberry coming between you and the woman in your life."

I smiled. "The expression is gooseberry I think, but you are here on the colonel's orders. I will tell Marie why you are here. Don't worry." There was acar waitng for Hera in the hospital carpark

Marie was waiting in her room. She wore a denim skirt and jacket, with a small bandana around her neck. Someone had given her perfume. The overall effect was like walking into a room where summer had just taken up residence.

"Drew," she said holding out her hand when she heard my footsteps. "They have dressed me. But I don't know what I look like."

"You look wonderful, darling. Wow!"

"Is 'wow' good?"

I laughed. "Yes, darling! Wow is good. It's what people say when you play Chopin. Now, my walking *wow*, we are going to Morar beach so you can see the sea when the bandages come off."

"Drew, there were footsteps behind you, but they were too heavy for Mi-Ling or Libby. Has someone else come with you?"

"Yes. Hera has been sent with me to act as a bodyguard. Colonel Carlisle's orders. But like you, Hera is a woman in love and she understands things. She won't keep close enough to ruin our big moment together."

Marie sighed, "On our honeymoon, my darling, can I get you all to myself, just you?"

"Done," I said. "Promise, just us." We said goodbye to the nurses and hospital staff. One of them asked, "Where are you going for the great unveiling?"

She looked friendly and interested, but I didn't think I had ever seen her before. Caught on the hop, I stupidly told her, "Morar Beach."

"Oh," she said "it can be breezy there." The others wished Marie goodbye and she got a package of eye drops and a course of antibiotics to be taken to ward off infection. As we turned to go, I noticed the unknown nurse on the phone.

Dr. Frazier ordered, "Take it easy for the first week. No knocks. Avoid falling or any kind of strenuous activity."

We went out to the car. Hera followed us in her car and I marveled at her intelligence and adaptability. It was incredible that she had advanced so far into the modern world when she had only just touched down in it.

We arrived at the beach after what seemed a long drive. As I pulled up and parked, I noticed that Hera's car was nowhere in sight. It didn't worry me. She hadn't been driving long and drove more slowly than I did. Besides; she had the coordinates to where we were going.

My heart beat nosily inside my ears. "*Soon,*" I kept telling myself. "*Soon I will look into Marie's lovely eyes and she will look back at me.*" It was a heady feeling.

We walked down to the beach. "I can feel the wind in my face," Marie said dreamily. "Soon, I get to see your lovely face, my darling!"

God, I prayed, *please let Marie see.* I gently unwound the bandages and they slipped off her lovely face and fell into the sand. She blinked. Her hands went to her eyes. "Drew," she whispered in a stricken voice, "I can't see! I can't see, Drew! I can't see."

"Don't panic," I said, trying unsuccessfully to hold back my tears. "Remember what Dr. Frazier said. It may take a little time until things get adjusted. Just wait, darling."

There was panic in Marie's voice and fierce dismay. "I can't see! It didn't work! I'm going to be blind forever! Oh! How cruel and unfair of everyone to lie to me! Why did you give me false hope?"

Marie broke away from me and ran. How she ran blindly without falling, I'll never know. I fell just running after her.

Suddenly, a figure rose up from behind a dune. He grabbed Marie and pointed a pistol at me. He smirked. "We haven't been introduced yet. I've wanted to meet my brother's murderer for a long time. Now you've added to that by killing my father and seducing my sister!"

He looked at Marie. "This must be your Polish tart – or so-called fiancée who can't see. Blind, and you were going to marry this?" He laughed, a horrible empty laugh without mirth – a laugh from the pit of hell. "We'll that's an insane idea whose time has passed." He mocked. "Surgery didn't work. What a shame."

He saw the question I wanted to ask and smirked at me again. "My girlfriend planted herself there as a nurse to keep tabs on you and report back to me so I can give you both what you deserve."

Still holding the gun on me with one hand, he spun Marie around and slammed his fist into her face with quick, short punches. When I started to jump forward to stop him, he pulled the trigger back. The gun clicked. "Better think before you do that, walking dead man."

To my horror, he pulled another pistol out of the waistband of his jeans and began to pistol whip Marie, not knocking her unconscious, but knocking her to the ground. "Just to make sure I undo any good the doctors did," he said savagely through clenched teeth. Marie took the abuse silently, tears running down her bruised face. It broke me.

"Kill me!" I yelled, "but leave her alone! Your fight is with me, not her! Stop, for God's sake, stop! I beg you."

"Keep begging," he leered. "I like the sound of begging! You beg just like my father did when you threw him over the rocks at the castle. He asked you for mercy but you gave him none."

"That's a lie! I tried to save your father! I went over the wall on a rope to help him and he…"

"Tell it to someone who cares," he snapped.

Marie held her hands over her eyes. Blood seeped around her fingers and I was terrified. What kind of damage had this insane madman inflicted on her?

"Blind forever," he mocked. "You'll never get to see what your *beloved* looks like. But don't worry tart. He won't live long enough for you to waste time thinking about." He kicked her savagely, then turned the gun and his full attention on me. "After I've killed you, then I will take your *fiancée* and give her a night she won't forget with a real man, a real man that can go time and again until she's begging him to stop."

"Drew," Marie said through swollen lips, "make him stop saying such horrible things. It hurts my heart."

He laughed and bent over her prone figure, still holding the gun on me and watching me intently as filth dropped out of his mouth and poured over Marie. She screamed so loudly that it startled even me. I realized that her screaming wasn't from terror – it was to guard her heart from hearing his filthy language, but it angered him and he started kicking her again.

I was helpless. He had two guns and control over Marie. I was unarmed. If I lunged for him, he would kill us both. Sometimes, a minute is an eternity. I tried to reason with him. "Please listen to me. Your father slipped. I tried to help him. You can ask…"

"I don't have to ask nobody. Professor Reynolds was there. He saw everything, you lying peace of scum! He saw your hate. Now how do you like hate, Major? Think of it when you're dead and I'm with your woman again and again until I ruin her. Then she'll go to a brothel, sex with a blind girl. Some men would pay extra for that."

My only chance was to rush him. I had to be quick or he would kill Marie. Of course, once he had killed me, Marie would probably be better off dead. I began a quiet count in my head, *one, two, three…*

Like a mythological creature, Hera rose from the dune behind him and grabbed the hair on the top of his head. Jerking his head back, she drew her knife blade across his throat, quickly and clinically.

The look on Joshua Bryant's face transformed from hate to sheer horror as he began to choke on his own blood. Hera wiped her blade on the inside of his shirt just before he collapsed into the sand.

Joshua writhed in the sand, coughing and choking as blood colored the pale sand around his head.

"Not so big now are you, big boy?" She kicked him. The Greek that followed was both sharp and angry and it didn't take much in the way of brains to guess that Hera was expressing feelings of Greek displeasure.

I sprinted over to Marie and lifted her up out of the sand. She sobbed against my shoulder. "Drew, my eyes! What has he done to my eyes?"

I turned my darling's swollen face toward me and cradled her against me, crying with guilt and frustration; guilt because I had let my guard down for a moment and this had happed to her; and frustration because I hadn't been able to stop the physical and verbal abuse against the woman I loved.

"It's okay, Marie, he's gone. He will never bother us again. I love you. I don't care that you can't see. The wedding is still on and we can..."

Her hand reached slowly up to my face and she touched my lips. "Drew," she whispered, "I think I can see you. Is this you?"

I was too stunned to speak.

Marie kept staring at me as if she were drinking in my features. A tone of wonderment crept into her soft voice, "I can see you! You're beautiful, Drew! I knew you would be beautiful! Oh! I'm the most blessed woman in the world..." her voice broke off and she repeated, "you are so beautiful! Why would someone as beautiful as you want to marry me?"

She took a few tentative steps away from me, looking down at her feet in amazement. "They belong to me," she breathed. She held her hands and arms up to her swollen eyes and examined them. "What color am I wearing?" she asked, looking around. "Drew! My colors! The colors of my clothes! God used the color of my clothes to paint the sky and the water. Is that what blue looks like?

She spun around, dancing along the beach as gracefully as her fingers danced across piano keys. "And this is grass! So this must be green! And this is sand. What color do you call that, Drew? Tell me! I need to know everything! I've waited so long!"

A song went through my mind, a lovely song written by Charlie Landborough about a blind girl, *What color is the wind, Daddy....I know each color shape and size, I see them all through my Daddy's eyes.*

As sore and wobbly as she was finally Marie could see the world for herself. She wouldn't need Mi-Ling to be her eyes. God had kept His promise. He always does.

Hera came over and pointed to the slowly dying man on the beach. "What do you want me to do with this?"

"Will he die?" I asked.

"Soon," Hera replied nonchalantly.

"We have to get him off this beach," I said. "Search his pockets. He must have a time car control that will take him back to where he came from. Perhaps they can save him if he gets there in time."

Marie hugged Hera, "Thank you, my friend. I will never forget what you did for me." Then she shot a mock scowl at me and told Hera. "You are very beautiful, I think. I haven't seen much yet of beautiful yet, but it doesn't hurt my eyes to look at you. Yet, Drew, he has not told me that he works with such a beautiful woman."

Hera laughed and displayed her engagement ring to Marie. "This is why. The engagement ring that keeps Mikey and me so much close. Excuse me while I look for a time control. I would leave this…" she lapsed into Greek, then back into English, "to bleed into the sand to death, only your Drew is too kind and wants to send him off for a chance to hurt us again. I must be getting old." She sighed, shook her head and rolled her eyes. Marie laughed.

Hera found the time car control. The car arrived. We were partly sheltered by a dune and it was a miracle that the beach was still empty. We opened the door, bundled Joshua inside, and pressed the button. The car vanished through the time portal. Did Joshua Bryant die? The answer is, I don't know and care even less. While God turned his battery of Marie into a positive outcome, I didn't think I could ever find it in my heart to forgive him for his physical and verbal abuse of her. Remembering it would sour my stomach for a long time.

With the danger from Joshua Bryant gone, Hera left us alone on the beach and returned to her car. "I drive reeel slow," she explained. "That's why I was late to get here, but not too late."

"Thank the Lord not too late!" I exclaimed.

Marie's eyes swept across every new sight on the horizon and each one delighted her more than the one before it. I found myself laughing joyously at her enthusiasm. "Mi-Ling was wrong," she said suddenly. "You don't have wrinklies." When she giggled through her swollen lips, music by Chopin could have sounded more lovely.

I don't know who moved first, but suddenly she was in my arms and later I was embarrassed to remember those passionate kisses on the beach. Surely not comfortable with a bruised, swollen face – and yet – the fire raging inside her had matched the desperation of the blaze inside me and our shared passion ignited a flame that we were just barely able to control. Whew! It was a good thing we were getting married soon!

We headed back to Foresterhill Hospital and the accident room. Dr Frazier was shocked and dismayed by Marie's injuries and we had to invent a story to cover up what really happened. He examined Marie's eyes delightedly. Her eyes followed the thin beam of light he played across her face and he finally satisfied himself that her sight had indeed returned.

"Yet with all this roughness and hurt…Someone up there must have been taking good care of you."

I smiled at him. "Yes, Doc, He is indeed!"

Because of the extent of her injuries, Marie was kept in overnight for observation. She was still fine the next day, so Dr. Frazier released her.

When we got back to HQ, Marie went in search of Mi-Ling and Libby to share her sweet surprise with them. I went to look for Hera. She was with Mike.

"Thank you, Hera. I'll never be able to repay you."

Her grey eyes regarded me. "You would have done the same for me. I am now glad that the colonel say that I accompany you. If you get tired of these time travel," she said thoughtfully, "you could go be gladiator – but you have to like crowds."

I laughed. "Thanks for your vote of confidence, Hera. But I rather think my place is with Marie and the girls."

Mike said, "I am very, happy for you sir."

"Your fiancée is some girl, I told him. "Take good care of her."

This time it was Mike who laughed. "Hmm…I don't know about that. It's a sort of mutual defense pact between us."

Over the next few weeks, Marie's bruises healed. Her sight held. She grew more beautiful by the minute. Then one day as I was going down the corridor at HQ I heard Lucy's voice in my heart or head — actually, I never figured out where it came from. "Drew, I'm so, so, so happy for you and Marie." The corridor filled with intoxicating perfume. What was it called, I wondered? *The Scent of Home? The Scent of Eternity?*

If I followed that lovely scent, would it lead me *home* one day?

CHAPTER 16 - The Road to Happiness

I went back to Marie's room and knocked. When I entered, I was glad to see Martha had finally made it back from her visit. "Don't look so surprised, young man," she told me briskly. "You didn't expect me to stay away and miss the wedding did you?"

I hugged her. "We're so glad you're back

I laughed. "We missed you as a friend, Martha."

"Well, Major, get used to missing me because when you two are safely married I'm getting my tea plantation." Then she turned back to Marie. "What's it like to be able to see, my dear?" Without waiting for Marie to answer, she said to me, "You know, she has tried on every possible color combination and looks good in them all."

"Do you think red suits me? Or is green better? What about blue?" Marie rattled off.

"What about our wedding, Mrs. Soon-to-be Faulkner?" I countered.

"We will have a family conference, of course," Marie said, spinning around the room with joyful abandon. "Now that Martha is back and the girls can help. What fun!"

She held up a multi-colored Kaftan dress in front of her and twirled around the room like a ballerina. "Weeeeee!"

"Then," she said, "you better go and prepare. After we get married, I can get you all to myself and love you till my bones creak."

Everything within my body seemed to leap in eager expectation of that

Marie smelled of hibiscus, herbs and hope - *The Scent of Home,* because my home would be with her.

Mi-Ling's anxious face peeked in through the door. "Papa?" she sighed,there were no further words. My relieved, joyful daughter was in my arms. As I kissed the top of her head, I realized how much I owed to her. I also knew that I loved Mi-Ling the way Jesus loved me. There was a shy movement at the door. I looked over the top of Mi-Ling's head. Libby stood quietly, hanging onto the edge of the door. I smiled at her and opened up my arms. With a squeal of joy, she joined Mi-Ling and Marie. Our family was complete.

The next day Marie asked, "How would you feel about a double wedding with Hera and Mike?"

"Great idea! We could do with a good celebration." As I thought about it, I wished Sir Charles Gray could be at the wedding. He was with the Lord, but even after all this time I missed him. He had made me believe in myself and set me on the road to the Lord Jesus.

There was much to do, much to see to and much to prepare for prior to the wedding. One thing that I wanted for our wedding was Reverend Thornton, the minister who had married Lucy and me and who had helped me through the tragic aftermath. Marie agreed. We laughed together about how to explain time travel to him. Actually, it turned out easier than I could have imagined. He remembered the way Bryant had appeared out of nowhere to murder Lucy. He was easy to convince.

When he met Hera, Reverend Thornton broke into Koine Greek, the Greek of the New Testament which had been Hera's native language. She decided he must have good Greek blood in him. But in spite of her enthusiastic friendship, the good Reverend did decline the offer of being taught how to use a gladius. He good-naturedly explained to Hera that in the ministry there was not a large demand for that skill.

CHAPTER 17 - The Night is Past the Time for Singing has Come

The morning of June 12 broke with bright sunshine. The day I had longed for so long had arrived. Angus was my best man. Anton, who had been busy on an unspecified mission, was Mike's best man. Mi-Ling and Libby were bridesmaids.

Angus brought Abigail through for the wedding. She looked lovely, as did Anton's lady love, Soila, from Finland. Soila wore an engagement ring, as did Anton, but that's another story.

We had traveled through to Mr. Thornton's Church near Bellefield. Bellefield lay half-burnt from the night Bryant attacked the house and Marie had shot in the dark skillfully and saved our lives.

Sebastian, wreathed in smiles, couldn't quit singing.

As we stood there, Angus and I, I saw someone else in the congregation and excused myself to go hug her. Mrs. Jamieson, my wonderful, kind landlady and friend from Foochow, China, beamed like a Cheshire cat. "By all that's wonderful, Mrs. Jamieson, it's so good to see you! You are a sight for sore eyes and as young as ever."

"Now, Major Faulkner, you always did have a way with words, but it is right pleased I am for you after all you have been through. May you both have a long and happy life. If you want a holiday in Foochow you are both welcome"

She put a small package in my hand. "Oooolong China Tea, the cure all of all cure alls. Sure, but what it cures you even when you are feeling fine."

"Thank you," I said, hugging her again. I thought of that clipper ship tea race between China and London and wondered if I would have done anything differently if I could go back and do it again. Probably not, but even in time travel hindsight is a great thing.

As I turned to walk back up to the dais, a stone with paper around fell at my feet, and unwrapping the paper I read.

Walking away from you in Balmoral that day was the hardest thing I ever had to do in my life, but for both of us it was the right thing. Drew, I will always be your friend. Look up in the balcony. In our hearts we will never need to say goodbye again. A long, happy, and blessed life to you and Marie. She is a lucky girl and you a blessed man. Amigos para siempre- con amore - Sun in Her Hair.

I looked up in the balcony and saw Meryl. She waved and smiled. She looked utterly lovely. But this time there were no *what ifs*. I smiled and waved back. This was not the ending, but the beginning for us all.

As I stood there waiting for Marie, Angus said to me, "I'm very happy for you, Drew. It's been a long, tough road for you, but today is payday. And no one deserves it more than you."

"Thanks, Angus. I owe you more than I can ever repay, like my life several times over."

He smiled at me and shook his head. "Between friends, there is no question of repayment. Thanks for watching my back."

Then I saw his face change. "Drew, Reynolds is sneaking out the back of the church."

It was not the greatest of news but was a reminder that the fight against evil and those who want to take our liberty never stops.

"I hope there are too many Vanguard operatives here for him to try anything just now," I told Angus. "One day he will overstep the mark just like Bryant did, but, Angus, please don't tell Marie."

The music began to play. How it got there I never found out - *We've Only just begun* by the Carpenters.

Then Marie came down the aisle. If there were words to describe how beautiful Marie looked, I didn't know them. She had chosen a wedding dress that looked like something from Romeo and Juliet. A short veil flowed from the top of her pillbox hat. Green lace-trimmed long sleeves added to the sense of beauty and mystery. She carried orange blossoms. Had she known that was what Lucy had carried?

Mi-Ling and Libby walked behind her. The girls were dressed in ivory - colored dresses. Both had black hair that fell in folds down their necks. They, too, carried orange blossoms. Only Mi-Ling could have known. I realized that

Lucy wouldn't have been jealous; she would have been pleased that Mi-Ling was finally getting her Amma.

It was Mi-Ling's smile that threatened to bring up tears from whatever well they usually hide inside. From the little girl I had seen in that hell hole in China, Mi-Ling had grown into a joyful and graceful young lady. Jesus had not only healed Mi-Ling, but had given her a future. Libby, too, had a future now, a chance to be the real her that had hidden in fear from the abuse and domination of her father. It had taken the real Father, the Heavenly Father, to set her free. She had been entrusted to Marie and me

Marie glided beside me and whispered, "How is my beautiful, shy, major?"

"You look stunning and gorgeous."

"Hmm…stunning is good and gorgeous is better, as you will find out."

I was vaguely conscious of Hera arriving beside Mike. She wore pale blue, her favorite color. You will forgive me if I don't put down along description of Hera. I had eyes only for my Marie. One thing for sure Mike looked like the cat that had found the cream.

Mike and I both wore our uniforms – but at a wedding, who comes to see what the groom wears?

Our reverie was interrupted by Reverend Thornton's voice.

"My friends, this is indeed a joyous day for us all, a time of celebration like the first long day of summer after a hard cold winter. God has brought happiness out of tragedy and joy out of pain. These young people are here to exchange vows and promises for the whole of their life together, and may that life be along and a blessed one…"

The next words I heard were, "I pronounce you to be man and wife. You may kiss your bride." I lifted Marie's veil and looked at her gorgeous face and sparkling eyes. The beauty of the music she played paled into insignificance with the way she looked. This was no dream. Marie was my wife for the rest of our lives together. I said in my heart and probably out loud, "Thank You, Jesus, for everything!"

The journal I had kept so faithfully through all my time travel adventures wasn't needed now. Someday, it might make a good book. For now, it would make a good gift for Mi-Ling. As Marie had already promised, we wouldn't need it on our honeymoon!

Then we were aware of Sebastian's voice, reading from another Book, from that beautiful celebration of human love in the Bible, Song of Solomon.

"For lo the winter is past
And the rain is over and gone
The flowers appear on the earth
The time of singing has come
And the voice of the Turtledove is heard throughout the land.

The time of singing certainly had come.

Lightning Source UK Ltd.
Milton Keynes UK
UKOW06f0626230415

250187UK00009B/158/P